Special Books by Special Writers

The Book: SOMEWHERE OUT THERE

Every now and then comes a book that defies convention, breaks the rules and still offers the reader all the excitement of romance. This is such a book. A wonderful story of adventure, romance and the endless possibilities that exist…somewhere out there.

The Writer:

Connie Bennett is a multipublished author. In addition to her eleven Superromance novels, she's written five single-title historicals and one title each for Harlequin American Romance and Harlequin Intrigue. Her books have been critically acclaimed. Honors include a *Romantic Times* Lifetime Achievement Award for Best Romantic Mystery, and in 1995 she was a finalist for Romance Writers of America's RITA Award.

D0401041

ABOUT THE AUTHOR

Connie Bennett is a multipublished author living in Missouri. In addition to her eleven Harlequin Superromance novels, she's written for Harlequin Intrigue and American Romance. She's also written historical fiction. Her books have been critically acclaimed. Honors include a *Romantic Times* Lifetime Achievement Award for Best Romantic Mystery, and in 1995 she was a finalist for Romance Writers of America's RITA Award.

As for being a UFO "true believer" herself, Connie has never personally seen a flying saucer, but she's spent a lot of time studying the sky and hasn't given up hope.

Connie loves to hear from readers. You may write to her at: P.O. Box 14, Dexter, MO 63841.

SOMEWHERE OUT THERE
Connie Bennett

Harlequin Books

TORONTO • NEW YORK • LONDON
AMSTERDAM • PARIS • SYDNEY • HAMBURG
STOCKHOLM • ATHENS • TOKYO • MILAN
MADRID • WARSAW • BUDAPEST • AUCKLAND

ISBN 0-373-70733-9

SOMEWHERE OUT THERE

SOMEWHERE
OUT THERE

PROLOGUE

June 14, 0015 hours/12:15 a.m.
Longview AFB, Tennessee

THE TENSION in the control tower had a life of its own.

It radiated from man to man, making the air vibrate and leaving no one in the silent room immune to its effect.

As one, they watched the radar scope as three blips inched across the screen. Two of the signatures were F-16 fighters that had just been scrambled from the base.

No one in the tower had the slightest idea what was making the third signal.

"Longview Tower, this is 212 Tango, flight of two. We have visual on the target." Captain Ryan Terrell's announcement from the cockpit of his F-16 sliced through the control room, edging up the tension another notch.

"Roger, 212 Tango. What do you see?" The sergeant at the radar scope never took his eyes off the three converging blips.

"Longview, it's a…little hard to describe," the pilot answered tentatively. "The target is small. Not much bigger than a commercial jet, and…well…it's not like anything I've ever seen before. Seems to be...uh...elliptical in shape, with an exceptionally bright band of colored lights intersecting the middle."

"Could they be landing lights, 212 Tango?"

There was a small pause. "If they are, they're not like any *I've* ever seen, Longview."

The sergeant glanced over his shoulder at the lieutenant colonel standing behind him, but the officer's stern face betrayed not a flicker of emotion. The sergeant turned back to the scope. "I copy that, 212 Tango. Maintain visual but do not intercept. Repeat...do not intercept."

"I don't think you have to worry about that, Longview," the captain replied dryly. "The target has increased its speed and we're barely keeping pace as— Holy—Longview, the target just made a ninety-degree turn to 360!"

The monitor corroborated Terrell's claim, but the sergeant couldn't accept what either of them were seeing. The "target" had just defied every known law of aerodynamic physics. "Say again, 212 Tango. You confirm a *ninety*-degree turn?"

"Roger, Longview! Attempting to track, coming up on 360."

"Do you still have visual?"

There was a moment of silence as Terrell completed a less dramatic turn than his target. "Roger, confirm visual."

"Maintain as long as you can." The sergeant shook his head in amazement and covered the mouthpiece of his headset. "Damn, that thing is moving fast. Those F-16s are at top speed, and they're eating dust."

"Just keep your eyes on the screen, Sergeant Nash," the colonel barked.

"Yes, sir."

"Colonel Munroe?" An authoritative voice cut through the tension. "What's going on? Why is my air base on alert?"

Lieutenant Colonel Bill Munroe snapped to attention and turned on his heel to greet his commanding officer. "General Avery, sir."

General Phillip Avery returned his officer's salute perfunctorily. "At ease, Colonel. Just fill me in."

"Sir, we've got a situation. About fifteen minutes ago our radar painted an unidentified aircraft flying at an altitude of twenty-five thousand feet and moving in excess of five thousand miles an hour."

Avery's silver eyebrows quirked upward skeptically. "Five *thousand* miles per hour?"

Munroe nodded. "Yes, sir. The vehicle relayed no automatic transponder signal and did not respond to verbal identification requests. When the craft slowed and began executing erratic maneuvers directly over the base, I ordered two jets to scramble and identify, and put the base on alert, as per your orders regarding nonresponsive aircraft, sir."

Avery nodded his approval. "Do they have visual on the target yet?"

Munroe hesitated for the first time in his narration, then repeated what the pilots had just reported.

If the general was alarmed or even surprised, it didn't show on his fleshy, implacable face. Munroe might just as easily have been reporting the sighting of a weather balloon. "Have you contacted NORAD? Are they showing the same bogie?"

"Not exactly, sir."

Avery frowned. "What the hell does that mean?"

Munroe lowered his voice. "NORAD went on Flash Alert at 2350, sir. Something very big tripped the fence in the upper atmosphere. They won't give me much information, but apparently they lost track of the bogie's signal. It just disappeared."

"That's impossible."

"That's why they're on Flash Alert," Munroe replied.

"And they're not reading any sign of our bogie?"

"No, sir. They're retasking all their satellites in a search for their own bogie. They don't have anything focused on this sector right now."

Avery's scowl was so deep that his silver eyebrows formed a continuous line over his pale blue eyes. The fence Munroe referred to was an electronic surveillance net in the upper atmosphere that extended nearly twenty thousand miles into space. Once something tripped it, all of the government's satellite surveillance equipment was brought to bear on the object, and unless it was immediately identified as nonthreatening, a Flash Alert was issued to the Pentagon, indicating a possible threat to national security.

It seemed incomprehensible that the two incidents—a NORAD Flash Alert and the bogie buzzing Longview—were unrelated, but General Avery wasn't paid to speculate. His problem was dealing with the situation at hand.

"What's our status now?" Avery asked, stepping toward the radar console to see for himself.

"Maintaining pursuit, sir."

"At what altitude, Sergeant Nash?"

A phone rang on the other side of the room, but no one at the console paid it any heed as the sergeant replied, "Twelve thousand feet, sir."

"Does the target appear to be attempting to evade pursuit?"

The sergeant shook his head. "No, sir. It made a radical ninety-degree turn, but considering the speed it's capable of, if it wanted to shake our aircraft it could do it easily."

"Sir..." Both the general and the colonel turned in response to the fresh-faced lieutenant behind them. "Sir, we have a call from Justin Powers, the tower chief at Knoxville Airport. Their radar painted our two aircraft and the bogie. They want to know what's going on."

"I'll handle it," General Avery said, moving brusquely across the room to pick up the phone. "This is General Phillip Avery. What can we do for you, Knoxville?"

"'Evening, General Avery. We're getting some unusual radar readings," the voice on the phone told him. "We saw something moving at an exceptionally high speed a few minutes ago, then it appeared that two of your jets went up in pursuit. What are you guys doing over there?"

"Just routine maneuvers, Chief."

"At five thousand miles an hour?" Powers asked incredulously.

The general forced a chuckle. "Chief, if you're showing speeds like that, I think you should have your radar checked. We've got two men up there on a routine training flight, but—"

"Only two?"

"That's right."

"Your radar doesn't show a third signature displaying erratic movements?" the Knoxville tower chief asked.

"Absolutely not. Have you considered the possibility that you're picking up meteor signatures?" the general asked genially. "You know, the Segrid meteor shower is supposed to provide a pretty spectacular light show tonight."

There was a moment of stunned silence on the phone line before Powers asked, "You're kidding, right? General, aside from the obvious problem of the size a meteor would have to be to show up on aviation radar, falling stars don't usually stop on a dime, alter their speed and change course at will."

Avery did not react to the chief's overt—and justly deserved—sarcasm. "But they can create anomalous readings on poorly maintained radar equipment."

"Our equipment is fine, General," Powers replied tersely.

"And everything is normal here."

There was another small silence before the chief asked shrewdly, "If everything is so normal, General, what's the base commander doing in the tower at midnight?"

Avery's jaw tightened in irritation. "Making a routine inspection, Chief. Now, I suggest you do a maintenance check on your radar because it's obvious that you've got equipment problems. If there's nothing else, good night." Avery slammed down the receiver.

"Trouble, General?" Colonel Munroe asked softly.

"Civilians are always trouble, Bill," Avery growled.

"Longview, this is 212 Tango! We have a second target! Repeat, we have a second bogie on an intercept course with Target One!"

Munroe and Avery hurried back to the radar monitor as Sergeant Nash responded, "Negative, 212 Tango. We show nothing on the scope."

"That's not possible, Longview," the pilot insisted. "This thing is huge—bigger than a football field! It has to show on radar!"

"Negative, 212. We've got nothing new on the scope. Can you get a lock on the second bogie?" Nash asked. Behind the sergeant, Avery and Munroe exchanged speculative looks that seemed to ask, "Could this be NORAD's bogie?"

There was a moment of silence as the pilot attempted to lock his acquisition radar on to the object. "Negative, Longview. I can't get a lock on. It's as though it isn't even there, but I see it!"

"541 Bravo, do you confirm 212's visual?"

A second voice, younger and not quite as controlled as the captain's, responded immediately, "Roger, Longview! I confirm! I confirm! It looks like…a Mother Ship trying to rendezvous with its scout craft!"

General Avery snatched up the nearest headset and barked into the microphone, "Can the chatter, 541! You're up there to report what you see, not jump to half-baked conclusions!"

"Yes, sir!" The response was more than a little insolent. "Sir, I report seeing an aircraft of unknown type and origin, in excess of four hundred feet in length and approximately that dimension in width. Sir! The craft is paralleling my own course, approximately two-hundred-and-fifty feet above my position, displaying three intensely bright white lights on its underbelly that seem to be lighting up the entire night sky. Sir!''

Avery's jaw quivered furiously throughout the staccato report. ''Who the hell is that pilot?''

''Lieutenant Mack Lewis, sir,'' Munroe replied quietly.

''Put him on report, Colonel,'' Avery growled.

Munroe hesitated. ''Sir... He's a good man. A little unseasoned, maybe, but this is hardly a routine—''

''General, Target One just made another ninety-degree turn and has increased speed!'' Sergeant Nash told his commanders. An instant later, 212 Tango made the same report.

''And Target Two is vectoring off, as well,'' the pilot told them. ''I'm staying on the big ship. 541 Bravo will track Target One!''

''Roger, 212 Tango.''

The officers in the control tower watched the screen as the F-16s changed course, moving in opposite directions—one in pursuit of the smaller aircraft, the other seemingly chasing nothing, because Sergeant Nash still couldn't get a radar signature for the craft Lieutenant Lewis had called the Mother Ship. Seconds ticked by like hours.

''Longview, this is 541 Bravo,'' Lieutenant Lewis reported, breaking the interminable silence. ''My target is making some radical course changes! Behaving ver...erratically... Can't kee...but attempting to...''

''Say again, 541 Bravo. Your transmission is breaking up,'' Sergeant Nash told him.

Static that shouldn't have been there crackled over

the speaker, and on the radar screen Nash watched in disbelief as the target executed an impossible one-hundred-and-eighty-degree turn—directly into the path of Lewis's oncoming F-16.

"Jesus, Longview, he's comi...ight at me!" Lewis shouted. "Attempting evasive..."

The transmission ended abruptly. No static came over the speaker. And no voice, either. Just cold, sickening silence. The officers watched the radar screen as the two blips converged with lightning speed. They connected, seemingly merging into one for a fraction of a second.

When they separated, the target signature executed another startling ninety-degree turn and accelerated, disappearing from the scope in the blink of an eye. The F-16 seemed to stop in midair.

"He's losing altitude!" Nash exclaimed. "541 Bravo, come in! Do you copy, 541 Bravo?"

Silence.

"541 Bravo, this is Longview Tower. Do you copy?"

More silence.

"541 Bravo—"

The signature of the F-16 vanished from the scope as though it had never existed.

"Oh my God," Nash whispered. "212 Tango, do you have visual on 541 Bravo?"

"Negative, Longview," Captain Terrell replied. "I'm still tracking Target Two."

General Avery grabbed the headset he had used earlier. "212 Tango, this is General Avery. Break off contact now! Return to base. I say again, break off contact and return to base!"

"Roger, Longview."

Silence enveloped the room as the single radar signature changed course.

"Sir..."

"Yes, Sergeant?" General Avery replied.

"Shouldn't we scramble search-and-rescue, sir?"

Avery collected himself. "Of course. See to it, Colonel Munroe," he ordered. "And when 212 lands, put that pilot into isolation for debriefing."

"Yes, sir."

Phillip Avery turned on his heel and left as the control tower sprang to life behind him. It would take a long time for the shock to wear off, but his men had duties to perform that would keep them occupied for hours. There would be time enough later to deal with their grief.

In the meantime, Phillip Avery had a duty to perform, as well. When he assumed command of this base three months ago he had been warned that something like this might happen, but he hadn't believed it. Even now, after what he'd just witnessed, he *still* didn't believe it.

But the fact remained: Longview AFB had just lost one of its pilots in an encounter with an Unidentified Flying Object.

The general reached his office, closed the door behind him and went to the phone to punch in a number he had been required to memorize three months ago.

The voice that answered at the other end said only, "Yes?"

"Get Brewster," Avery ordered. "We have contact."

CHAPTER ONE

12:34 a.m.
Clear Lake, Tennessee

THE SKY WAS a cloudless, ink-stained blue sprinkled with glittering stars. Every few seconds, tiny fragments of interstellar dust entered the atmosphere, blazed brightly as they streaked across the sky, then winked out as magically as they had appeared.

Lying on the grassy hillside in front of his mountain cabin, Kit Wheeler couldn't have asked for more from the light show. This ground-to-sky view wasn't the perspective of space that he'd spent most of his life dreaming of, but the former astronaut had had eight years to make peace with the fact that photographing the heavens with a high-powered telescopic lens was as close as he was ever going to get to exploring space.

He hadn't reached total acceptance yet, but he was working on it. Maybe in another decade.

A dazzling flash of three meteors rocketed in on their very predictable east-to-west trajectory, and Kit squeezed the shutter bulb of the camera that was fixed on a tripod next to him. Its panoramic lens and ultra-high-speed film were set to photograph any streaks of light that Kit was quick enough to snap, and he thought maybe he'd succeeded with that trio.

He hoped so, anyway. He was counting on the Segrid meteor shower yielding a number of good photographs. He needed at least one for the astronomy section of his new book, and he'd promised one to *Science Discoveries* magazine to accompany the article he was doing on new developments in high-speed film for night photography.

And of course, there was "Frontiers," Kit's science-and-technology update that was broadcast twelve times a day, every weekday on the Global News Network. Next Monday when he went back to his office at GNN headquarters in Washington, D.C., he hoped to be able to show his fans who had missed it that the Segrid meteor shower had been worth staying up for.

His fans.

Chuckling, Kit rolled the word around in his mind. He still had trouble comprehending it. He was a celebrity, and as far as he was concerned, a damn unlikely and undeserving one. How many scientists with doctorates in aeronautics and astrophysics had fan clubs? How many air force test pilots who'd washed out of the astronaut program before they'd made even one space flight got asked for autographs nearly everywhere they went?

It was truly an insane world, but through a combination of bad luck and good timing, Christopher "Kit" Wheeler had become the most recognized, respected scientist in the nation. From the time he was old enough to dream, all he'd ever wanted was to be an astronaut, and he'd sacrificed everything—including his five-year-old marriage—for the space program. But only weeks before his very first mission— the first shuttle flight following the horrifying *Challenger* explosion—Kit began experiencing vertigo during his Zero-G test flights and his career as an astronaut had ended. Just like that.

Years of hard work, swept away in an instant. A lifetime of dreams and aspirations squashed flat. Kit had been forced to find new goals and new ways to define who he was and what he wanted from life.

But that tiny flaw in his inner ear, which never troubled him unless he subjected his eardrum to unusual amounts of pressure, had also been a stroke of good fortune. NASA had allowed him to remain in the space program as a media spokesperson, which had brought him to the attention of the public. Even though he'd never made a space flight, he became the most recognizable astronaut since John Glenn, and that had captured the attention of the Global News Network.

A second career had been born, and though it wasn't what Kit wanted and it didn't come close to satisfying the hunger that had led him to NASA, it was a good career. A lucrative career. A career he knew he was damn lucky to have.

A cool breeze wafted up from the lake, scenting the air with a hint of pine; crickets, cicadas and an unusually vocal barn owl serenaded him. There was a silent radio behind him on the darkened front porch of the cabin, but he had no desire for any music other than the symphony being provided by Mother Nature.

A yawn caught up with him just as another meteor swept overhead and disappeared behind the hills surrounding the valley that had been named after its principal feature—a large, natural lake so clear it appeared to be as smooth and reflective as a mirror.

Kit, whose log-and-stone cabin was on the northernmost rim of the encircling mountains, loved to look down at it and watch the patterns of reflected stars mingling with the lights from Clear Lake Resort and the homes that ringed the lake.

His focus was on the sky tonight though, and when he saw the white-hot streak of light that came out of the northwest, Kit squeezed the shutter bulb out of reflex.

A fraction of a second after the camera clicked, he realized the streak of light wasn't a meteor.

This light was moving too fast, and it was at least twenty times brighter than any meteor Kit had ever seen. It was also coming in on the wrong trajectory, west by northwest, as though it had been poured out of the Big Dipper.

Puzzled, Kit sat up, never taking his eyes off the light that grew brighter by the second as it streaked across the sky. He snapped two more pictures, and just when it seemed that the light would disappear behind the mountains, it did the impossible.

It stopped.

Kit stared at the light that was hanging over the mountaintop like a star on a Christmas tree.

''What the hell is that?'' he muttered as his mind scrambled for an explanation. Longview Air Force Base was only a hundred and twenty miles southwest of Clear Lake. The military did have a few experimental jets that could fly as fast as that object had flown, but most experimental tests were done at bases in the desert, and Kit couldn't think of a single craft that would put out such a bright light.

Certainly none of them could stop in midair.

For all his study of astrophysics and his training in aeronautics, Kit didn't have a clue what could be generating the phenomenon.

But he could record it, he realized somewhat belatedly. Hurriedly, he repositioned the tripod, focused on the light and snapped off two pictures as quickly as the shutter speed would allow.

He was still looking through the viewfinder when the light started moving again. Not south this time, though, but slowly north.

Directly toward him.

He kept taking pictures as the light grew brighter and brighter...so bright that he had to reduce the shutter speed with every shot, to keep the film from being overexposed, and still it grew closer...larger... brighter.

Kit knew the instant it topped the crest of the mountain. The trees on the south slope of the valley began casting bizarre shadows, the lake below reflected the brilliant light and the little valley took on an eerie radiant glow as the object glided down the forested hillside.

Kit kept snapping pictures even as his mind rejected what he was seeing. The object was only a mile or so away from him now. He could see its shape clearly—a huge, flat chevron, somewhat similar to a stealth bomber. Only this was much, much bigger. Nearly two hundred yards long, with a wingspan about that wide.

Kit could see details, too...the shiny, smooth silver

surface of the object's outer skin...small rectangles glowing with light that seemed to come from within the craft, like soft candlelight shining through multi-paned windows...dark, formless shapes that cast strange shadows within those soft rectangles.

The craft settled lower into the valley and came to a stop, hovering over the lake. It was below Kit now, and its lights had dimmed as it made its descent. The forest was no longer casting shadows, and beyond the object, Kit could make out the lights of the marina on the other side of the lake.

His telescopic lens caught the whole bizarre, unbelievable scene, but his rational self told him that he would find nothing in the pictures but the boat dock and the dark, quiet tranquillity of the lake and valley.

This was a hallucination. Or maybe just a dream. A bona fide nightmare.

In fact, the Segrid shower probably didn't exist. His dreaming mind had invented it—just as it was inventing the Unidentified Flying Object that was hovering over the lake.

If Kit had believed in the existence of UFOs it might have been easier for him to accept what he was seeing. But he didn't believe in them. As a pilot, he'd seen strange lights before, but they had always been explained to his satisfaction. As a scientist, he rejected theories of visitors from other worlds. Oh, he believed that there were other forms of life in the universe, but he didn't believe they were visiting earth. That was a scientific impossibility, and people who thought otherwise were dreamers, science fiction writers or UFO crackpots.

What he was seeing now couldn't be an extraterrestrial spacecraft. Period. End of story.

But it couldn't be something from this world, either. Technology like this didn't exist on earth—not even in its most experimental stages. So this *was* a dream.

Yet he knew deep down that he was wide-awake.

The *thing* over the lake started moving again.

Kit clicked off another shot as the craft's lights began to brighten. It skimmed the surface of the lake, and then began to rise. Slowly, silently, it moved straight up, displaying three clearly defined lights on its underbelly. The higher it rose, the brighter the lights became, until they blurred into one intense ball like a white-hot sun.

And then, in the blink of an eye, it was gone.

Its disappearance took Kit's breath away, and he sucked in a great gulp of air as he scanned the sky. He looked in every direction, twisting to the north, then south, then north again, but there was nothing up there now that hadn't been there for millions of years.

"What the hell was that?" he asked the empty mountainside.

Kit came to his feet. "What was it?"

He turned to the northwest, where it had first appeared.

"Damn it! What the hell was that?"

1:39 a.m.
Georgetown, District of Columbia

IT WAS A NICE DREAM. No. Better than nice. It was wonderful…warm…comforting…and sexy. Yes, definitely sexy—which was one of the things that made it so nice. Brenna Sullivan hadn't had a sexy dream in longer than she could remember. Usually, her dreams were filled with hellish images of her father's tragic death on a lonely mountain road. She would wake up from them drenched in sweat, gasping for breath and awash in the pain of losing her only parent all over again.

That dream was so common Brenna sometimes dreaded going to sleep, but tonight there was no need to dread. Apparently, her subconscious had decided to give her a break from the recurring nightmare and provide her soul a little vicarious nourishment, instead.

And Brenna was enjoying the romantic interlude thoroughly. It didn't matter in the least that she couldn't see her lover's face. In fact, that seemed reasonable since she hadn't had a man in her life for years. She'd been too focused on her work. But tonight—in the dream, at least—there was no manuscript awaiting completion; there were no boxes of declassified documents cluttering her apartment; no covert meetings with government employees who would only speak to her off the record; no rampant paranoia; and best of all, no obsession to prove that her father's "accidental" death had been cold-blooded murder....

Nothing at all, in fact, but a wonderfully sexy rendezvous with a faceless lover. Unfortunately, her imaginary pleasure and nonexistent lover were banished by the discordant jangle of the phone beside her bed.

A half groan, half growl of frustration rumbled in her throat and Brenna rolled away from the irritating noise, trying to recapture the dream and call her lover back, but it was no use. The phone kept ringing.

"Damn," she mumbled, sleepily fumbling for the phone on the nightstand. It took a tremendous effort, but she finally succeeded in bringing it to her ear. "This had better be good," she muttered, her voice husky with sleep.

"Why aren't you on-line?"

Brenna knew she should recognize the voice, but forcing her brain into wakefulness required more strength than she had at the moment. She managed to pry her eyes open long enough to glance at her clock. "It's nearly two in the blessed a.m. Who is this?"

"It's Randall. Get it together, Bren. We've got work to do!"

Brenna groaned. Randall Parrish was her best friend, second-in-command and the closest thing she had to family. Twenty years ago he'd been an over-eager college kid when he signed on for a part-time job as her father's research assistant. Now he was the associate director of the Center for UFO Research. Brenna couldn't have run the place without him.

As much as she loved him, though, she wasn't at all shy about telling him what lousy timing he had. "Randall, you just woke me out of the sexiest dream I've had in years. Unless aliens have landed on the White House lawn, you're a dead man."

Brenna propped herself up on both elbows and waited for a barb about the sorry state of her love life, but her friend didn't take the bait. "They haven't landed at the White House yet, but they're buzzing

Longview Air Force Base. Is that close enough for you?''

Brenna bolted upright in bed. "Longview? Where is that? Tennessee, right?"

"Right. One hour ago, the base lost an F-16 that was playing tag with a UFO."

"Oh my God. Are you sure?" she asked needlessly. Randall always got his facts straight.

"Well, no one from the base is admitting that a UFO was involved, of course," he answered. "But the crash is verifiable. It started a fire just south of the Great Smoky Mountains National Park. Longview is setting up a search-and-rescue staging base at the Lion's Head ranger station even as we speak."

Brenna's pulse rate accelerated and her breath caught in her throat. "There was a midair collision? Are we looking at a downed UFO?"

She heard the hesitancy in Randall's voice. "Possible but not probable. We've got a reliable eyewitness report that says the UFO zipped off and only the jet went down."

Brenna pushed back her covers and slid to the edge of the bed. "Who's the witness?"

Randall chuckled with delight. "You're gonna love it—a solid, upstanding forest ranger named Dale Winston, who just so happens to be a much-decorated navy vet who flew fighters in Vietnam. He's going to be a hard witness to impeach."

"Oh, come on, Randall. Haven't I taught you anything? No one is hard to impeach when you have the full resources of the Department of Internal Security at your command. You'd better get hold of a copy of

Winston's service record before Brewster's people in DIS have a chance to butcher it.''

"I'll get on it first thing in the morning.''

"Is there any indication that Colonel Brewster has been called in?'' Brenna asked.

"Nothing yet, but you're the one with the Pentagon contacts and a U.S. senator waiting in the wings,'' he reminded her. "You gotta start making some calls, Bren, and quick. Sighting reports are coming in on the UFONet faster than the system can handle them. If that's any indication, this is going to turn out to be the biggest flap this country has ever experienced. It could be the one that breaks the conspiracy wide open.''

Brenna's pulse rate rocketed again at the thought of bringing to justice the man who had murdered her father, but she reined in her excitement quickly. Fifteen years of trying to expose the military's cover-up of its knowledge about UFOs had taught Brenna that patience was her most valuable asset—that, and her unquenchable thirst to see a man named Elgin Brewster pay for what he had taken away from her. Both assets had brought her to where she was now, and she knew what she had to do.

"All right, let's get plugged in,'' she said as she came to her feet. "Call Claudia, and I'll meet you downstairs at the office in thirty minutes.''

"We're on our way.''

The line went dead and Brenna sprang into action, her ridiculous, irrelevant, sexy dream completely forgotten as she began packing. If she was going to get to Tennessee before evidence started disappearing, she didn't have a minute to waste.

2:05 a.m.
Longview AFB

LIEUTENANT COLONEL Bill Munroe looked as though he was standing at attention even when he wasn't. His back ramrod straight, he watched from the edge of runway Baker as a cargo transport from Langley, Virginia, lumbered in for a landing. Behind him, a freshly fueled helicopter was taking off with more troops to fight the fire in the Cumberland National Forest, and a smaller Huey was on standby for the mysterious visitor who was arriving from Langley.

This night was getting stranger by the minute, and it was a long way from over.

Colonel Munroe waited without showing a trace of impatience while a ground crew rushed toward the Langley transport as it taxied to a standstill. The cargo bay in the belly of the great beast opened, and the ground crew held their places as seven men marched down the ramp in perfect chevron formation, like a small flock of geese playing follow the leader.

They started across the tarmac, and Munroe stepped out to meet them as the ground crew rushed up the ramp to unload equipment. Not one of the seven men approaching him was wearing a uniform, but Munroe snapped off a salute to the man in the lead.

"Lieutenant Colonel William Munroe, at your service, sir."

The leader of the flock returned the salute without breaking stride, and Munroe did an about-face, quickstepping to keep up as the new arrivals headed straight for the jeeps that were waiting. "Where's

General Avery?'' the leader asked, his voice surprisingly soft but unquestionably commanding.

"In his office, awaiting your arrival, sir," Munroe replied.

"And my helo?"

"Fueled and ready to depart as soon as you are."

The man from Langley nodded briskly. "Has SAR located the wreckage yet?"

"Yes, sir, but we won't be able to reach it until we bring the fires under control."

"What about Captain Terrell? Is he being held in seclusion for debriefing?"

"Yes, sir. And the tower crew has been segregated, as well, just as you ordered."

"Is there any indication that Lieutenant Lewis was able to eject?"

"No, sir," the lieutenant colonel answered, then made the mistake of volunteering, "And nothing to suggest that the unidentified bogie went down with the F-16."

The visitor came to an abrupt stop. The six geese flanking him read his mind—or maybe just his body language—and stopped in perfect formation behind him. Only Munroe was slow to react. By the time he ground to a halt, he had to do a one-eighty to face the other man.

When he did, the glacial cold of the visitor's pale blue eyes sent a chill down Bill Munroe's spine. "Colonel Munroe, let's be very clear on one thing. You had two men in the air on a routine training run tonight. Nothing more, nothing less. When we recover the wreckage, I have no doubt that we'll discover equipment failure, pilot error or possibly a combination of both were responsible for this terrible tragedy. But *there was no bogie tonight, identified or otherwise. Do you get my drift?*"

Munroe held the man's chilling glare unflinchingly. "Yes, sir. I understand."

"Good. Now, take me to General Avery." Colonel Elgin Brewster stepped out briskly, his silent flock obediently falling in behind.

CHAPTER TWO

IT WASN'T EASY to keep an even rhythm pounding along on the rocky trail, but Kit did his best. This was his favorite place to jog—the forested ridge that circled behind, above and back down to his cabin—but his heart wasn't in it this morning. He was trying to work off the anxiety that had kept him awake and moving all night long.

His pulse rate was up now, his thighs were burning, he was drenched in sweat, and the beauty of nature was all around him, but his stomach was still churning.

So much for the purgative effects of exercise on stress.

He had to slow down when he came to the man-high boulders that marked the final downhill stretch to the cabin. In fact, he had to vault over the lowest one just to reach the barely perceptible trail, and when he did, a flash of red at the bottom of the ridge caught his attention. He came to a stop, breathing heavily, bracing his hands on his thighs as he looked down.

Cy Coleman's fire-engine-red pickup truck was sitting by the cabin next to Kit's blue 4WD Mountaineer.

"Great," Kit said, gasping for breath. He wasn't ready for this. Cy Coleman was a retired printer who owned and edited the Clear Lake *Gazette*, a chatty, eight-page newspaper whose masthead boasted a circulation of 432. The paper operated on a hit-or-miss schedule during tourist season, with no particular rhyme or reason to when it might "hit the stands." If Cy had news, he put a paper out. If not…well, no one bothered to complain.

Unless Kit's close encounter last night had been a hallucination—as he was hoping—Cy had news today. Someone had probably told him that Kit was in town—maybe even that he intended to take pictures—and Cy wanted to know what Clear Lake's most famous part-time resident had seen.

Kit wasn't about to tell him. He wasn't telling *anyone* until he saw how those pictures turned out and got a few answers about that…*thing*.

He'd spent the entire night pacing, fuming, trying to rationalize the experience into nonexistence, to convince himself it was nothing but a hallucination.

His confusion had gone from bad to worse when he turned on the television for a little background noise and heard GNN's breaking news story: an air force jet had crashed in the mountains not a hundred miles southwest of Clear Lake.

The questions that had leaped into Kit's mind were unavoidable—had the pilot who crashed so close to Clear Lake seen the same amazing craft Kit had seen? Was the aircraft he'd seen last night somehow responsible for this tragedy? Or was it possible that the fire in the Cumberland National Forest hadn't been caused by the crash of an F-16 at all?

Could the craft in the middle of that forest fire be the one Kit had photographed?

Kit didn't want to believe it, but the two events—his sighting and the crash—had happened only minutes apart, so close in time that Kit wasn't even sure which had come first. The coincidence couldn't be ignored.

Knowing he'd never be able to rest until he learned the truth, he'd stopped pacing at 3:00 a.m. and started making phone calls.

Since then, he'd been to Knoxville, where he put the roll of film onto a private courier plane to Washington. His best friend, who owned a photo processing lab, had been waiting at the airport to pick up the film. Sandy Kirshner had promised to develop it immediately. Kit was supposed to call him about the results at 8:00 a.m.

He checked his watch. It was almost that, now, and hiding in the hills to avoid an unpleasant confrontation wasn't Kit's style. Whether he wanted to or not, he was going to have to talk to Cy Coleman. He jogged in place a couple of steps, then continued down the rocky path that cut diagonally across the hillside. The cabin vanished from view when the trail cut into a stand of pines, and by the time he emerged on the other side, Cy's truck was backing out of the driveway. In another second, it disappeared down the steep embankment that Kit laughingly called a road.

Cy was known for tenacity, so this was only a reprieve, but it was a welcome one. Kit panted a sigh of relief and jogged down the hill, sprinting the last hundred yards across his obstacle-free lawn around the cabin. He pounded up the steps onto the porch, stopped and propped his hands on his knees until his breathing came a little easier.

Drenched in sweat from head to toe, he stripped off his sweatshirt and used it as a towel to dry his neck and torso as he moved to the round cedar table and dropped into a chair.

The bold headlines of the newspapers that littered the table glared up at him: Air Force Jet Crashes In Smokys, screamed the Knoxville *Journal*. The Nashville *Leader* declared, Airman Dies In Jet Crash. And ironically, there were other headlines of interest in the papers, as well, like the one on page four of the *Leader* that announced, Meteor Shower Sparks UFO Scare.

In that tongue-in-cheek wire-service article, a respected Cal Tech astronomer had gone on record to state unequivocally that the hundreds of UFOs sighted across the Midwest last night had been nothing more than Segrid meteors and overactive imaginations.

Yeah, right.

Kit didn't know about the highway patrolman in Arkansas or the farmer from Georgia whose UFO encounters were described in the article, but what *he'd* seen bore absolutely no resemblance to any meteor he'd ever studied.

Kit took a liberal swig of water from the sport bottle on the table, then checked his watch again. It was eight on the money. Time to call Sandy.

He thought fleetingly about taking a shower first, but it would only be a stalling tactic. He had to call.

Kit heaved himself to his feet, turning toward the door, and that's when he saw it—the thin, folded-in-quarters newspaper that Cy Coleman had wedged into the screen door.

A sick feeling in the pit of Kit's stomach told him

that this day was about to go from bad to worse. He plucked the paper out of the door and read the big block letters that were written on the white sheet of notebook paper that obscured the front page:

TRIED TO CALL YOU EARLY THIS A.M. TO GET A STATEMENT BEFORE I WENT TO PRESS, BUT NO LUCK. CALL ME, OR I'LL ASSUME YOU WERE ABDUCTED BY THE UFO LAST NIGHT AND CALL OUT THE NATIONAL GUARD. HA, HA.

CY

Kit removed the note and flicked open the single sheet of newsprint. The two-word headline on the front page, printed in the biggest type he'd ever seen, loudly declared THEY'RE HERE! To prove it, there was a picture of the UFO right below it.

At least Kit assumed it was the UFO he'd seen last night. The photograph wouldn't win any prizes. It had been taken with a self-developing camera on film intended for daylight or flash pictures only, and the object was too far away for the flash attachment to have been of any use. The picture was also out of focus, as though the photographer's hands had been trembling.

Kit could empathize.

As vague as the picture was, though, he could make out the dark, triangular outline of the craft and the three lights that emanated from its underbelly. It was his UFO, all right.

He turned his attention to the article that bore Cy

Coleman's byline. Eight of his summer neighbors, including a lawyer, a banker and a local restaurateur, had been partying on the deck of David and Dana Boorman's pontoon boat when the craft appeared. They described its descent, the way it lit up the valley and then dimmed as it hovered over the lake. They described their fear, awe and disbelief, too.

Those people were as sane as Kit, and so were most of the others from up and down the valley who had shared their experience with Cy. "Well, if I decide to go public, there'll be a *few* people in the country who don't think I'm a fruitloop," he muttered as he scanned the rest of the article.

Halfway through, the name he'd dreaded seeing jumped out at him. Cy had written:

It is believed by many in the valley that the renowned GNN science correspondent and former astronaut, Dr. Christopher Wheeler, was in residence at his hunting lodge above the lake at the time of the incident. Witnesses state that Wheeler arrived in Clear Lake yesterday with the intention of photographing the Segrid meteor shower.

Though Wheeler was unavailable for comment this morning, if this report is true, his pictures of the unidentified aircraft would be remarkable and persuasive, since he told several people that he planned to use special film, and it is well known that Wheeler received training as a photographer during his tenure at NASA.

Kit let loose with a string of curses that would have shocked any of his viewers who bought into the all-

American-astronaut image he'd spent a lifetime cultivating.

Damn Cy Coleman! Didn't he know what this was going to do to Kit's life? So far, none of the major papers or TV-news outlets had drawn a correlation between the crash of that F-16 and the spate of UFO sightings, and it was such a bizarre theory that no one probably would. But both events were going to draw reporters out of the woodwork.

All the serious news media would be in the area investigating the crash. All the supermarket-tabloid paparazzi would flood the area to get the lowdown on the UFO sightings. The Clear Lake *Gazette's* circulation was minuscule, but eventually someone was going to run across a copy and want to know what Kit had seen—and photographed.

Unless Sandy Kirshner developed the film and found a roll of thirty blank negatives, Kit was going to have to decide whether he should deny the incident with an out-and-out lie, or go public and risk the destruction of his reputation—and possibly even his career.

Furious, Kit crumpled Cy's newspaper into the smallest, tightest ball his fist would make and threw it as hard as he could in the direction of the lake.

It would have been a more effective gesture of contempt if there hadn't been an opposing breeze. The paper ball fell a foot short of the edge of the porch and a timely gust of wind sent it tumbling back toward him.

It stopped inches from his feet.

"Great, Kit. You'll be pitching for the Yankees in

no time," he muttered as he bent to pick it up. "Which is good, because you're going to need a new career."

His telephone jangled inside the cabin.

"Oh, joy. That's probably CBS wanting a quote." He threw open the screen door and hurried inside, rehearsing what he'd say. "Why, yes, Mr. Rather, I did see something unusual last night while I was photographing the Segrid meteor shower. Four hundred and twenty-one meteors swept overhead, exploded and spelled out the lyrics of the 'Star Spangled Banner.'"

He ranted his way through the living room, reaching the phone in his office in the middle of the fourth ring.

"Hello?"

"Kit! Where the hell have you been? I've been calling you for an hour!"

It was Sandy Kirshner, and he wasn't calm. "I was out running," Kit said. "I thought we agreed that I'd call you at eight."

"You expected me to wait that long to talk to you after what I've seen?" his friend demanded. "What the hell is this thing?"

That had a familiar ring to it. "I wish I knew, Sandy. Obviously, the pictures turned out."

"I'll say. You can count the needles on the pine trees and the windows in that—" he stumbled over the words "—in that *thing* over the lake."

"The UFO." It was the first time he'd said the words aloud and they nearly choked him.

There was a short pause. "Is that really what it is?"

"I don't know what else to call it. It's an object, it was flying and I sure as hell couldn't identify it."

"That makes it an OFU," Kirshner joked.

The knot of tension in Kit's stomach eased a little. "Good point. I'd rather say OFU than UFO, believe me." Resigned to the inevitable, he sat at his desk and fired up his computer. "All right, Sandy. Let's get this over with. I'll give you my fax number and you shoot copies of the pictures down to me." He recited the number.

"Got it." Kit could hear movement in the background as Sandy readied the pictures for transmission. "What do you want me to do about the originals and negatives?"

Kit had given this a lot of thought. If he decided to come forward with his story, he was going to find himself defending the authenticity of those photos. He needed to be able to prove when he'd taken them and when he'd had them developed. "Do you know a notary public?"

"Sure. I do a lot of government contract work that requires authentication," Sandy replied.

"All right. Take the pictures and negatives to a notary and have him seal them in an envelope with the time, date…everything. Put them in a safe place until I come get them."

"When will that be?"

"I'm not sure. I'm going to start an investigation down here—check out the site of that F-16 crash, and talk to the brass at Longview."

"You think they're covering up the truth about what really happened? That there's a connection between this thing and the crash?"

"If there isn't, this is one mind-boggling coincidence."

"Is there any chance that the craft in the picture is something experimental the military is developing?"

"To tell you the truth, Sandy, that's what I'm hoping," Kit replied. "I'd have no problem coming forward if I discovered they were testing weird stuff over populated areas, even if they shouted 'national security' at me. My career might not survive, but my reputation would. Whatever I decide to do, I want those pictures protected."

"Why don't you just have someone from GNN come over and pick them up?" Sandy asked.

"I'm not ready for anyone at the station to know what I'm looking into. Some eager beaver might jump the gun and air them before I've figured out what that thing is."

"All right. I'll hang on to them, but don't take too long, okay? These things are spooky."

"How spooky?" Kit asked.

"You ought to know. You saw it in person."

"Sandy, I still don't believe what I saw."

"Well, maybe these will convince you. Here they come now."

An electronic beep warned Kit that he was receiving a transmission, and then his laser printer began its soft mechanical whine. Kit closed his eyes until he heard the first page fall into the paper tray. When he opened them, what he saw brought back all the wonder, disbelief and fear he'd experienced last night.

Even accounting for a loss of quality between the photo and the high-resolution facsimile, the picture was remarkable. Sandy had chosen to send the pictures out of sequence, starting with a shot of the UFO hovering over the lake. He hadn't exaggerated—it really was possible to count the tiny rectangles of light that Kit had assumed were windows. He could see the texture of the craft's surface, the lights from the resort boat dock that showed the size of the UFO in comparison...he could even see the craft's underbelly reflected in the lake.

"Have you got it?" Sandy asked him as the second photo began coming through.

"I've got it," Kit replied woodenly.

"Quite a sight, isn't it?"

"Yeah. It was."

"Kit..."

"What, Sandy?"

"Is this for real? It's not a hoax?"

Kit's stomach constricted painfully Sandy Kirshner had been his friend for years. He knew Kit as well as any man alive, and better than most. If Kit's best friend didn't believe him, what was the rest of the world going to think?

"Yes, it's for real," he snapped. "You know I wouldn't fake something like this. What would I possibly have to gain? You think I want to turn my life into a three-ring circus and make myself a laughingstock?"

"Hey, hey, hey," Sandy said quickly. "I wasn't calling you a liar, Kit. Calm down. If you say you saw it, I believe you. But you've got to admit that it's on the far side of bizarre."

"Believe me, I know that better than anyone—except maybe for the hundreds of other people across the state who saw it, too."

"What are you going to do about it?"

"I don't know, Sandy. But I'll be in touch. Just keep those pictures and negs safe until you hear from me, okay?"

"You got it, pal."

"Thanks for everything, Sandy. Give my love to Maura."

"Will do."

They hung up, and Kit picked up four more fax photos. Sandy was still feeding the others through, and Kit sat beside the machine, studying the pictures one at a time, until he had a full set of thirty replicas of the eight-by-ten photos Sandy had developed.

Working methodically, he put them in chronological order, starting with a ball of fire that had appeared over the mountain, and ending with a streak of light against a star-filled sky. In the middle were close-ups of the UFO that looked like something out of a science fiction movie.

Only it wasn't a Steven Spielberg special effect. It was real.

"Now, what the hell am I going to do about it?" Kit muttered as he shuffled through the pictures one more time, trying to convince himself to believe the unbelievable.

THE SALT LICK TRUCK Stop Café was crowded and noisy, but Brenna tuned out the clatter of dishes and the bellowing of bleary-eyed truckers vying for the attention of the waitresses. Newspapers were strewn across the table, and her considerable powers of concentration were focused on them. All of the bold headlines were similar: Air Force Jet Crashes In

Smokys, Airman Dies In Jet Crash. Even the small-town Salt Lick *Statesman* had a front-page article about the tragedy that had occurred shortly after midnight.

Brenna had read all the articles twice and could have quoted liberally from any of them if she had been asked—not that there was anything in them worth quoting. She was unimpressed by the accounts that were nothing more than elaborations of a curt press statement released by the public information officer at Longview Air Force Base. And she was even less impressed with the newspapers' satirical treatment of the UFO sightings that had been reported all across the Midwest.

"Hogwash! Pure de ol' hogwash, that's what this is!" The coverall-clad farmer in the booth in front of Brenna slammed his fist onto the table for emphasis, making the dishes rattle.

Brenna looked at him, more startled by the sentiment that echoed her own thoughts than by his booth-pounding outburst.

"What are you bellowin' about, Len?" a young, dark-haired waitress asked him as she hurried over with a pot of coffee to refill his cup.

"This article in the *Statesman*," he replied testily, waving the local Salt Lick paper under the waitress's nose. "Look at that. It says we're a bunch of kooks and crackers who don't know the difference between a shootin' star and a goldamn UFO. I *know* what I saw, damn it, and it wudd'n no shootin' star!"

"Where does it say we're kooks and crackers?" the waitress asked indignantly, snatching the paper out of his hand.

"Well...it don't say that exactly," Len replied sullenly. "But that's what it means. I'm gonna have me a long talk with Charlie Jacobs for printin' that trash, and don't you think I won't. I know what I saw!"

"It was a UFO? Really?" Brenna couldn't help asking, giving the farmer a friendly, inquisitive smile that she hoped would encourage him to confide in her.

Len swung his gaze over to her. His eyes narrowed with a hint of suspicion that Brenna was very accustomed to. She obviously wasn't a local, and she certainly didn't look like a lady trucker in her white silk T-shirt and gray pleated trousers. But she'd done this before and witnesses tended to trust her because she treated them with respect instead of reproach or disbelief.

Len apparently decided she was harmless, and finally replied, "Yes, ma'am, I did," with the conviction of a man swearing on a stack of Bibles. "So did my two boys, my wife and most of my neighbors. Not to mention, Dave Coombs, the deputy sheriff. The light was so bright it woke my wife up and she poked me in the ribs. We run to the window, and there it was, big as life."

A trucker at the counter swiveled his stool to join the conversation. "What did it look like?" he asked.

Len glanced at him suspiciously, but answered, "Just a big, bright light. It was movin' over the house real slow, goin' north, and when it got to Little Smoky, it just stopped and hung there, big as a harvest moon."

"Little Smoky?" Brenna questioned.

The waitress, whose name tag identified her as Cindy, dropped Len's newspaper on his table and stepped to Brenna's to refill her coffee cup. "That's what folks around here call the hills east of Salt Lick. I think just about everybody in town musta seen that light."

"Everybody except Charlie Jacobs," Len groused.

"Did you see it?" Brenna asked the waitress.

"Oh, yeah," Cindy answered eagerly. "Randy— that's my boyfriend—he was taking me home when we saw it come swoopin' over the town moving real fast. Then it slowed down and finally just stopped over Little Smoky. Randy stopped the car and we watched it for...oh, maybe a full minute before it dipped down and disappeared. Then it came back up, real high, and whizzed off."

"That must have been quite a sight," the trucker told her. "I was driving most of the night and saw lots of meteors, but I sure didn't see anything like that."

Len's craggy face rearranged itself into an even deeper scowl. "You callin' Cindy and me liars, mister?"

The trucker held up his hands. "Of course not. I just meant that I wish I'd been here. I've always wanted to see a UFO."

"Well, I ain't," Len said gruffly, picking up his newspaper again. "But now that I have, I don't appreciate some know-it-all egghead callin' me a liar. What does some astronomer in California know? He wudd'n here—how does he know what I saw?"

"Oh, don't pay no attention to that article, Len," the short-order cook behind the counter called out. "It's all just a government cover-up. They've had proof about UFOs for years, but they're afraid poor, ignorant farm boys like you and me would go nuts if we found out we were being visited by aliens.''

"Well, I don't know about aliens,'' Len grumbled. "But I know what I saw weren't no meteor. And I don't believe it's a coincidence that Longview lost one of its flyboys last night! 'Routine trainin' run,' in a pig's eye! That boy went down chasin' the light we saw—that's what happened, I'll bet you.''

"You're right, Len,'' the cook agreed. "But we'll never know about it. Our government can't balance the budget or get me decent health care, but it loves to spend big bucks keeping secrets.''

"Amen,'' Len replied.

Brenna couldn't help smiling. She'd heard the same sentiment expressed hundreds of times, and it never failed to amaze her. They had no idea how right they were. Of course, it wasn't the whole government; the agency responsible for perpetrating the UFO cover-up was buried deep in the intelligence community—but the conspiracy was very real. Like her father before her, Brenna had spent most of her life trying to prove it.

"I don't suppose any of you would be interested in making a formal report of your sighting,'' she said casually, looking from the waitress to the short-order cook to the voluble Len.

"Whadda ya mean, a report? What kind?'' Len asked, all narrow-eyed suspicion again.

Brenna dug into the soft-sided leather briefcase on the bench beside her. "Just a simple statement of what you witnessed,'' she explained, pulling a half-dozen report kits from one of the pockets. "I run the Center for UFO Research in Washington.''

"Government?" the cook shouted out, more as an accusation than a question.

Brenna laughed. "Not on your life. CUFOR is privately funded from the sales of the books I've written about UFOs. We investigate sightings like the one last night, and our goal is eventually to force the military-intelligence community to admit what it knows about UFOs. I'd really like to add your experiences to the others that we're compiling. Since midnight, we've collected reports from over a hundred people like you who saw unexplained lights in the sky."

"And you think you're gonna explain 'em?" Len asked.

Brenna held his suspicious gaze. "I'd like to, sir."

Len harrumphed and looked away. "I don't know about makin' no report," he growled. "Who's to say you ain't some fancy reporter, wants to put what I saw in the papers?"

"What do you care, Len?" the cook asked. "Nora'd be real impressed seein' your picture in the *National Inquisitor.*"

"I promise you, I'm not a reporter," Brenna said hastily as she slid out of the booth with the kits and placed them on the farmer's table with a reassuring smile. "Why don't I just leave these here? There's information on CUFOR and pamphlets about UFOs that I think you'll find very interesting. The report form is in there, and if you decide to fill it out, there's an envelope you can use to mail it to the center."

"I'll do it," Cindy said, snagging one of the kits off Len's table.

"Wonderful!" Brenna gave her a grateful smile as she returned to her booth.

"Cindy, your order's up! Stop gathering dust and get a move on," the cook yelled to the waitress, who scurried over to the counter to pick up three plates. As she turned, she nearly collided with a man in a baby blue jumpsuit with Arrowpoint Mountain Spring Water emblazoned on the back. She muttered an apology and the deliveryman took a seat at the counter.

"You folks talking about that UFO scare last night?" he asked.

"That's right, mister," Len said belligerently. "You wanna make somethin' of it?"

The man laughed lightly. "Not me. My cousin over in Witsett called and got me out of bed to tell me about the strange lights he saw. He was really spooked. He's not the only one, either. I've been on the road making deliveries for the last four hours, and everywhere I go I meet somebody who saw that light. And a woman over in Clear Lake even got a picture of it."

Len perked up—and so did Brenna. "A picture, you say?" Len asked.

"That's right." The deliveryman pulled a folded newspaper from his back pocket. "It's on the front page of the Clear Lake *Gazette*. A big article, too. It seems that a bunch of folks were out on the lake having a meteor-watching party, when this big spaceship came over the mountain and hovered above them. One of the women grabbed her camera and snapped off a couple of shots."

"Lemme see that," Len demanded, snatching the paper out of the man's hand. "Well, I'll be damned," Len muttered, then fell silent as he read the article.

"Can I clear these away for you, ma'am?" Cindy

had returned and was reaching for the empty plate that was half buried beneath the papers Brenna had been reading.

"Yes, please. I'll take my check now, too." While Cindy totaled her breakfast ticket, Brenna kept an eye on Len and the Clear Lake *Gazette*.

"Bigger than a football field, eh?" he muttered, obviously quoting from the article. "Well, this picture ain't real clear, but I guess it'll prove to those know-it-all scientists that what we saw wudd'n no meteor."

"Could I have a look at that, too?" Brenna asked politely, slipping out of the booth.

"Sure," the deliveryman answered, and Len handed the paper over to Brenna.

She looked at the photo. Len was right. It wasn't a particularly good picture. True believers in the existence of UFOs might herald the photo as proof, but Brenna knew a dozen debunkers who would be happy to denounce the photo as a fraud and make their claim stick.

She turned her attention to the article. More than a dozen solid, respectable citizens were quoted, but the meteor-watching party destroyed the credibility of the sighting. Debunkers would claim it was the result of excessive alcohol consumption, despite the fact that not everyone mentioned in the article had been drinking and the sightings were scattered throughout the valley.

Brenna read the article with a mounting sense of disappointment. The sighting had obviously made believers out of everyone in the little community of Clear Lake, Tennessee, but it wouldn't be enough to convince the rest of the world that UFOs existed. She had read accounts of dozens of similar incidents, and even though the article stated that other pictures had been taken by witnesses who were anxious to have their film developed, she didn't hold out much hope that their photos would be any more conclusive than the grainy one beside the article.

She would go to Clear Lake eventually and get the statements of these witnesses on record, of course, but nothing she read in the *Gazette* made the little resort community a high priority.

Until she caught sight of a name that changed everything.

Christopher Wheeler had been in Clear Lake last night to photograph the Segrid meteor shower. Christopher "Kit" Wheeler, the respected scientist, brave astronaut and charismatic reporter who had a square-jawed, Boy-Scout-next-door persona that was so clean it positively squeaked.

He was the one who had made science sexy with his all-American-hero persona and an uncanny ability to make complicated scientific theories comprehensible to the guy on the street.

If someone as respected as Kit Wheeler came forward claiming to have seen a UFO, he might be believed. If he had taken *pictures* of that UFO, there wasn't a debunker in the country who could claim they were fraudulent. Kit Wheeler was a perfect, unimpeachable witness that not even Elgin Brewster and his supersecret Department of Internal Security could denounce.

Oh, they'd try. Brenna had no doubt about that. If Wheeler had enough courage to report what he had seen, Brewster would do everything in his power to discredit him. As for Wheeler's photos...if DIS got hold of them, the negatives would be destroyed and the pictures would be doctored to make them look like obvious frauds.

Brenna couldn't let that happen. Those pictures and negatives had to be protected and preserved. So did Kit Wheeler. Brenna knew only too well what happened to people Brewster considered a threat. Her father had spent twenty years researching UFOs. Daniel Sullivan had been a respected journalist before the DIS went into action and made him a laughingstock, but her father hadn't backed down. He'd written best-selling books, cultivated intelligence sources and collected data.

And then, finally, fifteen years ago, after a lifetime of hard work, investigation and ridicule, he'd called Brenna at her college dorm to tell her that he finally had proof. He had been investigating reports that a UFO had crashed in Colorado, and this time he'd gotten his hands on hard evidence that the government couldn't possibly deny. His life's work was about to be vindicated and he was happier than Brenna had ever known him to be.

Twenty-four hours later, Brenna was standing on a treacherous mountain road surrounded by a group of solemn rescue workers as her father's mangled, lifeless body was brought up the mountain. A day after that, his car was painstakingly hauled up, too, but the "proof" that had cost Daniel his life had disappeared.

Proof in the form of a set of photographs.

If Kit Wheeler really had taken pictures last night, he was going to find himself in more trouble than he'd ever thought possible. Sooner or later, Colonel Elgin

Brewster's intelligence network would see this newspaper article and the colonel would come scurrying out of the woodwork like an insidious little cockroach, eager to learn what Wheeler was going to do with his pictures.

When that happened, Brenna knew she had to be nearby, no matter what she had to do or say to get close to Wheeler.

"Can anyone give me directions to Clear Lake?" she asked as she tossed the *Gazette* onto the counter.

"Sure can," the deliveryman said. He took a pencil and notepad out of his breast pocket and started drawing a map. "You gonna go UFO hunting over there?"

"Something like that, yes."

"Well if it don't come back, the fishin's real good up at that lake," Len assured her. "There's a bass-fishin' tournament comin' up this weekend—if you hang around long enough, you might catch a big one."

Brenna glanced down at the Clear Lake *Gazette,* but it was Kit Wheeler's square jaw and blue eyes she visualized. "That's what I'm hoping for," she muttered. "A very big one, indeed."

CHAPTER THREE

LONG BEFORE he saw it, Kit heard the vehicle coming up the road. The engine was laboring and the tires were crunching gravel, but it was obviously a four-wheel drive because anything less couldn't have made it this far.

He was on the porch, studying the faxes Sandy had sent, his hair still damp from his shower, and his mind still reeling from the impact of the photographs. When he heard the vehicle, he quickly collected the pictures and tucked them between the folds of one of the newspapers on the cedar table.

That was about all he had time for before the laboring automobile topped the rise. The vehicle, a silver Mountaineer with D.C. license plates, pulled to a stop beside his own Mountaineer. The tinted windows prevented Kit from getting a look at the driver. He stepped to the porch railing and waited with growing discomfort.

Those darkened windows made him nervous. He didn't recognize the vehicle, and he wasn't ready for reporters yet; although he couldn't imagine how any journalist could have learned about the article in the *Gazette* so quickly.

The suspense ended finally when the door opened on the driver's side. A second later, a woman stepped out, slipped the strap of a black briefcase over her shoulder and shut the door.

Kit became instantly aware of his bare feet, his torn blue jeans that were barely blue anymore and his even more faded cropped-off football jersey. He hadn't shaved, and he hadn't combed his hair yet, either. He liked to keep things casual when he was at the cabin, but this get-up was ridiculous—particularly when visitors like this came round.

The woman was gorgeous. No doubt about it. She was tall and slender, with shoulder-length auburn hair, aristocratic features and a complexion like porcelain. She was dressed simply—a plain silk blouse tucked into full-legged gray trousers—but she looked like a million bucks. All class and curves, with everything in just the right proportions.

Kit's libido responded appropriately to the sleek, stylish, beautiful woman—until he reminded himself that his cabin was way too remote for her to be just a lost traveler. She was here for a reason, and he tried to temper his instinctive masculine response with that thought. It would have been easier for him to take a flying leap off the mountain, flap his arms and fly down to the lake.

He hitched one leg up on the railing and sat with his body angled toward his guest, allowing himself to enjoy the view.

Brenna felt the full weight of Kit Wheeler's scrutiny as she stepped out of her Mountaineer and moved around it toward the porch. When she'd first pulled up, she'd cursed the clerk at the Pik-Yur-Pump gas station for sending her on a wild-goose chase. Then she'd taken a closer look at the jeans-clad man on the porch and realized that it *was* Kit Wheeler up there. Sort of. Brenna was accustomed to a slightly different version of the former astronaut.

He rarely did his GNN "Frontiers" segments in a suit coat, favoring sweaters in the winter and crisp, stylish cotton shirts in the other seasons; it was a friendly fashion statement that made him seem like "one of the guys" to men, and the desirable but conservative boy-next-door to women.

It definitely was *not* this bad-boy, sexy-as-hell, just-jumped-out-of-the-shower-and-couldn't-find-a-thing-to-wear hunk standing on the porch, looking at Brenna as though he liked what he saw, too.

For a fleeting instant, Brenna was reminded of the dream she hadn't been allowed to finish last night. She wouldn't be the least bit disappointed if she could go back to it, pull her phantom lover's face into focus and have it turn out to be Kit Wheeler's.

She was going to have to reevaluate her opinion of this squeaky-clean all-American hero. "Good morning, Dr. Wheeler," she called as she approached the porch. "You're not an easy man to find."

"That's one of the perks of having a mountain retreat," he replied with a smile. "I don't get many casual visitors."

"I can understand why. The attendant at the gas station warned me it was a rough ride, but she didn't say *how* rough."

He gestured toward her vehicle. "But you came well-equipped."

"I like to be prepared. I never know where my investigations will take me," she said as she reached the foot of the stairs.

"Investigations? Into what?" he asked suspiciously.

But his question barely registered because Brenna found herself looking up at the flat planes of Wheeler's abdomen beneath that cropped-off jersey. A narrow, tantalizing vee of softly curling hair disappeared into those disreputable blue jeans, and she had to force herself to remember why she'd made the treacherous drive up his mountain.

She dug into her briefcase for a business card. "I'm Brenna Sullivan," she said.

Kit reached down for the card and discovered that the gorgeous creature with the greenest eyes he'd ever seen wasn't a reporter. She was worse. "You're with the Center for UFO Research?" he asked incredulously.

Brenna had seen that skeptical, derisive look a thousand times and she hated it, but she'd stopped apologizing for her profession a long time ago. She nodded her assent, smiling sweetly. "Actually, I'm the *director* of the Center."

"What qualifications do you have to have to get a job like that?"

There was an unmistakable challenge in his gaze, which Brenna met without flinching. "An open, inquisitive mind," she said pointedly. "And a Masters degree in astrophysics from Cal Tech didn't hurt, either."

He nodded slowly. "Nice pedigree," he conceded.

"And I've had all my shots."

He smiled at her joke, and it was enough to take the edge off of "the look." "Welcome to Clear Lake,

Ms. Sullivan. Should I ask what brings you to this neck of the woods?"

"Only if you intend to play hard to get."

He folded his arms across his chest. "I don't know what you mean."

"Oh, please, Dr. Wheeler. Let's not play games." Brenna gestured broadly to their surroundings. "This isn't exactly the media capital of the world, but you have to know that something extraordinary happened in the skies over Tennessee last night."

Kit considered feigning ignorance, until he remembered the stack of newspapers on the table behind him. Unless he could keep her off the porch, she'd know he was lying. "I know there was a meteor shower, and that an air force jet crashed south of here."

"You also know about the flap over the Midwest, don't you?"

Kit's eyebrows went up. "Flap?"

"Multiple sightings of an Unidentified Flying Object."

"I recall reading something about meteors being mistaken for UFOs," he admitted cautiously.

She gave him a look that repeated her "Oh, please" as she reached into her briefcase and extracted a copy of the Clear Lake *Gazette* she'd purchased at the gas station. She held it up with the photograph facing him. "Do you recall reading about this particular UFO sighting?"

"Yes," he replied reluctantly. "But I'm a little surprised that you have. Do you normally read the *Gazette* over your morning coffee?"

"Only when I'm in the neighborhood. I ran across it at a truck stop in Salt Lick and noticed your name."

He fixed her with a hard glare. "Idle gossip travels fast."

Brenna wasn't the least intimidated. She moved up the steps and Kit came to his feet. Brenna still had to look up to meet his eyes. She held his guarded gaze steadily. "Dr. Wheeler, is there any truth to the speculation in this article?"

"I'm afraid I'm not prepared to answer any questions in regard to what I may or may not have seen last night."

"Meaning, you *did* see something."

"I am not prepared to answer—"

"Dr. Wheeler, I am not a fanatic, I'm not a tabloid reporter and I'm not visiting Clear Lake for the Sixteenth Annual Bass-Fishing Tournament," Brenna informed him. "The Center for UFO Research is an organization committed to the serious study of the phenomenon of Unidentified Flying Objects. I've written three meticulously researched, bestselling books on the subject, and I'm considered one of the foremost ufology authorities in the world."

She smiled disarmingly, and Kit suddenly felt his pulse rate quicken as she concluded, "Now, that may not put me in your league as a scientist, but I'm not a lunatic who spends her evenings baying at the moon."

Maybe not, but if she set her mind to it, she could probably turn a man into one, Kit realized. "I didn't mean to suggest that you were, Ms. Sullivan." In fact, he was downright impressed by her eloquence and her credentials. Obviously she wasn't just a garden-variety UFO nut—she was a very intelligent, articulate one. And beautiful—he couldn't ignore that factor, no matter how hard he tried. "If I was rude, I apologize, but I'm still not prepared to discuss what I may or may not have seen."

Brenna cocked her head to one side. "You don't believe that the public has a right to know that last night our air force lost a jet and its pilot in an encounter with a spacecraft of unknown type and origin?"

Kit held back a surge of excitement. That was exactly what he wanted to prove—or disprove. "Do you have any evidence to back up that assertion, Ms. Sullivan?"

Brenna smiled with satisfaction. She'd found Kit Wheeler's Achilles' heel; the man wanted information! Well, it just so happened she had some. "As a matter of fact, I do. And I expect even more within the next few hours."

"What evidence?" he demanded.

"Data collected by my staff in D.C., and reports filed with the Center."

"What data? What kind of reports?" he pressed.

Brenna hesitated. Her goal was a reciprocal exchange of information, not a one-sided disclosure session. "Let's slow down, shall we?" she suggested. "What do I get in exchange for telling you everything I know?"

"What do you want?" he asked with unconcealed suspicion.

"The truth about what you saw last night." Brenna set her briefcase on a chair and tossed her copy of the Clear Lake *Gazette* onto the cedar picnic table.

Right next to the stack of newspapers that hid Kit's fax photos. He held his breath, and fought the urge to snatch them off the table, out of her reach. "Why would what I saw be of any interest to you?"

"Please don't pretend naiveté, Dr. Wheeler. You're one of the most respected media personalities in the world. You have a background in aeronautics and astrophysics that will make it impossible for anyone to claim that you mistook a meteor or any other type of *known* aerial phenomenon for a UFO. And on top of all that, you have a television forum that reaches millions of viewers every day."

She took a step toward him. "In other words, you have the potential to be the most convincing eyewitness ever to sight a UFO—particularly if you have pictures to support your claim."

"I'm not claiming anything, Ms. Sullivan," Kit reminded her. "You are."

She smiled wryly. "Good point. Round one goes to Dr. Wheeler."

Kit did his best not to respond to her dry wit, but it wasn't easy. "There won't be a round two, Ms. Sullivan. I have no intention of making a statement to you or anyone else."

"Why not?" she challenged.

"Because I don't believe that little silver-skinned humanoids with big eyes and no mouths are paying social calls to Earth."

"You think all UFOs are terrestrial in origin or can be explained away as atmospheric phenomena?"

"That's right."

She tilted her head to one side and those emerald-colored eyes seemed to bore right into him. "Then you must be very confused by what you experienced last night.''

Kit sucked in a deep breath. It was a second before he said softly, "I was wrong. There was a round two, and you just won it.''

She had the good grace not to gloat. "So you admit you saw something.''

He frowned and recited, "I am not prepared to make a statement at this time.''

Brenna sighed with frustration and turned to her briefcase. His repeated "no comments" weren't getting them anywhere.

Every one of her feminine senses was vividly aware that Wheeler was watching her as she unzipped her briefcase and thumbed through her files. "Tell me something, Dr. Wheeler,'' she said, taking a new tack. "Has anyone else been here this morning to make inquiries about that article?''

"No, you're the first. Congratulations.''

That brought a ghost of a smile to her lips as she removed the file she wanted from her briefcase. "Here.''

"What's this?'' Kit asked, reaching for the thick sheath of papers she held out to him.

"Copies of just a few of the reports that have been filed with CUFOR since midnight. Most of them came off of the UFONet.''

Kit frowned. "A UFO computer network?'' he questioned.

"Yes, I travel with a portable computer setup, and my staff has been downloading these reports to me all night long. So far there have been over a hundred sightings reported on the UFONet alone. I haven't studied all of those—'' she gestured to the file he was holding ''—but I think you'll be surprised when you read them. There's one particularly detailed report made by a park ranger who actually witnessed the crash.''

Kit suddenly felt as though he was holding something priceless in his hands—something that might break if he so much as breathed too hard. He stepped to the table, sat and flipped open the file. ''I want to talk to that ranger,'' he said more to himself than his visitor as he began thumbing quickly through the reports.

''So do I,'' Brenna replied. ''And I also want to speak with the other pilot who was on that so-called routine training run. Not that I'll be able to. The air force has a habit of transferring personnel who witness unusual phenomena. Sometimes they even manage to 'misplace' the transfer paperwork. He'll probably be stationed in Germany by the weekend.''

Kit looked up from the documents. ''Are these reports the only proof you have?''

Brenna moved her briefcase onto the floor and sat across from him. ''No.''

''What else is there?''

''Why?'' she asked. ''Are you thinking of conducting your own investigation? Are you hoping to find a safe, logical explanation for what you saw last night? Something that doesn't challenge the laws of physics or your belief in an ordered universe?''

Kit met her penetrating gaze with equal intensity in his own eyes and voice. ''I want to find the truth. Whatever it is.''

''Then let me help you.''

Kit leaned back in his chair, studying the woman on the other side of the table. He ignored her beauty and completely disregarded what her smile did to his pulse. He would *not* make a decision based on attraction. The plain truth was, the last thing he needed was to have his name connected with what his former NASA colleagues called the "UFO lunatic fringe."

Granted, Brenna Sullivan didn't seem like a fanatic, and certainly Kit knew that not all people who believed in UFOs were nuts. Many were sober, well-meaning, upstanding—albeit misguided—citizens. At least, that's what he'd believed until last night. Now that he, himself, had seen something he couldn't explain, Kit had become one of those "misguided" people he'd always dismissed with a touch of arrogant disdain. He didn't like it one bit, either.

But there was a larger issue to consider. Ms. Sullivan wasn't just a UFO true believer, she was an investigator. Her organization had access to information that might be valuable to Kit's own search for the truth, and she seemed inclined to share what she knew—if Kit would share what he knew. She had baited a hook, cast it into the water and now she was waiting to see if he'd bite.

What was that joke she'd made about not being here for the fishing tournament? Bull. She was fishing, all right, and she was damn good at it.

"What do I get out of this if I tell you what I saw?" Kit was aware that his need to understand what he'd seen was overriding his better judgment.

"Access to everything my investigators at CUFOR are working on," she replied. "I'll tell you everything we know about this incident and I'll provide you with declassified government documents on other sightings that you can use as background for your story." She leaned forward, folding her arms on the table. "And I'll do everything I can to guide you through the minefield you're about to enter. You're in for a rough ride, Dr. Wheeler. You have no idea how rough."

"Oh, I think I do," he replied.

Brenna shook her head. "No, you don't. Right now you're worried about tabloid reporters and being made to look foolish in front of your friends and colleagues. Am I right?"

Kit squared his shoulders. "Wouldn't you be, if you were in my position?"

"Maybe," she conceded. "But you're only looking at the tip of the iceberg. Let me give you a piece of advice. Forget about what your colleagues are going to think and put those pictures on the air immediately."

"I haven't admitted to taking any pictures," Kit reminded her.

Brenna suppressed an exasperated sigh. "All right, *hypothetically speaking,* let's pretend that you did take pictures."

"All right. Hypothetically speaking, there might be pictures." He leaned forward, mirroring her position, and the air between them almost vibrated with the intensity of the connection they made. "Why should I air these mythical photographs before I conduct an investigation?"

"By making them public immediately, you'll be forcing the military to deal with the sensation the pictures will create. You'll have to defend their authenticity and handle attacks on your character and credibility, but the pictures and the report of your sighting will be public knowledge.''

"And if I wait to air them?''

"You may be regarded as a threat that has to be silenced.''

Kit leaned back heavily. "A threat? Isn't that a little melodramatic?''

"I don't think so,'' she replied evenly. "Right now, the air force is scrambling to find a nice, safe, logical explanation for that jet crash. If no one from a major media source draws a connection between the crash and the UFO sightings, the crash will be forgotten and the flap will become tabloid fodder for the rest of the country to chuckle over. Both stories will die a natural death in a matter of days.''

Brenna tapped the copy of the *Gazette* in front of her. "But this article makes you a threat, Dr. Wheeler. Make no mistake about it. If you don't go public with those pictures before the military finds out about them, they'll come after you in ways you can't even imagine.''

Kit's frown evolved into a deep scowl. "Do you know how paranoid that sounds, Ms. Sullivan?''

"Of course. But as the saying goes, 'Just because you're paranoid, it doesn't mean they're not out to get you.'''

"I think I've heard enough, Ms. Sullivan,'' he said tersely, coming to his feet. "If you're insinuating that there's some kind of government-sanctioned conspiracy to cover up the existence of UFOs, you can put your reports back in your briefcase and toddle off down the mountain. I don't buy it.''

Brenna knew she'd gone too far, but she had to

make him understand what was at stake. She stood and faced him squarely.

"Dr. Wheeler, whether you want to believe it or not, you're in trouble. As soon as you start investigating, you'll find out what it's like to butt your head against a wall of lies, denials and half-truths. In a few days, when you realize that you're being followed, you'll tell yourself that it's only your imagination, but you won't be able to convince yourself of that for long. They'll start chipping away at your sterling reputation with an ugly smear campaign, followed by bribes and finally threats. By the time they're done, you'll understand paranoia up close and personal."

She zipped her briefcase and slung it over her shoulder. "Then things will get really ugly. When that happens, give me a call. You've got my card." She whirled and started across the porch.

"Wait a minute," Kit demanded, coming around the table.

She stopped and turned slowly. "Why?"

Kit hesitated. Why, indeed? He didn't want anything to do with UFOs or government conspiracies, because he didn't believe in either. But when he reached down to pick up the file she'd given him, he caught another glimpse of the newspaper headlines. The boldest one said, Air Force Pilot Dies In Jet Crash. A smaller one read, Meteor Shower Sparks Rash Of UFO Sightings.

Whether he wanted to admit it or not, Kit already believed that the air force was lying about what really happened last night. If that wasn't a cover-up, what was?

It was just barely possible that Brenna Sullivan's

paranoia wasn't as unfounded as Kit wanted to believe. And it was more than possible that he needed help. Her help.

Brenna waited expectantly, watching the emotions that played across Wheeler's handsome face. He was trying to decide whether or not to trust her, and the battle raging inside him was fierce.

She knew she'd won even before he dropped the file folder and reached across the table to pick up a stack of newspapers.

When he finally looked at her, Brenna read grim resignation in his eyes.

"Can I count on confidentiality?" he asked her.

"Of course. Dr. Wheeler, my only motive for being here is a desire to see that the public learns the truth. You can make that happen. What good could come from betraying you?"

"None," he said succinctly. "And you'll assist my investigation?"

Brenna could hear her heart pounding in her ears. "In every way possible. I'll put the full resources of the Center for UFO Research at your disposal."

Praying that he wasn't making the worst mistake of his life, Kit flipped open the Knoxville *Journal,* extracted the full set of fax photos from between its folds and held them out to her. "Then look at these, Ms. Sullivan, and we'll talk some more."

Startled, Brenna hesitated a fraction of a second before reaching for the faxes, not even aware that she was holding her breath. She hadn't imagined that Wheeler had already developed them or that there would be so many.

Her briefcase slid onto the floor and she went

through the pictures one by one, stunned, fascinated and exhilarated at the same time. The emotions came almost too fast to identify, but one finally burst to the surface, drowning out the others.

That emotion was fear, because the pictures were gold. Sharp, clear, undeniable gold.

They were also terrifying, because Brenna knew that Elgin Brewster had killed at least once to get his hands on pictures that weren't nearly as startling as these.

CHAPTER FOUR

"MY, GOD..." Brenna slipped into the chair beside her as she finished her first pass through the pictures, having to remind herself to breathe.

"Have you seen anything like that before?" Wheeler was asking her. The question barely registered, and Brenna wasn't even sure it was the first time he'd asked it. "Are there reports of other people having seen it? What do you know about this thing? Ms. Sullivan? Ms. Sullivan!"

Brenna's gaze darted to Wheeler, then back at the pictures. She wasn't trying to be uncommunicative, she just didn't know what to say. His pictures were incredible, and Brenna's astonishment warred with an overwhelming urge to stress again how much danger he was going to be in if he didn't air them immediately.

The problem was, of course, that he'd never believe her. He'd already stated uncategorically that he didn't subscribe to UFO conspiracy theories. If she unloaded hers on him, he'd snatch the pictures out of her hands and order her off his mountain. The thread of trust between them was gossamer thin. Brenna couldn't risk breaking it. Whether he knew it or not, Wheeler needed her.

"I'm sorry," she finally managed to get out.

"These are the most amazing pictures I've ever seen. They're just...stunning."

"But do you know what it is?" he asked her.

Brenna made a concerted effort to pull herself together as she extracted a brochure from her briefcase. "It's a Type Six craft," she told him, opening the brochure to a graphic chart of ten basic UFO classifications—from saucer shapes to cigar shapes, to chevrons like the one in his pictures.

Wheeler took the brochure. "Okay, it's a Type Six. So what? Where does it come from?"

"I have no idea."

Wheeler's scowl deepened and Brenna realized that he was already regretting his impulsive decision to confide in her. "Well, who else has seen it?" he asked irritably. "Before last night, I mean?"

"This chevron-shaped craft is relatively new—sightings of it go back less than a decade. I can show you any number of sighting reports, but as to whether or not it's the *exact* craft that other people have seen, I have no idea."

"Well, what the hell do you know?" he snapped. "I thought you said you could help me."

Brenna tried not to take his anger personally. She understood that he'd been affected deeply by his encounter last night, and she felt a strong surge of sympathy. If her own world had been turned upside down as abruptly as his had, her fuse would have been short, too. "I know that you should take my advice and air these pictures immediately," she counseled him.

"I won't do that," he said tersely.

"I know. And you'll live to regret it," she predicted, then continued quickly with, "But since you don't believe that, let's move on. Where are the originals and the negatives?"

"In a safe place," Kit answered brusquely.

"Where?"

"A photo lab in D.C."

"Which one?" she pressed.

"A *safe* one."

Brenna cocked her head to one side. "'Safe' is a relative concept, Dr. Wheeler. Whether you want to believe it or not, a lot of people will be trying to get their hands on those pictures."

"Including you," he told her.

So that was the way it was going to be. "I wasn't thinking of me specifically," she said evenly. Wheeler regretted his decision to confide in her, and he was going to take his irritation with himself and the situation in general out on her. His distrust was going to make for an uneasy partnership, but Brenna could take the heat. "But yes, I want very much to get my hands on the originals—to isolate and protect them. If you don't have a secure, documented chain of custody in place, you'll be giving debunkers enough ammunition to successfully dismiss them as frauds."

"Only one person has access to the negatives, and he understands the importance of security," Kit said with a finality that closed the subject.

"All right," she conceded reluctantly. "The location of the pictures will be your secret until you're ready to go public."

"Gee, thanks," he muttered with a touch of sarcasm. "Now it's your turn. I want to see everything you've got on last night's...flap."

He used the word with such obvious hesitancy that Brenna had to smile. "Don't worry, Doc, you'll get the hang of it."

"I don't want the hang of it, I want information."

"And I'll deliver what I promised." Brenna glanced at her watch. "Why don't I brief you on the way to the crash site?"

That seemed to set him back a bit. "Now?"

Brenna nodded. "If we're both going to investigate, we might as well do it together, and we don't have time to waste. The government has had a special UFO recovery team down at the site since two this morning."

"Recovering what? That thing?" Kit asked with a nod toward the pictures.

Brenna was surprised and pleased. For someone who didn't believe in UFOs, he'd been astonishingly broad-minded if he'd allowed himself to consider that particular option. "We don't think so. The forest ranger, Dale Winston, reported what he called a near air collision between the jet and the UFO, but only the F-16 crashed."

"Then what's the recovery team recovering?" he asked.

"Anything that contradicts the military's version of what happened last night." *Or anyone,* she added silently. "What's it going to be, Dr. Wheeler? Do we work together, or not?"

Brenna watched as Kit reluctantly came to a decision. "Call me Kit," he suggested finally. "If we're going to be partners, we might as well be a little less formal."

Brenna would have been heartened by the invitation if he hadn't looked as though he'd just swallowed a bug. She answered his frown with a cheery smile. "Thank you, Kit. If you worked at it, do you think you could be a little less enthusiastic?"

He glared at her. "I have to change clothes. It won't take me a minute." He moved around the table and almost made it to the door, when he stopped suddenly. His gaze darted from Brenna to the pictures lying next to her briefcase.

It wasn't hard to read his thoughts. "That's okay, Kit," she said wryly, picking up the fax photos and holding them out to him. "I wouldn't trust me alone with them, either."

He took them and stood there a second longer, studying her with a puzzled expression on his face. Then he muttered a hasty "Thanks," and disappeared into the cabin.

Brenna didn't waste any time trying to interpret his behavior. It didn't matter whether Wheeler liked her or not. He'd agreed to a collaboration and that's all that counted.

Putting his temporary absence to good use, she gathered the UFO reports she'd shown him, stuffed them into her briefcase and retrieved her cellular phone from the side pocket as she hurried down the stairs to her car. Using her own phone was a necessary precaution. Her lines were scrambled so nobody could listen in.

When she punched in the number at the Center, Randall answered.

"Well, it's about time," Brenna said, breathing a sigh of relief. "I've been calling all morning and getting the machine. What's going on up there? Why was everybody out of the office?"

"Because this has been an unbelievable day," Randall replied. "Claudia got a lead on the possibility that the Knoxville airport picked up the UFO on radar. She's at a meeting with her FAA contact right now."

"That's wonderful. Make some calls to the airport directly. See if you can find anyone who was in the tower last night who'd be willing to talk to me," Brenna suggested as she opened the driver's door and dumped her briefcase onto the seat.

"Will do," he assured her. "And the next item of business... You'll be happy to know that your Pentagon friend finally called back. He said he had information, but he wouldn't give it to me over the phone. That's where I've been—I had to meet him on the Mall."

Brenna was more amused than surprised. Most of the contacts she had cultivated in the intelligence community demanded covert meetings, a guarantee of anonymity, and occasionally they even required the use of silly passwords. Sometimes their paranoia was justified, sometimes it was just for show.

Her "Pentagon friend," was on the flamboyant side, but his information was usually reliable. He was one of more than a dozen sources Brenna had called last night as soon as she had gotten on the road to Tennessee. "What did he have for us?" she asked Randall.

Brenna could almost hear her colleague smiling.

"You're gonna love it," Randall replied. "NORAD went on Flash Alert at eleven-fifty last night when something they never did identify tripped the fence over the continental U.S."

Brenna smiled, too. "Well, that would certainly be in keeping with everything else we've been able to piece together. Have you verified it from another source?"

"Not yet. I just walked in the door, but I'll get right on it. What's happening down there? Are you at the ranger station yet?"

"No. I had to take a little side trip."

"Why? Bren, what could be more important than proving what caused that crash?"

Brenna pulled the release lever on the rear cargo hatch, then moved around the Mountaineer to the passenger side as she gave Randall a shorthand version of what had just transpired.

"Holy cow!" Randall exclaimed softly. "Are you serious? Kit Wheeler, the former astronaut?"

"None other than. He took pictures of a Type Six craft, but he won't go public with them until he's conducted his own investigation. Fortunately, he's agreed to let us help him."

"Bren, that's fantastic! Was he hard to win over?"

Brenna remembered that infuriating sour-milk look on Kit's face when he read her business card. "So-so. He thinks I'm a nutcase."

"He doesn't believe in UFOs?"

Brenna laughed shortly as she stooped to disconnect the computer/printer/fax module that sat on the front seat. "Are you kidding? He thinks 'out there' is a baseball term meaning center field."

"Then why is he cooperating?"

"Because what he saw last night was so far beyond his level of comprehension that he doesn't know which way is up. Whether he likes it or not, he needs someone with my background to help him make sense of it."

"Correct me if I'm wrong, but it sounds as though you don't think too highly of him."

"It's hard to get all warm and fuzzy with someone who thinks you're a loony tune."

Randall must have heard something suspicious in her voice because he got very serious. "Bren, are you okay? Did he do something that got under your skin?"

Brenna flashed back on the sizzle of attraction that had flared briefly between her and Wheeler. It hadn't lasted long, and the distrust that had replaced it stung a lot deeper than it should have. "Don't be silly," she chided, shrugging off his concerns and her own disappointment. "You know me. I've got a hide like a rhinoceros."

"No, you don't," Randall said softly. "You just like to pretend you do."

Her friend knew her too well. "Don't let Wheeler hear you say that. I don't want to give him any more ammunition against me than he's already got."

"What ammunition?"

"Our profession. Haven't you heard? There's no such thing as a UFO."

Randall laughed. "My money's on you, kid. You'll make a believer out of him before the sun goes down. Now, what can I do to help from up here?"

Brenna circled to the tailgate of the vehicle. "I'm

going to make the entire CUFOR database available to him, but I have no idea what kind of computer setup he has here at his cabin. Go ahead and fax me the Net report and a statistical breakdown..." As she rattled off a list of documents she wanted, she lifted the hatch and began reorganizing the contents of the cargo area. It wasn't easy with only one hand free.

"What about the M.I.B. file?" Randall asked her.

Brenna shook her head. "No, he's not ready for the Men In Black yet," she replied. "He utterly rejects all possibility of a conspiracy."

"Only because you got to him before Brewster did," Randall said. "He'll change his tune in a few days."

"I know, but until then, I have to be very careful what I say to him or he'll tell me to get lost."

"You know, Bren, Wheeler's decision not to go public for a while could work to our favor," Randall said with a speculative note in his voice.

"How so?"

"Well, we know that the air force is going to cover up any connection between the flap and the crash of that jet. The more lies they tell, the bigger the cover-up will be."

"And the bigger the cover-up, the bigger the scandal—which might finally give Senator Hanson enough ammunition to demand a Senate investigation into Brewster's covert UFO operations," Brenna finished for him. "That's a very good point, Randall, but for Wheeler's sake, I'd still rather that he went public immediately. He'd be a whole lot safer—and so would his pictures."

"Speaking of which, how do you know they're going to be everything he claims? Where is he having them developed?"

"They're already done. I've seen fax photos of them, Randall. I wasn't guessing about what they depict. They're the most amazing UFO pictures that have ever been taken. But he won't tell me where the originals and negatives are. All I know is that they're at a photo lab in D.C."

"Not the TV station?"

"Apparently not." Brenna repeated Kit's exact words.

"Hmm... You know, Bren, there are a lot of private labs that do government contract work requiring high-security measures. Maybe Wheeler has a connection to one of those. That would explain why he's so sure they're safe. You want me to do some checking?"

Brenna didn't have long to think it over because Kit came sauntering onto the porch, pulling closed the big wooden door behind him. And this Kit Wheeler was more in line with what Brenna had expected from him in the first place. He was wearing tan trousers and a white cotton shirt with a short, stand-up collar and a tiny brown pinstripe running through it. His hair was combed, his square jaw was clean shaven. He had returned to his all-American-hero persona.

So why did Brenna still find him every bit as sexy as he'd seemed in his worn-in-all-the-right-places blue jeans and cropped-off jersey? She was going to have to get over this physical infatuation, and do it quickly, before she made a fool of herself over a man who didn't think her elevator went all the way to the top.

But damn it, he *was* sexy.

"Brenna? Bren, are you there?"

"Uh, yeah, Randall, sorry. I've got to run." Kit was looking at her questioningly, obviously wondering who she was talking to.

"What about the photo labs?"

"Do whatever you think best," she advised absently. "I'll check in later."

"Okay. Take care of yourself, boss."

"Will do."

Brenna snapped the phone closed and set it on the roof of the car. Having two hands free made her attempt to reorganize the cargo area a lot more effective. She shifted her suitcase and managed to clear the space she needed.

"What are you doing?" Kit asked as he came down the steps.

"Making room for you," she replied. "Grab that module out of the front seat, would you?"

He stopped by the open passenger door, his eyebrows rose inquisitively. "We're taking your Mountaineer?"

Brenna straightened and looked at him over the roof of the all-terrain vehicle. "You have something against women drivers?"

"Of course not. I just didn't remember that we had agreed you'd make all the decisions for both of us."

Brenna conceded the point to him. "Sorry, I wasn't trying to be pushy, but I am the one with all the equipment. If you'd rather transfer it to your Mountaineer..."

She left the offer hanging while Kit ducked his head into the front passenger area and looked over the back of the seat into the crowded cargo bay. "What is all this stuff?" he asked.

She pointed to each item as she ticked it off. "Report kits, evidence envelopes...extra forms, video equipment, brochures. A Geiger counter, magnetometer, field analysis lab equipment—" she flashed a wry grin at him "—my luggage...an emergency road kit and my survival kit. Among other things."

Kit stared at the mountain of scientific equipment. "All this for hunting UFOs?"

"Well, I don't really need the suitcase, but a change of clothes and a toothbrush comes in handy from time to time."

He grinned. "I can see that it would. What's the difference between an emergency road kit and a survival kit?"

"They cover entirely different kinds of emergencies," she said cryptically. "Now. Do you want to transfer this—"

"No, thanks," he said, cutting her off. "We'll take your Mountaineer." Being very careful, he picked up Brenna's portable computer unit, ferried it to the cargo bay and set it into the space she had cleared.

"Who were you on the phone to?" he asked as she began reconnecting all the ports on the computer.

"My office," she replied. "I gave my assistant, Randall Parrish, a list of documents I want him to send down for you."

"You didn't tell him about my pictures, did you?" Kit asked, concerned.

"Of course I did." She hurried on before he could start yelling. "Don't worry, I trust Randall completely. He would never do anything without my approval. Your secret is safe with us.''

"It had better be.''

Brenna ignored the implied threat and finished bringing her computer back on-line. "Okay, that's it. We'd better get moving.'' She slammed the hatch, retrieved her phone from the roof and started for the driver's seat.

"Follow the Yellow Brick Road,'' Kit muttered as he took his place riding shotgun.

As BRENNA NAVIGATED the snakelike road out of the valley, she briefed Kit on everything her organization knew about the sightings, including Randall's newest information on the NORAD Flash Alert and the lead they had on the Knoxville airport. She also gave him background on a recent spate of similar sightings that had been occurring around other military bases during the last few months.

"An extended period of intense activity over a wide area like this is called a wave, by the way,'' she informed him. They had just reached the highway and the driving was a little easier now.

"Occurring around military bases?''

Brenna nodded. "Just like last night.''

"That's interesting,'' he said thoughtfully.

"You think so?'' Brenna cast a quick glance at him. "What do you make of it?''

"Assuming that the sightings are credible and people are really seeing some type of aircraft, the most logical conclusion is that the government is doing widespread testing of something new.''

"Like the thing in your photographs?'' Brenna

asked, letting her skepticism show. "Is our technology really that advanced?"

Kit shifted in his seat. He couldn't decide which was making him more uncomfortable—this conversation, or the subtle, sexy scent of Brenna's perfume. "No. I don't think our technology is that advanced. But there's got to be a reason for the sightings."

"Preferably one that doesn't include UFOs?"

"That would make my life a lot simpler," he replied unapologetically. "Just don't tell me the sightings are caused by 'flesh-eating lizard aliens from planet Xenon' unless you can show me some proof."

"By proof, you mean…what?" Brenna asked. "A piece of UFO wreckage made from materials unknown on planet Earth? A joint announcement made by the leaders of the free world? The body of a space alien?" She took her eyes off the road long enough to pin him with a hard glare. "Or how about thirty photographs of stunning quality taken by a man whose integrity is beyond question? Would that convince you?"

Kit had never been backed into a corner quite so neatly in his life, and it infuriated him. "If you're going to drive, watch the road," he growled.

"Sorry." They both knew she wasn't apologizing for her driving. Brenna sighed deeply. "Look, Kit, I understand how difficult this is for you. You want a simple answer to a very direct question—What was that thing you photographed last night? But the sad truth is, you may never know what it was, where it came from, who made it or how it could do the seemingly impossible things it did. The best you may be able to hope for is to learn what it *wasn't*."

"That's not good enough."

"Too bad. I've been at this most of my life, and sometimes partial answers are all you get."

"Then why do it at all?" he challenged.

A very old, but still painful, memory flashed into Brenna's mind, and she saw the mangled wreckage of her father's car being hauled out of a mountain ravine as clearly as if it had happened yesterday. "I have my reasons," she said quietly.

Kit waited for her to elaborate, but she didn't. Instead, Brenna cocked her head in the direction of her briefcase behind her seat. "If you really want answers, why don't you start by reading those UFONet reports I showed you back at the cabin? They're in my briefcase."

"All right." Kit twisted until he could reach it.

"Taken as a whole, they should give you an undistorted view of what happened last night," she went on. "Would you mind reading them aloud? I haven't had time to study them myself. I was driving all night."

"Sure."

Kit retrieved the forms and started reading the first narrative account with all the sincerity of an adult reading a bedtime fairy tale to a toddler, but by the time he'd finished the first few reports, his tone had changed. Brenna's staff had downloaded only the most credible eyewitness accounts to her computer, so the statements Kit was reading forced him to sit up and take notice.

One had been filed by a physics professor from the University of Tennessee at Knoxville. Another had been signed by the teacher and all nine members of her astronomy class at a private high school in Lexington, Kentucky. Yet another report had been made by a state patrolman in Georgia.

Every report Kit read was filed by a sober, thoughtful, respectable citizen, and most of them were just as overwhelmed and confused by what they'd seen as Kit had been.

After he read the first two dozen, Kit had to stop. He needed a chance to assimilate what he was reading.

"Spooky, isn't it?" Brenna asked. "Dozens of people with absolutely nothing in common, scattered across a half-dozen states, witness the same phenomenon at almost exactly the same time.... Bright lights that streak across the sky, stop without warning and change direction in a fashion that defies all known laws of aerodynamics...."

"If you're asking whether I have an explanation for it, the answer is no," Kit said irritably.

Brenna's patience had started wearing thin. She was getting tired of being snapped at. It wasn't *her* fault he had seen a UFO. "My question was rhetorical," she replied as sweetly as she could manage.

"But none of this—" he waved the reports in the air between them "—proves anything."

"They do add credibility to your sighting," she reminded him.

"Not necessarily," Kit said, shuffling through the reports. "Granted, the professor from Knoxville, the woman from Ashville and several others described a huge ball of white light. That's an appropriate depiction of what I saw when it was some distance away, but most of these describe a small, saucer-shaped UFO with a band of colored lights around it. That can't possibly be the craft I photographed, which means that less than half of these reports provide any kind of support for the Clear Lake sighting. In fact, these reports actually confuse the issue."

"Unless we can prove that there were two separate UFOs up there last night," Brenna countered.

"Whoa! Hold those horses one damn minute! I'm having trouble accepting the existence of the thing I saw with my own eyes. Don't expect me to buy into a second one," he advised her.

"I don't expect anything, Kit. We'll collect the data and see what conclusions we can draw from it."

"Fine. But the conclusion won't have anything to do with *two* UFOs. I guarantee it!"

"Fine."

His pronouncement put an end to conversation.

Thirty—mostly silent—minutes later, they reached the turn-off to the Lion's Head ranger station. A knot of military and civilian vehicles congested the intersection, and Brenna slowed the Mountaineer to a crawl, inching along behind the others who were headed for the ranger station.

Dense forest closed in on them as soon as they turned onto the winding service road. The pace picked up, and nearly a mile later they came around a bend and discovered a military roadblock, complete with barricades and armed guards.

Beyond the roadblock, near the crest of a ridge, Kit could see the log-and-stone ranger station as well as the phalanx of vehicles that surrounded it, but joining them looked impossible. The sentries at the barricade were turning back more cars than they were admitting.

"Now what?" Kit asked as Brenna stopped the

Mountaineer at the end of the queue of vehicles. "Any idea how we're going to get past that?"

"This? Oh, this is only the baby roadblock. It'll be a piece of cake. Have you got your press credentials?"

"Uh, yeah." The car rolled up another notch as Kit retrieved his wallet from his back pocket. "Right here. What are you going to do?"

"What I usually do. Improvise."

"Could you be a little more specific, please? This may not be politically correct, but if I can't be in control of a situation, I'd at least like to have a clue about what the hell's going on."

"Sorry. Having a partner takes some getting used to."

"Just tell me what you're going to do with my press credentials," he said as he handed over the wallet.

Brenna pointed to a cluster of vehicles that were barely visible on the far side of the ranger station. "See those vans in the clearing a little beyond the parking area?"

Kit squinted. "Yeah."

"See what's on top of those vans?"

He grinned. She was right—it was going to be easy. "Okay. I get it." He looked at her. "Why do I have the feeling that you've done all this before?"

"Because I have. Many times." Thick, smoky air gushed into the Mountaineer when Brenna rolled down her window, and Kit confined himself to shallow breaths until they reached the head of the line.

"'Afternoon, Private." Brenna offered a smile that reflected respect and professional reserve toward the soldier who stepped to her window.

"I'm afraid you'll have to turn back, ma'am," the stern-faced young man told her. "This is a restricted area. Military and emergency vehicles only."

"And media, as well, I believe," she said pleasantly, using Kit's ID card to gesture toward the cluster of television vans that were equipped with satellite dishes and antennae. "This is Dr. Christopher Wheeler, with the Global News Network. We're to meet a crew from the Atlanta bureau at the Lion's Head ranger station. Would you happen to know if his team has arrived yet?"

Brenna held up Kit's identification for the private to read, but he barely looked at it. Instead, he was focused on the face of the celebrity in the passenger seat. "It's a pleasure to meet you, Captain Wheeler," the soldier said respectfully.

"Thank you, Private, but it's just plain Kit Wheeler now," he replied.

"Yes, sir, Mr. Wheeler."

Kit raised his eyebrows. "The GNN crew?" he prompted.

"Oh, yes, sir. They're here, sir. The GNN van came through this morning just after I assumed my duty station. You can go ahead and join them."

"Thank you, Private." Brenna put the car in gear and edged between the barricades.

Kit looked at her in astonishment. "How did you know that GNN was sending a crew up from Atlanta?"

Brenna flashed him a grin as she returned his ID. "I didn't. Some days I just get lucky. Keep an eye out for that GNN news van, will you? As long as they're here, we should make use of them. I'd like to see all the footage they've shot this morning."

"Why?"

"Because I want to know everything the military has said." *And who said it,* she added silently.

"I'm sure that can be arranged," Kit replied, a frown creasing his forehead. "Listen, Brenna, I haven't discussed my investigation with my boss in Washington yet, and I don't plan to until I have a better idea of what we're dealing with. Obviously, I'd rather no one knew why I'm here."

Brenna looked at him with one raised eyebrow. "Oh? Just how do you expect to ask questions about last night's flap without mentioning UFOs?"

"I'm here to interview Dale Winston. If he wants to bring flying saucers into his story, that's up to him. I don't know exactly how a UFO investigator like you operates, but in this instance you're keeping a low profile. Understood?"

Brenna didn't take kindly to being ordered around, but she had agreed to play by Kit's rules. "Don't worry, Kit, I won't say anything that might damage your reputation or call anyone's attention to the questionable company you've started keeping," she promised. "But how are you going to explain your presence?"

Good question. "I don't know. I guess I'll do what you usually do." He flashed her a grin so smug that she wanted to slap it off his face. "I'll improvise."

CHAPTER FIVE

"WELL, as I live an' breathe, if it isn't the eminent Dr. Christopher Wheeler, golden boy of the Global News Network." Janine Tucker's roots in the Deep South never showed when the attractive field reporter was on camera, but off camera was a different story. Particularly when there was a man around. The moment she spotted Kit navigating the maze of vehicles in the makeshift parking lot, her Southern-belle gene surged from recessive to dominant and the accent the broadcaster had worked so hard to lose came back at full strength.

That was the first thing Kit had learned about the ambitious newswoman when he met her shortly after she joined the GNN team three years ago, and it still held true.

"Hello, Janine. It's good to see you again," Kit said, taking the effusive greeting, her come-hither body language and a lingering kiss on the cheek in stride. "Jan, this is Brenna Sullivan. Brenna, meet Janine Tucker, one of the rising stars of the Atlanta news bureau."

The two women greeted each other with a polite handshake, but by not clarifying his relationship with Brenna, Kit had guaranteed a certain amount of speculation. Janine was a very territorial lady, even when she was defending something that wasn't hers and never had been.

"Who's doing camera for you today, Jan?" Kit asked, hoping to forestall any questions the reporter might throw at him.

They were standing next to the white GNN van with the side cargo door wide open, but there was no one inside the equipment bay. "Stu Clendennan," Janine replied. "He's off somewhere trying to find something interesting to film. We've been here all day, and all we've got to show for it are a couple of deadly dull press conferences. So what brings you to this colossal waste of time?"

Kit coughed and waved his hand at the smoke-heavy air in front of his face. "Would you believe I was just out for a breath of fresh air?"

Janine apparently caught the scent of a story because she barely cracked a smile. "Ha, ha, funny. No kidding, Kit. What are you doing here? Did you know the pilot who crashed?" Her seductive drawl had vanished completely.

Kit shook his head. "I doubt it. Have they released his name yet?"

"No." Janine was frowning now. "Is there something the military isn't telling us about this accident?"

"I'm not even sure what the military has said," Kit replied evasively. "Have they let you onto the crash site?"

She regarded him suspiciously, but answered anyway. "Not yet, but that's why all the news crews are still hanging around, twiddling our collective thumbs. The military has agreed to take us back to the site so we can get pictures right after this next press conference.''

"Which will be when?" Kit asked.

"One o'clock." Janine checked her watch. "About forty minutes from now."

Kit didn't know whether to be relieved or disappointed. If the military was letting cameras in, it meant there was nothing to see but the wreckage of a downed F-16, not something experimental and not a UFO. All of which meant he didn't have a prayer of finding physical evidence to support his own sighting.

"Who's been doing the talking for the military?" Brenna asked, drawing Kit away from his thoughts. He scowled at her, but she ignored him.

Janine didn't look too pleased about being questioned by Brenna, either. She gave Brenna a sharp, inquisitive look, but answered, "A Longview public affairs officer, Lieutenant Latimore, has handled all the briefings, but General Phillip Avery is supposed to be speaking at the next press conference."

"Is there any chance that we could get a look at the footage from those earlier briefings?" Brenna asked.

Janine gave her a you've-got-to-be-kidding look, then pinned Kit with a glare that said she'd had enough, "Okay, Kit, what's going on? Is GNN cooperating with another news source and nobody told me?" she asked with a vaguely accusatory gesture toward Brenna.

Kit fought an overwhelming urge to strangle Brenna. Damn it, she'd agreed to keep quiet! He'd have made that request for her, eventually. Probably. "No, of course not," he told Janine hastily.

"Then who's your friend, and why is she pumping me for information?"

"Brenna isn't pumping you, Janine. The truth is...she's helping me do background research on a story I'm putting together."

"A story about what?"

Kit hesitated. "I really can't go into it, but I promise you, it's nothing you'd be interested in pursuing."

"If it's got something to do with this crash, you couldn't be more wrong," Janine argued. "This story was brain-dead before we got up here from Atlanta—the forest fire fizzled out because of all the rain we had this spring, and the military hasn't let us anywhere near the wreckage. So far, the only exciting footage we've shot was of a news crew that got arrested for trying to sneak through the military cordon."

Kit forced a sympathetic smile. "Well, I'm sorry your story is a dud, but there's nothing I can do to spice it up. I was at my cabin when I heard about the crash, and thought it might tie in to something Brenna and I are working on," he said. "But I tell you what... You let us take a look at the footage you've shot today, and if we learn anything that would help your story, I'll let you know."

"Sure you will," Janine said skeptically.

Kit gave her his very best smile. "Hey, Jan, come on! Lighten up. I'm a science correspondent, not a reporter. I'm not out to scoop you on a story, I promise." When she still looked hesitant, he played his trump card. "Listen, if it'll make you feel better, I can call Ross Jerome in the D.C. office and have him authorize it.''

Janine's ultimate goal in life was to occupy an anchor desk at GNN's central bureau in Washington, so the inference that Kit would tell the executive news director that she was being uncooperative was enough to send her into retreat.

"No, no. I don't mind you looking at our footage," Janine assured him. She climbed into the back of the news van, and slipped into the bolted-down chair in front of the mobile editing console.

There were two video cartridges on the console, their cases labeled with today's date in grease pencil. As Janine popped the first tape into a slot and hit a rewind button, Kit and Brenna squeezed in behind her. Kit pulled a short stool from beneath another equipment console and offered it to Brenna, then knelt beside her.

"What, exactly, are you looking for?" Janine asked, glancing over her shoulder at Kit.

Now *there* was a good question. What, exactly, *was* Brenna hoping to see on the tape? Kit wondered. He thought back to what she'd said in the car. "I'd just like to get the military's official story."

Janine twisted around even farther to look at him, almost knocking Brenna off her stool. "You mean, there's an *unofficial* story?"

Kit's glance darted to Brenna. Was he imagining it, or was there a smug glint in her gorgeous green eyes that said, *You talked yourself into this one, buddy. You're on your own.* Smug or not, she gave a little shrug, and Kit decided he was tired of dancing with his colleague from Atlanta.

"Janine, just show us the film, okay? I swear, if you knew what I was working on, you'd run for the hills as fast as those long, sexy legs would carry you."

The reporter's Southern-belle gene surged again, sending the temperature in the van up at least five degrees. "You really think my legs are sexy?" Janine asked coquettishly.

She had no way of seeing Brenna behind her rolling her eyes heavenward, but Kit did. He ignored her as best he could. "Yes, I do," he told Janine. "Now, could you run the tape, please?"

"All right." Janine swiveled toward the console and cued up the tape. An image of the lush Appalachian Mountains appeared on one of the two monitors. It was barely possible to make out the distant forest fire through the heavy cloud of smoke.

If Janine was uncomfortable in the close quarters, with Kit looking over her right shoulder and Brenna over her left, she gave no indication of it. Kit, on the other hand, was keenly aware of his proximity to one of the women, and it wasn't the coquette from Atlanta.

Brenna's shoulder was pressed against his, and he could easily distinguish Janine's brassy perfume from the subtle, sultry scent of Brenna's. The distinction was made easier, of course, because he'd suffered with that tantalizing scent every minute of their long drive up here. He hoped like hell it didn't take Brenna long to learn whatever it was she wanted to know.

Scrunched between Janine, Kit and a stack of empty equipment cases with uncomfortably hard edges, it was also a struggle for Brenna to concentrate on the images that flashed across the screen, but having an agenda helped.

She recognized the first hillside shot as a view from the road where she and Kit had gotten their initial look at the scorched mountains. A helicopter swooped overhead, and a big prop plane unloaded a stream of chemicals on the distant fire.

From there, the video recorded the scene of chaos at the ranger station…fire engines, a backhoe… transports coming and going…endless shots of not much of anything, just as Janine had claimed. Then the press conference started, and Public Information Officer Lieutenant Lawrence Latimore predicted that the fire would be under control by midday. Brenna tapped her ear as she strained to hear the interview, and Kit reached around Janine to hike up the volume a bit.

"Janine? Yo, Janine! Where are you?"

"In here," the reporter called out to Stu Clendennan, a grizzled, bearded, twenty-year veteran of the TV news game. A second later, the cameraman stuck his head into the van and registered his surprise.

"Kit? What are you doing here?"

"Just in the neighborhood, Stu. Good to see you," he said.

Stu looked quizzically at Janine, who gave him an I'll-explain-it-later wave of the hand as she vacated her seat to Kit and climbed out of the van. "What's up?"

"Bad news," Stu replied.

Brenna leaned in closer to the screen and barely heard the conversation going on behind her.

"Rumor has it that they're not going to let everyone go back to the crash, after all,'' Stu was explaining. ''They've decided to take one pool camera back and do a live feed to all the stations.''

''How are they choosing the pool cam?'' Janine asked.

''By lottery.''

''Wonderful! What's bad about that? If we lose, we can head back to Atlanta and find a real story!'' Janine checked her watch again. ''Ooh, it's getting late. We'd better get over to the ranger station pronto if we want a good spot for the briefing.'' She looked inside the van. ''Kit, you about done in there?''

Kit, who'd found the outside conversation more interesting than the boring, unedited video footage, nodded to Janine. ''Yeah, I think—''

Brenna expressed a contrary opinion with a short but effective poke in the ribs that neither Janine nor Stu were in a position to see.

''I think I'd like another few minutes, if you don't mind,'' he amended, fighting the urge to massage his ribs.

''Okay, just lock up when you finish,'' Janine requested.

''Will do.'' A second later, Kit and Brenna were completely alone.

''All right, that's it,'' he said, swiveling toward his increasingly irritating partner. ''What the hell are you looking for?''

''I'm not sure, but as they say in the movies, I'll know it when I see it,'' she replied, not taking her eyes off the monitor. ''If you're not interested in watching, could I have the front-row-center seat, please? I'm getting cramps in places I didn't know I had."

"Oh, all right," Kit said grumpily, but actually he was relieved. Once Janine had vacated the van, all of his senses had riveted on Brenna and that damn sexy perfume of hers. He'd be happy to trade positions so that he could put a little distance between them.

He slid off the seat, turning it toward Brenna, then pulled her stool out of the corner. Unfortunately, it was so short that he could almost rest his chin on his knees as he watched the video monitor. It wasn't another five minutes before he was squirming in his seat.

To capture Brenna's attention, he reached out and punched the pause button.

"What did you do that for?" she demanded.

"I've got an idea," he said. "Since I don't have a clue what we're looking for, why don't we split up? I'll go see what General Avery has to say while you do this. The media should start clearing out right after the press conference and we can meet up and go looking for our forest ranger. How's that for a plan?"

Brenna nodded and resumed watching the tape. "Anything that will keep you from breathing impatiently down the back of my neck is a plan worth implementing."

"All right. Don't forget to set the lock on the door if you leave before I get back. And for God's sake, keep a low profile."

"Yes, sir." She gave him a crisp salute, and the van swayed sharply as he climbed out. Then she turned back to the video footage. Latimore's press conference had just ended, and Stu had returned to shooting anything that looked military and that moved. The footage was so boring that Brenna finally resorted to the fast-forward button. There were lots of shots of trucks and equipment passing through the roadblock she and Kit had cleared, as well as a bigger, more menacing barricade farther down the road.

There were shots of rangers coming and going from the station, and the minor altercation Janine had mentioned when a camera crew tried to circumvent the cordon. Brenna slowed the film to normal speed to get a better look at that action, and that's when she saw what she'd been looking for.

There, deep in the background behind the newsmen being arrested, were four men in nondescript fatigues escorting a khaki-clad ranger across a field to a helicopter. The ruckus with the camera crew drew the attention of the men crossing the field, and one of them stopped to look over his shoulder.

It was Colonel Elgin Brewster, the senior investigator for the Department of Internal Security, and the current head of Project Chariot, a super-secret, DIS-financed inquiry into the existence and origin of UFOs. No one knew who had started Chariot or how Brewster had come to power, but if there was a conspiracy to cover up what Chariot had learned, Elgin Brewster was the heart and soulless soul of that conspiracy.

On the monitor, Brewster stopped, and the ranger did, too. They exchanged a few apparently heated words, then one of Brewster's minions grabbed the ranger's arm and shoved him onto the waiting chopper. There wasn't a doubt in Brenna's mind that ranger being carted away, apparently against his will, was the same one who'd filed a report on the UFO-Net.

Brenna checked the time in the lower right-hand corner of the video screen. Dale Winston had been taken away for debriefing at eight forty-eight this morning. How long he'd be held would be up to him. Brewster would let him go as soon as the man signed a statement admitting that he was mistaken about what he'd seen. If he didn't sign...

Brenna didn't want to think about it. As far as she knew, it had been a long time since Brewster had killed to silence a witness, but she never discounted the possibility because she knew that he was capable of it. Besides, there were lots of things short of murder that a man like Brewster could do to destroy Dale Winston.

This was a whole new ball game now. Brenna had to find a way to get Winston out of Brewster's clutches, and do it quick.

AT TWENTY MINUTES after one, General Phillip Avery, commander of Longview AFB, appeared on the steps in front of the ranger station flanked by a lieutenant colonel and two aides, with the sullen-looking district ranger bringing up the rear. Avery took the podium, gazed out over the densely packed sea of media members and proceeded to bore everyone with a speech three times as long as it needed to be.

Essentially, all he did was confirm that the forest fire had been brought under control—in record time, thanks to the joint efforts of the military and the forest service. He also released the name of the downed pilot, Lieutenant MacKenzie Lewis, and announced that the CBS network affiliate had won the lottery to take a camera feed back to the crash site.

By the time Avery finished, Kit was wishing he'd stayed with Brenna. Anything would have been preferable to being squeezed like a sardine near the front of the media mob. He was relieved when the general finally threw the floor open to questions.

At least twenty voices all shouted at once, and Avery pointed at a reporter from the local CBS affiliate. "Have you recovered the body yet?" the newsman called out.

"Yes," General Avery confirmed. "And Lieutenant Lewis's family has been notified, of course."

"Was he married?" someone else yelled, just before a second voice chimed in, "Did he have any children?"

"Yes, to the former. No, to the latter," the general replied.

"Did Lewis and his wife live on the air base?"

Avery had to glance over his shoulder at the lieutenant colonel behind him before he could answer, "Yes, they did. And I'm sure you can understand that we want to protect the widow's privacy as much as possible."

"Do you have any idea yet what caused the crash?" Janine Tucker shouted at the officer.

"No. As we stated in the earlier briefings, this was just a routine training exercise. It was a by-the-numbers flight right up until seconds before the crash. We'll be doing a full investigation, obviously, once we've collected all the wreckage."

"So you suspect a mechanical problem, not pilot error?"

"We're not ruling out anything at this point."

Someone yelled another question, and Kit leaned toward Janine's ear. "Ask him about the instructor," he whispered.

Janine frowned up at him questioningly. "What?" she mouthed.

"It was a training run. That means—oh, never mind. Let me borrow that," he said, taking the microphone out of Janine's hand. Kit hadn't wanted to call attention to himself, but realized how silly that was. As soon as he got an opening, he called out, "General Avery, sir, what about the instructor Lewis was flying with? Who was the flight commander and what did he report occurred prior to the crash?"

Kit's question was long enough that Avery had plenty of time to pick him out in the crowd, and the general registered considerable surprise when he realized who was questioning him. "I'm sorry, Captain Wheeler, but that information is restricted as part of the ongoing investigation."

The response was a creative way of saying "no comment," but it was a reasonable answer. Kit tried again. "You won't release the identity of the wing commander?"

"No," Avery replied.

"Well, when will you be releasing a transcript of the conversation between the pilots and the control tower? You have recovered the black box, haven't you?" Kit asked.

"Yes, we have, but it will be up to the investigation

unit out of D.C. to determine whether a transcript release would be appropriate.''

Another disappointing but reasonable answer. Before Kit could come up with another question, someone behind him called out, "General, where were you when the crash occurred?''

Avery frowned. "I don't think that's relevant, but it so happens I was in my office catching up on some paperwork.''

"General! General!'' A woman's voice rose commandingly above the cacophony of questioners, and Kit caught his breath. It sounded an awful lot like Brenna. In fact, it sounded exactly like Brenna.

He swiveled his head, looking for her, but even when she shouted out her question he couldn't find her in the dense crowd. She was obviously at the back of the pack.

"General, is it true that one of the rangers stationed here at Lion's Head claims to have witnessed an encounter between your jet and an Unidentified Flying Object?''

Kit felt the pall that came over the entire assembly—he felt it all the way to the marrow of his bones, in fact. Five seconds of dead silence reigned supreme as everyone registered their shock, then there were one or two chuckles on his side of the crowd, and an outright laugh on the other side.

Everywhere Kit looked, reporters were shaking their heads and trying to hide who-let-her-in smirks.

All in all, there seemed to be only two people who weren't amused by the question—Kit and General Phillip Avery. Both men were fighting mad, and of the two, Kit was doing a better job of hiding it. Of course, he didn't have to answer Brenna's stupid question.

"UFOs?" Avery said imperiously. "This is a serious situation, miss. The air force has lost a fine young flyer, and I have no intention of demeaning his memory by acknowledging nonsense about flying saucers and little green men."

Kit jockeyed for a better position, trying to see where Brenna was when she called out again, "I'm not interested in little green men, General, just the forest ranger who witnessed the crash."

Avery rolled his eyes to the heavens. "It was night. How could there have been an eyewitness?"

"Why don't we ask the ranger? He was last seen at eight forty-eight this morning in the company of—"

"I don't have the slightest idea what you're talking about," Avery claimed, his voice booming into the microphone to drown out the final words of Brenna's sentence. "As I said before, this is a serious situation and I won't disgrace the memory of that dead flier with this kind of nonsense. Legitimate members of the press may direct any other inquiries to my public affairs officer! This briefing is concluded."

And with that, Avery turned sharply on his heel and marched back into the ranger station.

"Jeez, UFOs... Can you believe it?" the reporter in front of Kit muttered as he turned away from the dais. He looked up at Kit, shaking his head. "I had to show my press credentials, driver's license, two credit cards and promise them my firstborn male child to get past the roadblock. How did that nut get in here?"

Janine laughed. "Hey, these days, anyone can get a press pass from a rag like the *Inquisitor*. Isn't that right, Kit?"

"What? Oh, right," he agreed, though he wasn't quite sure what he'd agreed to. He was livid! What the hell had possessed Brenna to make a stupid grandstand play like that? He'd asked her to keep quiet and this was how she'd responded—by disrupting a military press conference in front of a hundred of his colleagues.

And where had she come up with that garbage about the ranger's disappearance? She certainly hadn't shared that information with him. The little troublemaker had blindsided him, that's what she'd done! He should probably thank his lucky stars that she hadn't blurted out his name and told everyone what he'd seen last night. When he got his hands on her...

But first he had to find her.

"You know, Kit, that woman's voice sounded familiar. It wasn't your friend, was it?" Janine asked as she disconnected her microphone from Stu's camera setup and began coiling it around her hand.

Kit managed what he hoped was an expression of surprise. "Of course not. It didn't sound at all like her to me. Anyway, I left Brenna back on the other side of the building."

Janine was craning her neck, looking through the dispersing crowd. "Well, I didn't see this woman, but I sure would like a chance to talk to her."

Kit frowned. "Why on earth would you want to talk to some UFO kook?"

"Because that general got awfully hot under the

collar when she started pressing him about the missing forest ranger," Janine answered.

"Don't tell me you believe in UFOs, Janine," Stu said.

She ignored his skepticism. "Hey, if there really is an eyewitness to the crash, that's news worth reporting—UFO or no UFO. I'll consider anything that might give this story a pulse."

"Don't waste your time," Kit advised her. "Ross would never approve a UFO angle based on information this slim. Listen, thanks for your all your help. It was really good seeing you again," he said, giving her a swift peck on the cheek. "I'd better catch up with Brenna. So long, Stu."

He barely gave his colleagues a chance to acknowledge his hasty goodbye before he hurried off. Jostling his way through the dispersing reporters, he finally broke free of the pack and worked his way quickly around to the GNN van.

Brenna wasn't there. So where was she? Damn it, why hadn't they agreed on a meeting place when they decided to separate?

He zigzagged through the sea of media vehicles toward the road where she had parallel parked her Mountaineer. That was the next most logical rendezvous point, and sure enough, Kit finally spotted her. She was unlocking the door of the Mountaineer.

And she wasn't alone.

Two uniformed, rifle-toting soldiers were standing on either side of her, and Kit was certain she hadn't requested a military escort.

But was she being arrested or just evicted?

"Brenna!" he called out. She was too far away to

hear him, but she turned at just that moment to speak to the soldiers, and Kit could tell that she saw him. He broke into a jog, not certain whether he was going to rescue her or murder her when he got there.

Brenna made that decision for him, though. The second he started running, she hurriedly climbed into the Mountaineer, started the engine and drove off without a backward glance, stranding Kit a hundred miles from his cabin.

"Murder. Most definitely murder," he murmured as he stood in the road glaring after his so-called partner.

CHAPTER SIX

IF SHE'D WANTED TO, Brenna could have come up with several methods of ditching the two privates who had evicted her from Lion's Head. They were nothing more than green-as-grass noncoms who'd been ordered to get rid of the loudmouthed UFO nut by the swiftest, most discreet means possible.

The officer who'd given the order was probably going to find himself hip deep in scalding water when *his* superiors learned that he'd ordered her evicted rather than detained, but Brenna wasn't about to point that out to anyone. Once she'd made the media aware that there was an eyewitness and he was missing, her only goal had been to quietly disappear.

To that end, the two privates had been quite helpful. When they had demanded her press credentials, rather than give them her name and show them the ID she carried from several respectable science magazines, she smiled sweetly, apologized profusely for crashing their party and offered to leave immediately. And they'd offered to escort her without ever learning her name.

It was all very nice, friendly and exactly what Brenna wanted. She had to get away from Lion's Head before someone higher up ordered her detained, which would mean interrogation, intimidation and a search.... Which she could not afford at the moment because she had a videocassette in her briefcase that contained footage she'd copied from the GNN master tape showing Brewster with Winston. If Brewster got his hands on that, her copy would disappear and before the day was over, GNN's original would go missing, as well.

Departure was definitely in order, and quickly. That was why seeing Kit come charging toward her hadn't been good news. Obviously he hadn't found the note she'd left for him sealed in an envelope on the dashboard of the GNN van—*Sorry. Low profile impossible, will explain later. Meet me at junction of Highway 260 and County Road 89.*

He looked madder than a hornet, and she had to get away before he reached her and made a scene in front of the soldiers. Chances were good that at least one of the cameras at the press conference was Brewster's. He hadn't been there in person—he was probably off somewhere interrogating Dale Winston—but eventually he'd learn that she was the UFO nut who'd disrupted the media briefing. If these soldiers connected her to Kit Wheeler, Brewster would learn about that, as well, and start wondering exactly what the nature of that connection was.

And what Brewster wanted to know, someone always managed to find out for him. It was inevitable that he'd learn about the *Gazette* article and Kit's photographs, but sometimes, in the game Brenna and Brewster played, a few hours could make a big difference. At the moment, she was out in front of the colonel, and she intended to stay that way for as long as possible.

She drove away, watching Kit in her rearview mirror, as he came to a standstill, staring after her in disbelief. That was okay because the two privates went off in the other direction without noticing the celebrity only a stone's throw away from them.

She breathed a sigh of relief as the distance between her and Kit widened until she could no longer see him. But she wasn't out of the woods yet. There was another hurdle coming up. General Avery probably didn't know her name yet, but if he wanted her detained he might have relayed her description to the sentries at the roadblock.

Traffic was restricted to one lane, and a half-dozen vehicles were lined up in the exit lane waiting for oncoming traffic to clear the roadblock. Brenna couldn't tell whether the sentries were questioning the departing drivers or not, but she couldn't take any chances.

Her pulse pounding, she pulled in behind a big transport truck and dipped into the utility pocket on the back of her seat to retrieve a banana-yellow baseball cap.

Working quickly, she gathered her hair into a ponytail, poked it through the vent at the back of the hat, and pulled the brim firmly onto her forehead. Then she popped open the utility compartment between the bucket seats and selected the sunglasses she wanted from the assortment of four pairs.

She slipped them on and checked the effect in the rearview mirror. Perfect. In the bright yellow cap, and fashionable but horribly gaudy red sunglasses with rhinestone frames, Brenna didn't look like someone who was trying to make a quiet escape without being noticed.

If they stopped her at the barricade, and questioned her, this wasn't much of a disguise, but sometimes it didn't take much of one.

The line of oncoming traffic finally passed and the transport began to move. Brenna put the Mountaineer in gear and stayed as close to the bumper of the big truck as she dared, gliding slowly toward the barricade—and right on past it.

They weren't stopping traffic. No one was looking for her. Yet.

Now, if only dealing with Kit could be as easy as donning a pair of retro fifties sunglasses and a ponytail.

THERE WAS an ancient abandoned gas station at the intersection of Highway 260 and County Road 89. At one time, there had also been a grocery store, a bait-and-boat shop and a few houses, but all that remained now were rotting wooden skeletons, a rusted out pickup truck and a lot of weeds.

All in all, it couldn't even be called a wide spot in the road anymore. The traffic on 260 wasn't required to slow down at the intersection, and the stop sign that sat at a rickety forty-five-degree angle on CR 89 was almost as rusted as the pickup. The whole junction had become invisible to the people who lived and worked in the area, and it was so insignificant that strangers would have no reason to notice it, either.

But Brenna wasn't a casual traveler. She had trained herself to be attuned to her surroundings because she never knew when something as mundane as a weedy gravel driveway in front of an old gas station would prove useful.

Tucked under the portico that had once sheltered two gas pumps, Brenna locked herself in the Mountaineer and settled in for what she knew might be a lengthy wait for Kit. She was certain he would catch a ride with his friend Janine, but there was no telling how long it would be before the GNN people left.

She checked in first with Randall and instructed him to launch a telephone campaign on behalf of Dale Winston. He was to enlist several of the freelance ufologists Brenna sometimes employed and have them make calls at regular intervals to Longview AFB and Lion's Head, requesting to speak to Winston. They were to keep it up all day—and all night, if necessary.

Randall, in the meantime, would start leaving messages at Winston's E-mail address, and hopefully the missing witness would establish contact with CUFOR as soon as Brewster released him. Beyond that, there wasn't much else they could do but wait.

With their battle plan established, Randall proceeded to give her a quick update on what he'd accomplished this morning. He hadn't had any luck finding a second source to verify the Flash Alert, but Claudia had arranged a meeting between Brenna and Justin Powers, the air traffic controller who'd been in charge of radar operations last night at the Knoxville airport. She and Kit were to meet him tomorrow morning after he finished work.

Once Brenna and Randall had exchanged updates, they signed off quickly, and Brenna settled in with her computer to wait for Kit. A steady flow of reporters fleeing Lion's Head slowed traffic to a turtle's pace, but Brenna ignored the passing parade. She was so absorbed in reading UFONet reports that she was actually startled when a flash of white directly ahead of her caught her eye.

She looked up and there was Kit, stalking toward the Mountaineer. Behind him, the GNN van was pulling back onto the highway. Kit couldn't see her through the tinted glass, of course, but she could see him, and he wasn't happy. In fact, he looked downright murderous.

With the greatest reluctance, she clicked the ignition over one notch to activate the electrical system and unlock the passenger door for him, but Kit didn't go to Brenna's right. He came left, to her door, glaring at the spot where he could only assume she was sitting.

And he was right. He found that out as soon as he yanked open the door.

"Get out of there!" he commanded.

Brenna stared at him in disbelief. "And if I don't?"

"Don't push me, lady. I've never resorted to physical violence against a woman before, but you're making it a tempting possibility."

If she'd believed for one second that she was in any danger, wild horses wouldn't have dragged her from the Mountaineer, but she recognized Kit's anger for what it was. He needed to vent some frustration, so she'd let him. She swung her legs out and stood, but Kit was close enough that she couldn't step away from the door.

"Okay. I'm out. You happy now?"

"Oh, I'm delirious," Kit snapped. "What the hell did you think you were doing back there?"

Brenna sighed and prayed for patience. "I'm sorry I had to leave you, Kit, but I didn't want you to make a scene in front of those soldiers and draw attention to our association."

"Then why didn't you think of that before you made your grandstand play at the press conference?" he demanded.

Brenna frowned. "Did someone connect us? Someone from the military?"

"No, but they very easily could have." He took a few agitated paces away from the door as he told her, "Janine thought she recognized your voice, and all the way down the mountain she kept after me like a bloodhound. I denied it, but she's convinced you're the mystery woman from the press conference."

"What did you tell her about why I left?"

"Oh, I did great with that," he said sarcastically. "I told her you had an errand to run, and when she didn't buy that lame explanation, I said we'd had an argument and you'd left to give yourself some cooling-off time."

"Did she believe it?"

"No, but she accepted it. Thanks to you, I'm turning into a regular Pinocchio!"

Brenna's patience finally ran out. "Hey, buster, I'm not the one who told you to lie about why we came up here," she snapped, advancing on him so that he had to back up a few paces. "You're free to tell the truth at any time!"

"I will!" he retorted. "But in my *own* good time, not yours! I thought you understood that! You were going to abide by my terms, remember? I don't recall anything in our agreement about making a scene in front of the press!''

"Well, I'm sorry, but I had to ask those questions," she told him.

"You had to stir up trouble! And for what? A bogus story about a missing eyewitness?"

"It wasn't bogus! I saw the ranger on the GNN video. He was being taken away by—'' She stopped in midsentence.

Oh, boy. Now what? she asked herself, doing mental gymnastics. If she told him the ranger was being detained by special intelligence agents known colloquially among ufologists as the Men in Black, Kit would strangle her on the spot.

What was she supposed to tell him? She had to decide quickly, because he was waiting impatiently with his hands on his hips and his jaw clenched.

"By who?" he demanded to know.

"Whom," she corrected absently.

Kit threw his arms into the air. "Will you forget my grammar and tell me what the hell is going on! *Whom* took the ranger away?" he asked sarcastically. "And how do you even know what Winston looks like?"

"I just knew, all right?"

"That's not good enough!"

"I recognized the men he was with," Brenna admitted finally. "I've run into them on other investigations."

That calmed Kit down a bit. "Who are they?"

"They're with that special UFO recovery team I mentioned."

"Well, so what? What if Dale Winston is being questioned by government investigators? We'll get his story after they finish with him. You didn't have to make an announcement to the world."

Brenna shook her head. "You are so naive. They're not taking a statement from Winston because they want to put it on the six o'clock news. They found out he's talking about what he saw, and they'll do whatever it takes to make him recant. By the time they get finished with him, we'll be lucky if he admits his name is Dale Winston."

Kit looked at her as though she'd just dropped in from Mars. "Has anyone ever suggested that maybe you've watched one too many episodes of 'The X-Files'?"

Brenna sucked in an angry breath and blew it out again. "I spoke up at the press conference because I wanted Winston's detention to be a matter of public record. By the time you get ready to air your story, you'll be glad I did. Trust me."

"Trust you? After what you did today?"

"Believe it or not, Kit, I took the most conservative action available, and I did it all without exposing you to anyone—with the possible exception of Janine Tucker. And since you've already proven that you can control her with just the threat of a phone call to your boss, your exposure as a result of my action is exactly nil. You should be thanking me instead of taking out your frustrations on me!"

"If I'm frustrated, it's because you lied to me. I'm not going to thank you for that."

"When did I lie?"

"You said you didn't know what you were looking

for on the GNN tape, but you did, didn't you? You were looking for those men, right?"

Brenna nodded. "Yes."

"Well, would it have hurt you to tell me that?" he asked.

"Kit, I have to be very selective about what I tell you, because you don't want to hear the truth."

"What truth?"

Brenna shook her head. "Ask me that question again after you've talked to Winston."

"That's not an answer."

"Well, it's the best you're getting from me," she informed him coldly. "I could hand you the truth gift wrapped on a silver platter, and you wouldn't believe it."

"Try me."

"No. You're going to have to learn it for yourself." She advanced on him, but Kit held his ground this time. They ended up toe-to-toe with Brenna glaring up at him. "And you've got a choice to make right now, Kit. You can have me as your own personal tour guide on this roller-coaster ride, or you can do it all alone—whichever you prefer—but if you decide you want my help, we're going to lay down a few new ground rules."

"Such as?" he asked defiantly, clearly ready to reject any ultimatum that she issued.

"First and foremost, you're going to stop treating me like I'm a one-eyed half-wit whose choochoo doesn't go all the way around the bend!"

"That is not how I've been treating you," he argued.

"Oh yes it is."

Brenna could tell by the guilty shifting of his eyes that she'd scored a point. "Well, you haven't exactly been the model of courtesy and respect, yourself," he reminded her.

"That's because you offend me, Kit," she said in all seriousness, her voice taking on a hushed resonance.

That took him by surprise. "I offend you? How?"

"Last night you saw a miracle. The sky opened up to you—so close that you could almost reach out and touch the universe, and you can't take five seconds away from worrying about your reputation to let the wonder and majesty of it sink in. I've waited most of my life for an experience like that, and to you it was worse than a plague of locusts."

"Well, forgive me if I'm a little hesitant to jump on the God Bless UFOs bandwagon, but I've built a career on science, not science fiction," he growled. "It may not mean much to you, but my reputation is all I've got, and that *thing* is going to destroy it!"

"I've got a reputation, too, Kit, and you might be surprised to know that not everyone in the world thinks I'm a crackpot. In fact, I've got a few friends in places that would surprise the hell out of you."

"I doubt that."

Brenna ignored his sarcasm. "Kit, if you'll stop fighting what happened last night and open that narrow mind just a little, you'll see that we're not adversaries. We're allies, and if we're going to work together, we're going to have to start acting like it."

They glared at each other for a very long moment.

"Is that your ultimatum?" Kit asked her. "You want my respect?"

"I'll settle for you giving me the benefit of the doubt once in a while," she countered. "I wouldn't want to put too much of a strain on you."

Kit took a step back, and it was a while before he answered. "I'll think about it."

"Oh, goodie."

He shook his head in disgust, and moved around her toward the Mountaineer, heading for the door Brenna had left open. "Get in," he ordered, pointing toward the passenger side.

Brenna stayed where she was. "What are you doing?" she demanded.

"I'm driving us back to Clear Lake so you can get a room for the night at the resort. I'll let you know tomorrow whether we're still partners."

She regarded him a moment, then told him in the calmest, most matter-of-fact voice she could manage, "Tomorrow I'm meeting with the air traffic control supervisor from Knoxville to discuss the incident report he filed this morning with the FAA."

Kit stopped at the door and stared at her for a long time as his anger waged war against his hunger for knowledge.

"We're still partners," he finally announced gruffly.

Brenna smiled and stepped toward the door.

"And I'm still driving," he added.

CHAPTER SEVEN

KIT STEPPED to the edge of the porch and looked out over the darkened mountainside. It was the same landscape that Kit had known since he was a boy, but his world was different now.

One of the biggest changes in it, he had to admit, was the addition of a smart, sassy, beautiful woman who irritated the hell out of him because she represented everything that had happened to him last night. He couldn't look at Brenna without seeing that *thing* in the sky. She was a constant, in-your-face reminder that the universe probably wasn't what he'd believed it to be.

But that didn't make her responsible for the upheaval in his life, he'd finally realized on their mostly silent drive back from Lion's Head. And it certainly didn't mean she deserved the kind of antagonism he had subjected her to today.

She'd been right to demand a little respect, and Kit was now doing his best to accommodate her—in more ways than one. Thanks to the fishing tournament, the only vacant room within forty miles of Clear Lake was Kit's guest bedroom.

He'd offered it to Brenna as a gesture of peace, and the truce seemed to be working satisfactorily. On their way to the cabin, they had stopped briefly at Cy Coleman's office, where Kit had reassured the newspaperman that he hadn't been abducted by aliens and Brenna handed over a box of UFO report forms, which Cy promised to distribute for her. The retired printer had also promised that he'd try to get the locals to stop giving strangers directions to Kit's summer home.

Back at the cabin, they'd scavenged a light supper from Kit's almost-bare larder, and then Brenna had provided him with enough UFO background reading material to keep him occupied through the millennium. While he began studying an encyclopedic history of sightings written by Brenna herself, the author had stepped outside to watch the sunset.

Now it was dark, and she was out on his lawn, reclining on her elbows, her legs stretched out, ankles crossed, and her face turned up to the sky. The light from the cabin touched her just enough to add a shimmer of gold to her hair whenever she moved her head.

It turned a little to the left, as though she was tilting her head toward a sound—toward him—just before she said, "Had enough light reading for one night?"

"Yep. I made it as far as the sightings of Saint Gregory in A.D. 584 before my eyes started crossing from lack of sleep. I'll pick it up again tomorrow. You're a very good writer."

"Thanks."

Night sounds filled a long silence as the two human inhabitants of the mountain studied the sky. Kit was pretty sure they were doing the same thing—looking for some trace of last night's UFO. But where Brenna was undoubtedly hoping it would put in another appearance, Kit was praying it wouldn't. He wasn't ready for a repeat performance.

It was finally Brenna who broke the silence. "I don't bite, you know," she told him.

Kit grinned and ambled down the stairs. "Maybe not, but you've got a wicked bark. You certainly flayed the skin off my hide this afternoon."

"Just returning the favor."

He joined her on the gently sloping hillside and stood for a moment looking down at the lake. "This is where I took the pictures."

"I know," Brenna replied. "I found the holes where the tripod dug into the earth."

"You don't miss much, do you?"

Kit could feel her bristling defensively even before she said tightly, "I'm an experienced investigator. I'm not going to apologize for it."

"Truce. Truce, remember?" Kit said as he sat next to her. "That was just an observation, not a call to arms. I swear."

Brenna flashed him a sheepish grin. "Sorry. Bad habit."

"No, it's my fault," Kit replied. "You wouldn't know it by my behavior, but I'm not usually an ogre."

"I don't think either one of us was at our best today," she conceded. "I'm all for starting from scratch. How about you?"

"Done," he agreed.

Brenna returned to her stargazing, and Kit leaned back, mirroring her relaxed pose. Now that they'd gone from truce to full-fledged peace treaty, he felt no particular need to entertain his visitor, and they shared an oddly companionable silence for several minutes.

Finally, in a voice so hushed it seemed in perfect harmony with the night sounds, Brenna said, "What's your earliest memory, Kit?"

The question caught him completely by surprise. He had to think way, way back, and when he did, he couldn't help chuckling. "A tubby yellow plastic airplane barely big enough for a toddler to ride in—like a kiddy car, but with wings, you know?" He glanced at Brenna; she nodded and smiled, but never stopped her lazy inspection of the sky. "I couldn't have been more than four, but I remember being in that airplane with someone pushing me so fast that everything was whizzing by—"

"And you loved it so much, you knew then and there that someday you'd fly a real airplane," she finished for him.

Kit laughed. "No, it scared me so bad I cried like a baby every time my dad dragged it out of the closet. They finally gave it away to my aunt Louise when her daughter Danielle got old enough to ride it."

Brenna laughed with delight. "Well, if that didn't make you want to be a pilot, what did?"

"Actually, I never really wanted to be a pilot," he replied reflectively. "I wanted to be an astronaut. Knowing how to fly was just a means to an end. John Glenn's space flight... If you're asking what shaped my life, that's the memory you really want to know about. I was only six years old, but I knew right then that I wanted to be just like him." Kit paused a moment, his gaze focused on Arcturus, the brightest star over their heads. "And I *almost* made it."

Kit saw Brenna turn her head toward him, and he could actually *feel* her looking at him. "You did make it, Kit. You're every bit as famous as John Glenn."

Kit frowned at her. "I didn't care about his fame. Glenn was a pioneer. A hero. He *earned* the respect and admiration this country will always feel for him. I didn't earn anything, Brenna. I'm just a NASA washout the media turned into a flavor of the month."

There was no bitterness in his voice, just the regret that comes from losing something precious. Brenna knew all about that kind of loss, and she felt her heart reaching out to him. "Cut yourself some slack, Kit. Don't you think a willingness to be a hero counts for something?"

"No."

"Well, what do you call taking failure and turning it into success?"

"Something that should be carved on my tombstone?" he suggested lightly. "'Here lies Kit Wheeler. He couldn't make it into orbit, but he looked good on camera.'"

Brenna didn't laugh. She still had vivid, deeply entrenched memories of the *Challenger* disaster, the ensuing investigation and the tense but triumphant flight of *Discovery* that followed it two years later. Before the *Challenger* launch, space flight had come to seem routine; after the explosion and those seven tragic deaths, it would never seem so again.

Brenna hadn't realized it until now, but Kit Wheeler's presence was woven very tightly into her emotions and memories of the entire incident.

"Don't put yourself down, Kit. You represent some very important ideals to the American people," she said earnestly. "You didn't make a space flight like your hero, John Glenn, but you showed a different generation of children the meaning of courage in the face of crushing disappointment. When you lost command of the *Discovery,* you didn't slink off to sulk. You held America's hand while we prayed that *Discovery* wouldn't turn into another *Challenger.* You personified those *Discovery* astronauts and made them real to us. You helped us understand the depth of their heroism."

Kit was more than just surprised by Brenna's eloquent defense of him—he was deeply moved. "Thank you."

"No, thank *you,*" Brenna replied.

Their eyes met, and a moment of genuine admiration and appreciation passed between them. Then it turned into something more. The faint golden light from the cabin cast a halo around Brenna, making her almost too beautiful to be from this world.

The desire to kiss her didn't creep up on Kit; it hit him like a runaway freight train, stealing his breath and sending an undeniable ache to his loins. It would have been so easy to lean across the scant distance separating them and match thought to action, but he didn't. He couldn't. His life was too complicated as it was. Something told him that kissing Brenna Sullivan might send everything spinning *completely* out of control.

But the desire wouldn't go away, and Kit realized that it had been with him all day. This was just the first opportunity he'd had to recognize the feeling for what it was. His rational self warned him that he should get up immediately and beat a judicious retreat before he did something he might regret, but he couldn't force himself to leave. There were too many things he needed to know about Brenna, because understanding what made her tick suddenly seemed very important.

"Okay, your turn," he said, hoping he didn't sound as hungry as he felt. "What's your earliest memory?"

Brenna shifted, returning her gaze to the sky, but the connection between them remained. "This. Being in a strange place, studying the night sky, waiting for something to come. If there was a flap anywhere in the world, my father and I would move there. During the day, he'd interview witnesses and investigate the sightings. At night, we'd watch the sky."

"Your father was a—" Kit hesitated, trying to remember what she'd called herself this morning.

"Nut?" she suggested lightly.

"A ufologist."

Brenna gave him an appreciative grin. "You really are making an effort, aren't you?"

He grinned back. "That crack you made this afternoon about me being narrow-minded really hurt. That's not the way I perceive myself. But we were talking about you," he reminded her. "Your father was a ufologist?"

"One of the first," she confirmed. "He wrote four books in the sixties and seventies. All of them became bestsellers, which is how we could afford to move all over the world investigating the UFO phenomenon. I never lived in the same place for more than a year or two until I went off to college."

Kit thought about his own stable, ordinary suburban upbringing in Minnesota. "That's a tough way to grow up."

Brenna gave a little shrug. "In some ways it was, I guess. But my father made it a wonderful adventure. By the time I celebrated my sixteenth birthday, I had seen more of the world than most people see in a lifetime."

"What did your mother think of all that moving around?"

"She died of breast cancer when I was five. I don't remember much about her," Brenna replied. "I did have a stepmother for a while, though. And *she* hated the moving. They met in Missouri when Daddy went there to study the Piedmont Flap in 1973. By 1978, she'd had enough. They divorced when Daddy decided to move us to Switzerland so he could investigate a wave of sightings. I wasn't particularly sorry to see Paulette go."

Kit smiled. "Wicked-stepmother syndrome?" he guessed.

She shook her head. "Not wicked, just hypercritical. Nothing I did was good enough for her. She wasn't a bad person, though. She was just in the way."

"Where is your father now?" Kit asked. "Is he with CUFOR, too?"

Brenna's smile faded and she rolled back onto her elbows. "No. My father died in a car crash while I was in college."

Kit didn't have to see her eyes to know what a painful memory that was for her; he could hear it in her voice. "I'm sorry. You were so close... Losing him must have been a terrible blow."

"More than you can possibly imagine."

She sounded far away, and Kit felt a little sliver of her sadness. It reminded him how lucky he was that his own parents were still alive and well. "What about the rest of your family? Brothers or sisters?"

"Neither. It was just Dad and me most of the time."

"Husband? Lover? Sweetheart?" he asked lightly, and watched her beautiful profile as she left the sad thoughts about her father behind and smiled.

"Never. Not lately... And I don't kiss and tell. In that order." She faced him again and that web of sensual awareness between them came back in full force. "What about you? I see your name every time someone publishes a list of the top ten bachelors in the country.... You have any plans in motion to get off that list?"

Kit shook his head. "Not at the moment."

"But you were married once, weren't you? I seem to recall reading that somewhere."

"We divorced about ten years ago."

"What went wrong?" she asked him.

Kit groaned and moved onto his back with his hands cradled beneath his head. "You want the long answer or the short one?"

Brenna propped her head on her hand. "Whichever you want to give me. I'm not picky."

"The short answer, then," he announced. "Summed up in three words—the *Challenger* explosion."

"Oh," Brenna said softly. "She wanted you to quit the program."

"And I wouldn't," he said with a nod. "That's a

gross oversimplification, of course. Our problems went way back. We hadn't been married six months when Laurie decided that being the wife of a test pilot—even one on the fast track to NASA—wasn't all it was cracked up to be. She complained constantly about the danger, but I think most of the problem was that our life wasn't as glamorous or romantic as she thought it would be.''

"So the *Challenger* tragedy was the last straw," Brenna guessed.

"Yep. She issued an ultimatum. I leave the program or she'd leave me.'' He gave a short, humorless laugh. "The irony, of course, is that I was forced to quit the program anyway. I gave up on my marriage for no good reason.''

"There was no chance of reconciliation?"

"Hardly. Laurie was no longer available by then. She remarried two days after our divorce became final.''

"I'm sorry."

"Oh...don't be," he said. "I have a feeling it was inevitable. The marriage was out of sync almost from the very beginning. Or we were, at any rate.''

"Do you think you'll ever try it again?"

"Marriage?'' Kit turned toward Brenna and propped his cheek on his fist. "I hope so. I've always pictured myself with a wife, and maybe even kids. What about you? No desire to juggle a career and a husband?''

Brenna's smile lit up the night. At least, that's the way it seemed to Kit. "You're calling what I do a career?'' she asked with an airy laugh. "You really are trying to be nice, aren't you?''

"Hey, when I call a truce, I do it right," he declared with mock earnestness, then grew genuinely serious. "Now stop dodging my question. Why haven't you ever married?"

"A combination of a lack of motive and opportunity. I never met the right man at the right time. Mainly because I have a very one-track mind," she admitted somewhat belatedly.

"But you don't have anything against marriage in general?"

"Of course not."

They chatted on in the lazy, meandering fashion of two people just getting to know each other, discovering a mutual affinity for contemporary country music, action/adventure movies and a good mystery novel. They disagreed on their other literary preferences, though; with Kit naturally preferring science fact, while Brenna came down on the side of science fiction.

That led them to a discussion of astrophysics, and they argued at length over a controversial new theory on the nature of dark matter that had been put forth by one of the world's leading astrophysicists.

It was an invigorating conversation, and an eye-opening one for Kit. Despite his degrees, he wasn't really a scientist. He made his living reporting the breakthroughs of real scientists, but he was essentially an outsider in that community. His day-to-day world was broadcasting, and though he knew a lot of wonderful people in that field, there weren't many of them who knew how to define the parameters of a protostar.

Brenna had an educational background and interests comparable to his, but she was an outsider in the scientific community, too. It gave them a lot more in common than Kit would have imagined.

"Then I suppose you use Lowenstein's theorem as a basis for your belief in extraterrestrial life," Kit commented. Their discussion had slipped into a debate about yet another controversial theory—this one having to do with planetary evolution. They were sitting up now, and Brenna was absentmindedly weaving blades of grass and clover buds into a chain as they talked.

"I think his theory makes a lot of sense," Brenna replied. "You don't think he's on to something?"

"On the contrary. He's probably right. But it doesn't in any way substantiate interplanetary space travel," he added quickly.

Brenna looked at him with surprise. "I never said it did."

"Well, how *do* you explain UFOs?"

She smiled wistfully as she stretched to reach the nearest flowering clover. "You're not going to like this answer, Kit, but frankly, I don't even try to explain them. I don't know what's up there or where it comes from. I'm just trying to prove that *something* exists."

"You're right. That's not an acceptable answer."

"But it's a reasonable one," she countered. "For all of man's pretensions about understanding the physical world, we're still in the dark ages—scientifically speaking. There's just too much that we *think* we understand, but don't."

"But you do believe that unexplainable UFOs are extraterrestrial, don't you?"

Brenna shook her head. "Not necessarily. There

are a lot of other theories out there. They could be from a parallel universe, or they could be time travelers from our own future. Some researchers believe UFOs are cohabitants of this planet, with a vast civilization hidden in the depths of our oceans.''

She grinned impishly. ''Or they could be flesh-eating lizard aliens from the planet Xenon.''

Kit chuckled. ''You're a big help.''

Brenna shrugged. ''I'm sorry, Kit. I know you're frustrated by what you saw last night and you want answers very badly. I wish I had more to give.''

''So do I.''

As they looked at each other, that desire to kiss Brenna welled up in Kit again. Actually, it had never gone away—it waxed and waned in direct proportion to his self-control. She was beautiful, intelligent...warm, and witty... Did her bizarre profession and outlandish beliefs really matter so much?

Brenna yawned and stretched languorously. The golden light from the cabin silhouetted every one of her luscious curves, and at that moment, her beliefs mattered not at all.

''Ooh, that's it for me,'' she said as she recovered from the yawn. ''It's been a pleasure debating you, Kit, but I need to turn in.'' She tossed away her clover rope.

''That's probably a good idea,'' he replied, trying to ignore the way his pulse had quickened. ''If we're going to meet Justin Powers in Knoxville in the morning, we'll need to get an early start out of the valley.''

Brenna yawned again as they stood and began meandering toward the porch. ''Kit, if I haven't said it yet—thank you for your hospitality. You didn't have to open your home this way. I appreciate it.''

"It's no problem," he assured her. "I couldn't let you sleep in your car."

"It wouldn't have been the first time," she said wryly as they reached the porch stairs.

"Well, you're welcome here for the duration of our investigation." He stopped and smiled at her. "We made it through the first day without killing each other. We can probably survive a few more."

His sexy, infectious grin quickened Brenna's pulse. And it wasn't the first time tonight by a long shot. "Who knows, we might actually end up liking each other," she said, feeling a little out of breath.

Kit tilted his head and quirked one eyebrow. "Or worse."

Brenna grinned. "What could be worse than liking each other?"

"Liking each other too much."

He took a step closer, and Brenna's smile faded. He wasn't joking. He was testing the waters, trying to find out how she felt about the sexual attraction that had been sparking between them all day long.

So how did she feel? She was going to have to decide fairly soon, because the hum of tension between them was growing more compelling with every heartbeat. Her choices were limited—retreat, surrender or attack.

Or stall. Stalling was always good.

She held her ground as he took another step toward her. "Kit, what are you doing?"

"Getting an answer to a couple of questions that have been bugging me all day." One more step closed the distance between them, and another slight movement brought Kit's mouth to Brenna's.

She caught her breath but didn't even consider pulling away when his tongue brushed her lower lip, then her upper one. In fact, her soft sigh encouraged him to explore farther, and he did, with explosive, breathtaking results. Before her brain could catch up with her body, Brenna found herself in Kit's arms, with her own wrapped around his shoulders.

It wasn't until she heard a soft, eager moan and couldn't tell if it had come from her or Kit that she moved her hands to his chest, pulled away from his kiss and snatched her senses out of his control.

Breathless and stunned by the intensity of the passion that had blossomed in only an instant, she took two steps backward. When her eyes met Kit's, though, the hunger in them made her want to throw herself into his arms again. Somehow, she restrained herself.

"What—" It was more a croak than a word. She cleared her throat and tried again. "What question was that supposed to answer?"

Kit took a step toward her, but made no attempt to touch her. "Does Brenna Sullivan taste as good as she smells? Are her lips as soft as her smile? Would kissing her be as disastrous to my peace of mind as I think it would be?"

His husky whisper was every bit as erotic as his kiss had been. "Did you get your answers?" she asked breathlessly.

"Yes, she does. Almost... And very definitely. In that order."

Brenna took in a deep, much-needed gulp of air and expelled it in a rush. "Kit—"

"Getting involved isn't a good idea?"

"Right." Her mind was scrambling to collect rational arguments. "We're in the middle of an investigation, and we need to keep focused on that. Plus, we're very different ideologically."

"True," he admitted, though he looked for all the world as though he might kiss her again at any moment.

"Then there's the fact that I have an agenda, Kit. I have definite goals in my life that don't leave a lot of room for romantic relationships."

"What goals?"

He was looking at her lips when he asked the question, and Brenna was having trouble thinking. "Just...goals. They're private. And on top of all that, I'm not even sure you *like* me."

A frown creased Kit's brow. "Don't be ridiculous. Of course I like you."

"Really? Attraction isn't the same thing as affection, Kit. Just because we have chemistry doesn't mean we have to cook up any experiments."

Kit took a step back, and the web of sexual tension between them vanished like gossamer on the wind. "Do you really think I don't like you, Brenna?" he asked.

She shrugged. "I honestly don't know, Kit. There were moments today—"

"When I was angry, true," he said, cutting her off. "I was also surly and obnoxious, but that's no reflection on you. I *do* like you, Brenna. You're intelligent and you're tough... You're patient, you know how to laugh, and you can stand up for yourself as well as any woman I've ever met. That's a lot to like. It's even a lot to admire.''

Brenna was almost speechless. ''Thank you. That's quite a testimonial.''

''You can also be stubborn, high-handed and pushy,'' he added.

She chuckled. ''Gee, thanks.''

''Just doing my part to keep your ego in check,'' he said with a grin. ''But do you like *me,* or do I still offend you?''

Brenna felt a flush of shame creep into her cheeks. ''Sorry. That was a pretty nasty crack, wasn't it?''

''Indeed it was.''

''No, you don't offend me,'' she informed him. ''You do, however, frustrate me. But so do most skeptics.''

''I'll try to do better,'' he promised.

''And I'll try not to be so pushy.''

''And we'll agree to table the issue of romance until...'' He raised his eyebrows expectantly. ''When?''

''Hell freezes over?'' she suggested lightly.

He shook his head and grinned. ''I'd prefer something in this century, please.''

Brenna grew serious. ''Why don't we table it until you've had a chance to decide how you feel about what happened to you the other night? That way, your confusion about the UFO question won't get tangled up with any emotions we might start to feel for each other.''

Kit nodded. ''Wise as well as beautiful.''

''And pushy.''

"Exactly."

He gestured toward the cabin, and they went inside, and adjourned to their respective rooms. But despite their newly negotiated treaty arrangement, it was a long time before either of them went to sleep.

CHAPTER EIGHT

"WE'RE MEETING him here?" Kit asked.

Puzzled, Brenna looked around the trendy café that Justin Powers had designated as their meeting place. There wasn't much of a crowd at this time of the morning, and it appeared to be a college hangout, but she didn't see anything worth objecting to.

"What's wrong with it?" she asked Kit.

"It's..." He looked around suspiciously. "Well...you said that Powers was reluctant to meet us. This isn't exactly what I visualized as a covert rendezvous point."

Brenna laughed. "What? You were expecting an alley behind a seedy skid-row bar?"

"Of course not. But after that rigmarole we went through this morning with my fax photos—"

"Rigmarole? We put them in a safe place. What's the big deal?"

He lowered his voice another notch and leaned toward her. "They're hidden in a secret compartment in the back door of your Mountaineer. Doesn't that seem a little...James Bondish to you?"

"Maybe, but they're a lot safer there than in your cabin," she replied. "Don't worry, though. It's a little early in our investigation for skid-row alleys. When we get into the real cloak-and-dagger stuff, I'll let you know."

Brenna chose a booth that gave her a good view of the entrance and laid out a leather notepad and matching pen-and-pencil set from her briefcase. A tanned, athletic-looking, college-age waitress arrived and solemnly took Brenna's order for a double mocha-caf latte, but when Kit ordered, "A cup of coffee, black," the girl gave him a look that suggested he should have his head examined or find another restaurant. She turned away, and Kit shook his head.

"Do I look as old as she just made me feel?" he asked.

"Not to me," Brenna replied with a smile. "But then, I'm an old crone compared to her."

Kit laughed shortly. "Brenna, even when you're old enough to *be* a crone, you won't turn into one. Beautiful women who know how to smile never do."

A blush crept up Brenna's cheeks. "Thank you."

"You're welcome."

This was the second time this morning that Kit had paid her a compliment. Brenna couldn't decide if he was flirting with her despite their agreement not to get romantically involved, or if he was just trying to reassure her that he liked her. Either way, she had discovered that she liked his compliments and the way they made her feel.

"Your Mr. Powers is late," Kit said, checking his watch. "You don't think he changed his mind, do you?"

"Anything is possible," Brenna replied as she stowed her briefcase on the floor next to the wall. "Claudia's contact in the FAA said things happened so fast yesterday that he couldn't keep track of what was going on. Powers filed an incident report at the end of his shift, but by midafternoon all traces of his report had been expunged from the National Daily Flight Status Log, and a computer lockout had been placed on all communications coming out of Knoxville. Obviously, the FAA is very determined to keep anyone from finding out that Knoxville tower personnel saw what went on between those F-16s and the UFO.''

"Whoa!" Kit said, a frown beginning to shadow his face. "We don't know anything of the kind yet. All we know for sure is that Powers filed a report that's being investigated. Why don't we get the facts from him before we start leaping to conclusions?''

Brenna considered arguing with him about the conclusions they could draw from the existing information, but she decided against it. Last night seemed to have brought about a positive change in their relationship, but Kit was no closer to accepting his close encounter, or to the realization that he was in the middle of a widespread cover up of the incident. Arguing with him wasn't going to change his mind.

"You're right, Kit. We don't know why Powers filed an incident report or why it has disappeared," Brenna conceded solemnly. "We should wait until we talk to him instead of making guesses.''

Kit's mouth twitched a little at both corners. "You're humoring me, aren't you?''

She grinned. "It seemed like the nice thing to do.''

"Thank you. I appreciate it. I so rarely win an argument with you that every little victory counts.''

"Glad to be of—'' She stopped abruptly when one

of the oak-and-stained-glass doors at the entrance opened, and a man in his late thirties paused nervously to look around. He was wearing a wrinkled white shirt, no coat, a loosened tie, and even from across the room, Brenna could see the dark patches under his eyes. But his exhaustion was more than just that of a man who'd been working all night on a stressful job.

"I think this is our guy. Hang tight," Brenna said, coming to her feet. The man saw her and straightened his tie as he moved across the room. "Justin Powers?"

There was no smile of relief or welcome on his face. "That's right. You're Brenda Sullivan?"

"Brenna, no 'd.'" She extended her hand. Powers accepted it, but reluctantly. "I have a table over here. I can't tell you how grateful I am that you agreed to this meeting," she said, leading him to the booth.

"I shouldn't have," he replied, glancing around nervously. "In fact, I wouldn't have if that woman, Claudia, hadn't said Kit Wheeler would be with you."

As Brenna and the air traffic controller reached the table, Kit stood and extended his hand. The two men exchanged greetings, with Powers muttering something about what an admirer he was, and Brenna did a little subtle manipulation to get their reluctant witness into the seat Kit had just vacated.

She resumed her own seat with Kit beside her this time, and all she had to do to keep an eye on the entrance was look past Powers's left ear. If anyone followed Powers inside, she wanted to know about it.

The waitress brought their coffees, and Powers

shook his head at the young woman, muttering something about not needing any more caffeine. She dropped the check on the table and departed.

"I really shouldn't be here," Powers said again once they were alone.

"Mr. Powers, nothing you say will go any further than this table if that's the way you want it," Brenna assured him.

"Oh, that's what I want, all right. I could lose my job for talking about this."

"You've been threatened?" she asked.

"More or less. I've been warned that the report I filed yesterday morning is under investigation, and it would be in the best interests of my career not to discuss the incident with anyone."

Brenna wasn't surprised to learn that. She'd expected it, in fact. "Have they invoked national security yet?"

Powers shook his head. "No. And frankly, I don't think they will because it would mean acknowledging that something happened. From what I've seen so far, I think they're going to try to make me retract my report and deny everything."

"Will you?"

"If it's the only way to save my career? Of course I'll deny it."

"Wait a minute." The conversation was moving way too fast for Kit. "Why don't we back up here. Deny what?" he asked the air traffic controller. "What happened Thursday night?"

Powers frowned in confusion. "We caught a UFO on radar. What did you think happened?"

Brenna cast a sidelong glance at Kit, but he didn't

return the look. Probably didn't want to see the I-told-you-so smile in her eyes, she guessed.

"Go on," Brenna encouraged him. "Please tell us everything you can."

Nodding, Powers took a deep breath and launched into a terse rendition of the extensive actions he had taken after something peculiar—an anomalous radar signature—had been spotted by controller A. J. Conchlin while the third man on their shift—Jim Nak-amura—was taking his break.

"What was it doing?" Brenna asked.

"Anything it damn well pleased," Powers said crossly. "It went down, it went up. It went slow, then it would put on a sudden burst of speed and come to a stop on a dime. I've never seen anything like it. Eventually, it descended to fifteen hundred feet, and I swear, it had to be right on top of Longview at the time."

"Did you see the Longview jets scramble?" Kit asked.

Powers nodded. "Yeah. The F-16s showed up on our screens as 212 Tango and 541 Bravo."

"Which one was Lieutenant Lewis?" Brenna asked.

"He was 541 Bravo."

"How did the bogie respond to the F-16 launch?" Kit inquired.

Powers shook his head as though he still couldn't believe what he'd seen. "It went straight up to ten thousand feet, then took off like a bat out of hell— I'm talking zero to five hundred miles per hour in an instant."

Powers went on to describe the game of cat-and-mouse that the "unidentified" played with the slower, less maneuverable air force jets. "And that's about the time I got Jim Nakamura back onto his scope so that I could call Longview. When I talked to General Avery, he—"

Kit frowned and leaned forward in the booth. "Wait a minute. You called Avery in the tower *before* the crash?"

"I most certainly did. I heard what he said at the press conference about being in his office, but he was lying. He was in the tower," Powers said bluntly, then went on to relate the particulars of his conversation with the general. "He even suggested that *meteors* were causing our anomalous signatures."

Powers shook his head in disgust. "When I asked him why the base commander was in the tower if everything was so normal over there, he got all huffy and practically hung up on me."

Kit directed a frown at Brenna, and she realized that he wasn't accepting Powers's story at all. On this particular issue, especially, it was the word of a stranger against that of an air force general, and Kit— a former air force pilot—was coming down squarely on the side of the military.

"What happened after this alleged conversation with General Avery?" Kit asked, earning a scowl from Brenna. Powers was a reluctant witness at best. If Kit scared him off with his skepticism, she'd kill him!

"It wasn't an *alleged* conversation," Powers replied angrily. "It happened. And it was less than a minute later that the two fighters split."

"Split?" Brenna queried.

He nodded. "Separated. Bravo—Lieutenant Lewis—stayed on the bogie, and Tango peeled off on a one-hundred-and-forty-degree tangent *away* from the bogie...away from Lewis...away from the base—it was like he was heading nowhere and trying to get there as fast as he could go."

"That doesn't make sense," Kit argued. "A mission commander would never desert his wingman in the middle of a chase without a damn good reason."

"Well, this one did," Powers retorted, then went on to describe Lieutenant Lewis's chase and its tragic results. There was an ache in his voice, and Brenna felt a deep pang of sympathy for the man who'd been a silent, long-distance witness to a tragedy he couldn't control or even influence.

"Tell me something," she said after a quiet moment had passed between the three of them. "Did any of the air traffic you were juggling report seeing anything?"

"Yeah. Three of them. Two commercial pilots and one civilian reported seeing unexplained lights."

"Did all three describe the lights in the same way?"

Powers looked at her in surprise, as though he was amazed that she would know that. "No, they didn't. An L-1011 en route to Atlanta and the pilot of a private Lear described a strobe effect of colored lights in a single band around something solid. Given their locations, that had to be the bogie we had on our scope," he explained. "But right about the time we picked up Tango and Bravo, a DC-10 out of Houston cruising at *fifty thousand* feet reported a ball of intense white light *above* it. They couldn't have been seeing the same bogie, but the DC-10 flight crew was positive about the sighting.''

Brenna looked at Kit again, and again he refused to acknowledge her.

"How long did they maintain visual?'' he asked Powers tersely.

"Less than a minute. It crossed their path on a downward descent and they lost it.''

"Did they file reports?''

"Yes. But they've been suppressed just like mine.''

"So there's nothing to substantiate any of these sightings?''

"No.''

The men locked stubborn gazes, and Brenna fought the urge to kick Kit under the table. "Can you draw me a map?'' she asked, sliding her notebook over to him. "I'd like to get a feel for where the bogie was in relation to the civilian pilots who spotted it,'' she told the tower chief.

Powers took the mechanical pencil she handed him, but he was shaking his head as he started sketching out the locations. "This won't mean much because it's not three-dimensional.''

"Just mark the altitudes,'' Brenna suggested. "That'll help me piece it together later.''

Powers stopped and looked at her. "For what? I told you, none of this is on the record.''

"I understand that,'' Brenna said soothingly. "But you're not the only person involved in this sighting. If some of the others want to talk…''

Powers shook his head. "They won't. I guarantee it. The bosses upstairs want this buried, nobody is going to buck them.''

"Not even you?"

"Especially not me."

"I don't believe that," Brenna said, leaning forward and meeting Powers's eyes dead on. "You didn't come here today because you wanted to meet Kit Wheeler, and you haven't put up with his skepticism because you're a fan. You're here because you want somebody to know the truth. You want to tell your story because there's a cover-up going on and you don't want the truth to be buried."

Powers chewed his bottom lip, but he didn't look away from Brenna's direct gaze. It was a long moment before he finally replied, "Maybe you're right, but that doesn't mean I'm ready to risk my career by giving you permission to use any of this."

Kit leaned forward, too. "Then what you've told us doesn't mean anything, Powers. It's just a fairy tale."

"I know what I saw, damn it," the controller argued. "I know what the other guys in the tower saw and what those pilots described!"

"Then give me some proof!" Kit demanded.

Powers shook his head. "I can't. I'm sorry. I did my job and filed all the appropriate incident report forms at the end of my shift. I turned over a copy of the voice recordings of my communications with the pilots, and a copy of the radar scope tape. I did everything by the book, exactly the way it's supposed to be done, and I'm probably going to be crucified for it! If my bosses want the truth buried, I won't make things worse for myself by calling them liars."

"Then don't let them lie," Brenna begged. "Give

us copies of your reports, the audio communications, and the scope tape.''

"I couldn't even if I wanted to," Powers told her. "When I got to work last night, my reports had been deleted from the computer, the master audiotape for Thursday night had been 'accidentally' erased and the radar tape was missing.''

"Then give us copies of your private backups," Kit said quietly.

Brenna looked at Kit in surprise, but Powers nearly dropped his jaw into the table he was so shocked. "How did you—" He shook his head. "What... Why would you think I made backups?''

"It's common practice," Kit replied. "I've known several ATCs and every one of them makes a copy of anything he includes in an official report. You did, too, didn't you?''

"That's pure speculation on your part," Powers replied nervously.

"But he's right, isn't he?" Brenna pressed, excited by the possibility that a second set of tapes existed.

Powers drummed his fingers on the table nervously as he shook his head. "No.''

"Then there's no hard evidence to support anything you've told us," Kit said with disgust. "It's a fairy tale and you're just wasting our time.''

"Fine. Believe what you want," Powers replied hotly. He scooted to the edge of the booth and stood. "I shouldn't have come here. It was a big mistake.''

"Powers, wait!" Brenna scrambled after him, forcing Kit to stand quickly to make way for her. "Wait.''

The ATC paused, but didn't look at Brenna. "Look, you can pressure me all you want, but—"

"I'm not going to pressure you, and I'm not going to call you a liar," she swore, throwing an angry look at Kit. She reached for Powers's hand and pressed a business card into it. "Just hang on to this, okay? Put it someplace safe. If you call from a pay phone, you can reach me any time at any of these numbers and no one will ever know. My cellular phones are scrambled and we sweep the hard lines at the Center regularly to be sure they're not tapped. Be sure and use cash, not a phone card. If you change your mind about going public, or if you need help, call me."

Powers was frowning at her. "I won't."

"Never say never," Brenna advised him. "You may discover that sometimes it's *safer* to get the truth out in the open."

He let her warning sink in and looked for a moment as though he wanted to say something, but he didn't. Instead, he gave Kit a terse nod and hurried out of the café.

Brenna and Kit watched him go, then resumed their original positions on opposite sides of the booth. Brenna sat very still for a second, trying to conquer her anger with Kit. She failed.

"Were we playing good cop/bad cop and you just forgot to tell me?" she finally asked.

"I was approaching the witness objectively."

Brenna's answering snort of laughter was decidedly unladylike. "Oh, please. If you'd been any more objective he'd have punched you out for calling him a liar."

Kit shook his head in disgust. "I take it you bought his whole story? Brenna, he didn't offer a shred of evidence, and he openly admits that he plans to deny everything he told us!''

"That doesn't mean he was lying," she asserted.

"We can't even prove that he talked to us."

"Wrong," Brenna said, reaching under the table to retrieve her briefcase. She produced a tape recorder from one of the pockets, picked up the silver pen that had been lying on the table the whole time and held it toward Kit like a microphone—which it was. "Testing, one, two, three…"

"You recorded him?" Kit glowered at her. "Why didn't you tell me you were going to do that?"

"I didn't know how you'd feel about taping him without his knowledge, and I didn't want to argue about it," she replied unrepentantly, slipping the recorder back into her briefcase. "Don't get in a snit over this, okay?"

"A snit?" Kit wiped his hands over his face in frustration. "God, you are the most infuriating woman. You know, Brenna, that was a nice little speech you made yesterday about wanting more respect, but it works both ways. You're going to have to start trusting me."

"Trust you to what? Keep quiet and not tell anyone about the pictures you took or the things we're learning? Oh, I trust you on that score, absolutely! But trust you to have an open mind on the subject of UFOs?" She shook her head. "Sorry, Kit, but I haven't seen any evidence that you're even *trying*."

"You're wrong. Last night…"

"Kit, loosening up enough to kiss me senseless does not qualify as being open and broad-minded about anything but sex."

"Let's leave the kiss out of this," he said sternly.

"All right. But that still doesn't make you open-minded."

"Try me," he demanded.

She studied him for a long moment, then nodded. "Okay. What do you make of the fact that Tango deserted Lieutenant Lewis in the middle of the chase?"

"I don't know what to make of it," he replied. "It doesn't make sense."

"It does if you think about it logically."

Kit spread his hands and leaned back. "Dazzle me."

Brenna leaned forward intently, accepting his challenge. "Tango left Lieutenant Lewis because the chase was joined by a *second* unidentified craft equipped with stealth technology that rendered it invisible to conventional radar."

Kit gritted his teeth. "Come on, Brenna! Get real. I told you, I wasn't going to buy your two-UFOs-for-the-price-of-one theory."

"But it's the only scenario that fits the facts," she argued. "Those two pilots were chasing a little saucer-shaped UFO with a band of colored lights, when the big UFO you photographed appeared. The large ship caught their attention, then sped off in another direction. That's why the pilots separated. The team leader followed the mother ship, and Lieutenant Lewis stayed on the smaller scout."

Kit's jaw was set as rigidly as a block of granite. "It's also possible Tango could have experienced equipment failure that sent him off course."

"And night blindness, too?" she retorted. "Suddenly Tango couldn't see those pretty colored lights in front of him *or* the F-16 flying alongside him? Gee, it's a miracle *he* wasn't the one who crashed. How did he make it back to the base alive?''

Kit glared at her. ''Sarcasm isn't going to prove anything, Brenna.''

''No, but it's the best weapon I've got against a close-minded skeptic who won't accept facts even when they're right in front of his face.''

''What facts?'' Kit demanded. ''So far, our investigation has amounted to one big goose egg. You roped me into teaming up with you by using an eye-witness forest ranger as bait, but he conveniently disappeared, kidnapped by some clandestine 'recovery' team no one but you seems to have seen. And today you bring me to a college hangout where our mystery guest spins a swell yarn, but offers not a shred of evidence to prove his story—or who he really is, for that matter! For all I know, Dale Winston doesn't exist, and Justin Powers is the star of the Knoxville Repertory Theater's stage adaptation of *Close Encounters of the Third Kind!*''

Brenna couldn't have been more shocked if Kit had slapped her. She'd been accused of manufacturing evidence before and it was always infuriating, frustrating and sometimes even painful. But this was different. Those attacks had been professional, engineered by Elgin Brewster to discredit her, or by small-minded debunkers who made a living telling the world that people like Brenna were fruitcakes.

But Kit's indictment was different. It was personal. The man who had taken her into his arms and kissed her last night thought she was a liar and a con artist. So much for his professed "admiration" for her.

Moving very slowly and deliberately, she collected her notebook, Powers's unfinished sketch and her briefcase as she said too calmly, "That's quite a scenario you've concocted, Kit. Thank you. I never realized what a brilliant manipulator I am. And multitalented, too. The institute I run is really the Center for UFO Research and Acme Talent Agency, all rolled into one."

"Can the sarcasm, Brenna."

"Oh, but I'm just getting started," she said, her calm beginning to desert her. "I want to make sure I understand exactly what you're accusing me of. I baited you with phony UFO reports, then scripted and directed the performance Powers just gave.

"Did I also arrange for you to see a UFO? What did I do? Construct it out of *Star Trek* model kits and hang it by invisible wires over Clear Lake?"

"Brenna, stop it," Kit commanded, flushing. "I'm sorry I—"

But Brenna was too angry to listen. "Did I also arrange for that *Gazette* newspaper article so that I'd have an excuse to come looking for you? How brilliant of me! Of course, I guess it was just a stroke of sheer luck that Lieutenant Lewis crashed that jet. Or did I make *that* happen, too?"

"Damn it, stop," Kit said again. "I apologize. I'm sorry. I know you're not manipulating me."

"How do you know?" she snapped as she scrambled out of the booth and came to her feet. "How do you know *anything* at all, Kit? With inquisitive minds like yours feeding information to the American public, it's a miracle schoolchildren don't still think the earth is flat!''

She turned on her heel and stalked off, leaving Kit sitting there, fighting the urge to follow her. Instinct told him he was better off waiting. She needed a minute to cool down, and he needed time to frame an apology that she wouldn't fling back in his face.

What he'd said to her had been so unfair; a knee-jerk reaction. Actually, her theory did fit the facts—*if* he was willing to believe that Justin Powers was telling the truth. Which he wasn't willing to believe. Not yet. He needed proof. Data. Solid, incontrovertible evidence.

So far, the only thing that came close was his own sighting and the roll of film that supported it. And since *he* didn't believe what he had seen, how could he expect anyone else to?

Damn! Kit slammed his fist on the table, making the coffee cups rattle on their saucers. Why couldn't he just accept what he'd seen with the same calm that Brenna did? Why couldn't he believe that Justin Powers was exactly what he appeared to be—a basically decent guy who had witnessed something extraordinary for which he would probably be crucified.

Why couldn't he just fly back to Washington right now, pick up his pictures and negatives from Sandy Kirshner, toss them onto Ross Jerome's desk at GNN and be done with it? Let Ross air the damn pictures and let people say whatever they wanted to about them—about *him*... Let them call him a hoaxer, a fraud, a charlatan, a deluded lunatic... What did he care what the rest of the world thought about him?

Actually, he cared a lot. Maybe too much. But

could anyone blame him? What good was a reporter who lacked that one all-important attribute—credibility. Without it, Kit would find himself looking for a new job before the month was out.

The only way to make his pictures public and maintain his credibility at the same time was to back up his own sighting with hard evidence. Which brought him right back to where he'd started, all tangled up with a beautiful spitfire in the middle of an investigation he didn't want any part of.

Damn. Why couldn't life be simple? Why hadn't he stayed in D.C. this weekend? Why couldn't he have met Brenna Sullivan in the bar at Luciano's or at a party given by mutual friends? He could have invited her out for dinner and gotten to know her without the pressure of feeling his life crashing down around him. If they'd met like two ordinary people, he would have proved to her by now that he wasn't such a bad guy once you got to know him.

But it hadn't happened that way.

"Is everything all right, sir?" The waitress came up behind him, pulling him away from his gloomy thoughts. "Can I get you something else?"

"No, thanks," Kit said, coming to his feet. "I have to catch up with my partner."

He settled the bill and hurried out to the parking lot, hoping she hadn't gone off and left him as she had the day before. Sure enough, there she was, leaning against the tailgate of her Mountaineer, her ankles crossed, her arms folded across her stomach, her briefcase lying on the roof behind her. She didn't look happy, but she didn't throw anything at him, either.

In fact, when Kit got close enough to see her eyes,

he realized that she was more hurt than angry. Tough-as-nails Brenna Sullivan wasn't as tough, or as bulletproof as she seemed. Seeing the hurt in her eyes made him want to reach out for and protect her, but right now he was the only one she needed to be protected from.

That was the moment Kit realized what he felt for Brenna was more than just sexual attraction. She challenged him intellectually. She touched him emotionally. Now she was bringing out his primal hunter/protector gene. He was moving into dangerous waters, and the weird thing was, he didn't mind.

As he reached the car, he shoved his hands into his pockets because it was the best way he could think of to keep himself from taking Brenna into his arms and getting his face slapped.

He stopped in front of her, his gaze meeting hers squarely. "Are you getting sick of hearing me say I'm sorry?"

"A little."

"Then how about an explanation?"

Brenna sighed heavily. "I understand more than you think I do, Kit. I've dealt with a lot of people over the years who had their lives turned upside down because they saw something they couldn't bring themselves to believe in. I'm not unsympathetic to what you're going through."

"I know that. But if I accept that these things exist, Brenna, then I've also got to accept that our science is literally light-years off course. I'll have to accept that there's something in the universe, other than God, who's more powerful than we are. I'll have to ask who they are, what they want…what they can do.

"Everything I thought I understood about this world will have to go out the window and be replaced. But by what? Even you admit there aren't any answers to those questions," he said. In response, he saw a small softening in her eyes, but it was a long way from total forgiveness.

"So you took a page from the history of ancient Rome and blamed the messenger for the message?" she asked quietly.

"I'm sorry. I was thrashing around, hoping to find an answer that was a little closer to home than Alpha Centauri. You were the nearest target."

"Well, I don't like being target practice, Kit. And I don't like playing games."

Kit frowned, confused. "What games?"

"That 'Gee, you're sexy when the sun goes down,' game you were playing last night. But you sure change your tune in the light of day."

"That wasn't a game, Brenna. We made a connection last night."

"Well, we broke it today," she said, turning to snatch her briefcase off the roof.

"No, we didn't," he argued, taking her arm to keep her from retreating. "You wouldn't have been hurt by my stupid accusation if you weren't feeling the same things I'm feeling."

Brenna glared at him defiantly, tolerating his hold on her arm because she didn't want to give him the satisfaction of playing tug-of-war. Besides, it felt more like a caress than a restraint, and the impact of it curled inside her like something warm and inviting.

"Oh? What is it you think I'm feeling?"

"That deep-down-in-your-gut sensation that only comes when you meet someone special. It's there whether we want to admit it or not."

Brenna was experiencing the sensation he described, and a number of others that were equally potent. The chemistry between them was breathtaking.

Why did they have to be so damn different? Letting Kit Wheeler get too close was just begging for trouble!

So why was he getting closer and closer with every beat of her heart?

"This...sensation. You're admitting that you've got it?" she asked him with a touch of suspicion.

"Yes."

"It's not just indigestion?"

Kit grinned. "No. How about you?"

She sighed heavily. How could she lie when he was flashing his sexiest grin and she was looking directly into his perfect blue eyes. "I feel—" The muffled trill of her cellular phone interrupted her. She dug into her briefcase for it.

"You feel what?" Kit pressed.

She held up one finger, indicating that he should wait while she answered her phone. She flipped it open and thumbed the button. "Acme Talent Agency," she said sweetly.

Kit rolled his eyes, and on the other end, Randall said, "Brenna?"

"Randall! Good morning. What's up?"

"Good news. What's up with you?" he demanded. "What is this Acme—"

"Never mind. It's a long story. What's your news?"

"Dale Winston, our errant forest ranger, just made contact. He's mad as hell about the way he was treated by the military, and he's ready to talk."

"Hallelujah!" Brenna practically shouted. "It's about time we got a break."

"I'm faxing the directions to you even as we speak," Randall informed her. "What happened with Powers?"

Brenna fished out her keys and unlocked the hatch so that she could get at her computer. "It's a long story. I'll call you back and explain everything as soon as Kit and I get on the road. Bye for now."

"What's happened?" Kit asked.

She opened the hatch and retrieved Randall's fax from the computer tray as she replied, "Not much. The forest ranger you accused me of inventing just surfaced." She slammed the door and looked at Kit triumphantly. "Shall we go interview him?"

"All right, but first tell me what it is you feel?" he insisted.

Brenna looked at him innocently. "I feel elated that a witness who wants to go on the record has come forward to talk to us."

"You know what I mean," he said as she breezed past him, headed for the driver's door. "You were going to admit what you feel for me."

She glanced over her shoulder. "I was?"

Kit shook his head in disgust as he moved around the car. "Oh, never mind," he muttered. "Get in the car and drive."

Chuckling merrily, Brenna did as he commanded,

and less than a minute later, they were pulling out of the parking lot. Neither of them noticed the plain black sedan that pulled out a moment later and stayed at least two cars behind them all the way to the freeway—and beyond.

CHAPTER NINE

DALE WINSTON WAS the kind of witness Brenna had learned to love over the years. He was a tough, plainspoken man of few pretensions—a man who believed in doing what was right and who refused to allow himself to be intimidated by anyone or anything. He was only a few years short of retirement, but even the threat of losing his pension wasn't going to shut him up.

His wife, on the other hand, was a nervous woman who couldn't be blamed for treasuring security above freedom of speech. Winston had been returned to his home only a few hours after Brenna had confronted General Avery at the press conference yesterday, but Annalee Winston had thrown a fit when her husband announced his intention to answer the E-mail messages Randall had been leaving him.

The battle had raged all night, and this morning Winston had declared victory. As near as Brenna could tell, though, Annalee hadn't really surrendered so much as she'd been bulldozed into submission. As her husband recited his experience, with Brenna's video camera rolling, Annalee sat off to one side, wringing her hands and chewing on her lower lip.

At least twice, Brenna heard her mumbling something that sounded like, "Never shoulda give 'im that computer for Christmas."

Someone else who'd rather shoot the messenger than accept the message.

The message itself, though, was pretty straightforward. A few minutes after midnight, Winston had been driving home from Lion's Head when he'd seen a strange, pulsating light coming from the west. He'd pulled into a Scenic Overlook parking area, and as soon as he shut off the engine, he heard the familiar drone of a fighter-jet engine.

As he watched, the bizarre blob of colored lights suddenly poured on a short, dazzling burst of speed. A second later, a pinprick of fire flashed a mile or more *behind* the lights, and the former navy pilot had recognized it instantly as the flash of a jet afterburn. A second later, he heard the unmistakable roar.

With his heart in his throat, he'd stared as the UFO came to an impossible sudden stop, then reversed course into the path of the jet. For an instant, the two seemed to merge into one, then the UFO flashed up so quickly that it was nothing but a streak against the sky.

A stark silence had been followed by the gut-churning whistle of an enormous metal projectile hurtling toward the earth. The jet zoomed past Winston, disappeared behind the hills to the east and exploded on impact, sending a giant fireball into the sky.

He sounded the alarm to mobilize the Lion's Head fire crews, but the air force search-and-rescue teams had arrived by helicopters and taken control before Winston's people had assembled. All Forest Service personnel had been ordered to stay clear of the crash area and Winston had gone home.

At four that morning, the air force changed its mind about wanting the ranger's help, and Winston had been called back to work. He'd recounted his UFO sighting to anyone who'd listen, and he'd been completely stunned when three men in camouflage fatigues had demanded that he accompany them to Longview for a debriefing.

What followed was nearly six hours of uninterrupted attempts at humiliation and intimidation. Locked in a small, windowless room, Winston had recited his story again and again. If his account deviated in even the slightest detail from one telling to the next, his interrogators accused him of inventing the facts as he went along, but if two recitations sounded too much alike, they accused him of having rehearsed his performance.

Then he was shown a copy of his UFONet report and he'd had to defend every section of it. They treated him as though he was a criminal for even knowing about the existence of the UFONet, and with broad smirks on their faces, they'd asked if he had any alien-abduction stories to relate.

Through it all, Winston had remained unshakable about what he had seen, and they had finally resorted to veiled threats about his retirement pension. Only unstable people saw UFOs, they claimed, and our government couldn't afford to employ unstable citizens, even in noncritical departments like the Forest Service.

Winston had told them in no uncertain terms what they could do with their threats, but he'd really been shaken by the time they returned him home without a word of apology.

"Is this one of the men who interrogated you?" Brenna asked, taking a photo from a file that she'd set in front of her on the coffee table right after she arrived.

The look of fury on Winston's face was all the answer she needed. "That's him, all right," the ranger said. "Never did give me his name, and he wasn't wearing a uniform or insignia, but if he's not military now, he was in the past. He was clearly in charge."

"His name is Elgin Brewster. He's known as the colonel," Brenna told him. "But I've never been able to ascertain what branch of the military he's with. He's one of those unique people who travels in military conveyances and occasionally flashes ID showing that he's with the Department of Internal Security, but about whom the government claims to know absolutely nothing."

"Well, he's the bastard who tried to put the fear of God in me. Begging your pardon, ma'am," he said, tossing the picture back on the table. Kit, who was sitting beside Brenna on the sofa, reached for it.

"I wish you'd shown me this before, Brenna," he said as he examined the picture. "I have some contacts that go pretty high up. I'll see what I can find out about him."

Brenna started to tell him not to waste his time, but thought better of it. He might get lucky, and if not, he'd learn another valuable lesson about the difficulties of investigating UFO sightings.

She offered Winston the opportunity to add to his

statement, but there didn't seem to be anything else. Kit had no more questions, so Brenna shut off the video camera and began putting it away.

Winston had some questions, though. "Are you the one who got me released?" he asked. "My boss told me that the commanding general from Longview got really upset when someone asked about me at the press conference. Was that you?"

Brenna nodded as she nestled the video camera into its molded foam bed. "I don't know if I had anything to do with your release, but that was me at the press conference. You were accidentally caught in the background of a videotape clip as you boarded the helo, and I was serving warning to Brewster that I knew he had you in custody."

"Well, thanks. That may be the only reason I got out of there as quick as I did. This guy, Brewster, was with me when one of the others came in and whispered something to him. I got the feeling that the you-know-what had hit the fan, but I had no idea what it was about. Knowing what I do now, I think it had something to do with what you said at the press conference."

Brenna grinned at him. "Or it could have been the phone calls I arranged to have flood into Longview on your behalf."

Winston smiled at her, displaying twinkling blue eyes and deep, craggy dimples in his weathered cheeks. "You know, I've read all your books and followed some of your investigations on the UFONet. You're the best at what you do, and I've always admired that. I admire you a whole lot more now."

"Thank you," Brenna said simply.

"If you don't mind my asking, where did you pick up your interest in UFOs?" Kit asked the former navy man.

"Nam," he replied promptly. "My carrier was anchored in the bay at Nha Trang in 1966."

Brenna stopped what she was doing. "You were a witness to the blackout?"

"Yes."

"What happened?" Kit asked him.

"A huge white ball of light came out of the north and hovered over the base for nearly four minutes. It lit up the valley like daylight, and every electrical system for miles—including the carrier's—failed. Then it flew straight up and was gone within three seconds. As soon as it was dark again, the power came back on."

"Did you suffer any burns?" Brenna asked him.

"No, I was on board the ship, and none of us got cooked. But a couple of my buddies who were on the base came back that night looking like they'd been sleeping in the sun all day."

"Maybe they had," Kit suggested before he could censor the thought, and was surprised that Brenna didn't give him a dirty look. Instead, she and Winston exchanged a coded "ignore him, he's a skeptic" look before the ex-fighter pilot replied.

"That would have been kinda hard, Captain Wheeler. I saw them both right before they left. It was already sunset, just two hours before the UFO appeared."

"Oh. Sorry if I sounded too skeptical."

Winston nodded. "That's okay, Captain. I've followed your career for years, too, and I never pegged you for a believer."

"I'm working on it," he replied with a tight smile. "And it's Kit. I haven't been a captain for a long time."

"All right, Kit," Winston said proudly, obviously pleased to be on a first-name basis with the celebrity.

When Brenna finally finished dismantling the video equipment, she thanked Winston profusely and gave him the same set of phone numbers she'd forced on Justin Powers. Kit took the heavy video case, Brenna picked up the tripod, and Winston escorted them to the door, saying their goodbyes as they went.

"Goodbye, Mrs. Winston," Brenna said, turning in the doorway to look at the nervous woman.

"You know what's gonna happen if Winnie's story gets out, don't you?" Annalee Winston said as she came to her feet. "Winnie will lose his job and his pension. But you got what you came for, so I don't guess that matters much to you, does it?"

"Annalee!"

"I'll do everything I can to protect your husband, Mrs. Winston, but we need his statement," Brenna replied. "Someone has to put a stop to the kind of intimidation tactics Elgin Brewster used on your husband."

"And you think you can do that?"

"I've spent a lot of years trying, and thanks to your husband, I'm closer than I've ever been."

"Well, you'd better be, 'cause my Winnie has worked hard to get where he is today, and I don't want to see him lose it all," Annalee said. Tears began seeping out of the corners of her eyes, and she hurried out of the room. Winston apologized for his wife, and after another round of goodbyes, he hurried off to check on her.

"This is nuts," Kit said as they moved across the porch and down the stairs. "That poor woman is frightened out of her mind."

"She has a right to be," Brenna responded.

Kit frowned at her. "Oh, come on. You can't be suggesting that those people are in any danger. This Brewster person certainly isn't going to kill to silence Dale Winston, and it's not as easy as you might think to knock a government employee out of his pension."

"That depends on how much power you have and how high the stakes are." They reached the curb and Brenna glanced right and left to check for oncoming traffic. "Brewster has a lot of power, and the stakes are higher than—"

"What is it?" Kit asked when she suddenly stopped talking.

"I'm not sure. Maybe nothing," she said with a shake of her head as she stepped off the curb. The Winstons' home sat in the middle of the block in the attractive Dearbourne residential neighborhood, and she had parked the Mountaineer on the opposite side of the street. There were other cars parked intermittently along the curb in both directions, but it was the black sedan with tinted windows two blocks down that had caught her eye.

Outwardly, she'd given it only a split second of attention, but all her senses were keenly tuned in to it as she opened the hatch and they stowed her equipment.

"Here." Brenna tossed her keys to Kit, then slammed the hatch.

He looked at her suspiciously as they moved to opposite sides of the car. "You're voluntarily giving up your autonomy? Why?"

Brenna forced herself not to look back at the sedan. "Because I have something to tell you and you can't go ballistic if you're behind the wheel."

Kit stopped at the door. "What?"

"Just drive." She slid in, buckled up and pulled down the sun visor. Her hair was a mess, but that was the least of her worries at the moment.

"I don't think I've ever seen you primp before," Kit commented mildly as he started the engine.

"And you're not seeing me primp now," she countered, glancing over her shoulder. "As you pull out, I want you to keep an eye in the rearview mirror. About two blocks back there's a black sedan with tinted windows. See if it pulls out, too."

Kit looked at her in disbelief. "You're not going to tell me we're being followed."

"I'm not telling you anything. I'm pointing out a car. You drive us back to the lake and draw your own conclusions."

"All right." He put the car in gear and pulled into the street. The sedan didn't move. "Sorry, Mata Hari. No cloak-and-dagger today."

Brenna didn't comment, but she did smile with satisfaction when Kit made a left turn at the first intersection and the sedan edged into the street. A few seconds later, it made the same left turn.

"Coincidence," Kit decreed, but Brenna could tell he wasn't at all sure about that.

He was even less sure twenty minutes later when they left the rural backroads for the interstate and the sedan was still behind them. He didn't see it continuously, of course, but every time he thought he could tell Brenna she was imagining things, he'd catch sight of it again, always a few cars behind.

Brenna had turned up her visor some time ago. "Still there?" she asked.

"What's so odd about someone from Dearbourne driving to the interstate?" he asked, still not quite willing to give up.

"Take this exit," Brenna instructed.

"We just got on the highway."

"And so did our friends from Dearbourne. If we don't have any reason to get off, why would they? Besides, we'll need gas to make it all the way back to Clear Lake. Might as well do it now."

Kit took the exit. So did the sedan. He turned left off the access ramp. So did the sedan. He pulled into the first self-service station he came to.

And the sedan went right on by.

"Aha!"

"Just wait," Brenna advised him. While Kit pumped the gas, Brenna went into the minimarket and returned a few minutes later with soft drinks for both of them. There was still no sign of the sedan as they navigated back onto the northbound freeway, but they hadn't been driving five minutes when Kit spotted it several cars back.

He finally gave up pretending they weren't being followed. He was stubborn, not stupid. "I suppose you know who this is," he said.

"I'm pretty sure they're Brewster's men."

Kit ran one hand down his face. "I can't believe I'm about to ask this. We're just under surveillance, right? We're not in any, you know..."

"Danger?"

"Yeah."

"Not at the moment," she reassured him. "Actually, this was pretty predictable. It makes sense that Brewster would watch Winston to see who he contacted. I'm sure I wasn't a surprise to the colonel's men, but you undoubtedly were. They're probably trying to figure out what my connection is to you."

Kit remembered the warning Brenna had issued when she was trying to convince him to show her his pictures. Learning that he was being followed was the first of several increasingly unpleasant possibilities she had predicted. "Do you think that Brewster got hold of the *Gazette* article?"

"If he doesn't already, he will eventually, now that he knows you're investigating the crash. He'll make contact with you soon to find out whether the speculation in the article is true."

"You say that with such certainty," Kit said, his voice filled with exactly the opposite. "Don't take this the wrong way, Brenna, but it's as though you've known exactly what's going to happen every step of the way."

"I know how Brewster operates, Kit. I've been down this road with him a lot of times."

"Is that why this thing between you and Brewster seems so...personal?"

Brenna leaned her head back on the headrest and closed her eyes.

"Brenna?" he prompted.

"At the risk of sounding egocentric—not to mention paranoid—let me say that Elgin Brewster would like nothing better than for me to drop off the face of the earth." Brenna raised her head and looked at Kit. "And I fully expect that if I get too close to exposing his petty dictatorship, he'll try to make that happen."

Kit raised his eyebrows and nodded. "You're right. That's paranoid."

"Would you change your mind if I told you I have the ear of a U.S. senator who believes that certain factions within the government have been spending millions of tax dollars to finance UFO investigations despite repeated denials that no such investigative body exists?"

"Then why doesn't he sic the General Accounting Office on Brewster, or call for a Senate hearing?"

"Oh, Kit, please. You have bona fide pictures of a UFO that you're afraid to make public because it could ruin your reputation. If you were up for reelection, how anxious would you be to run around Congress shouting about UFOs?"

Kit bowed his head in acquiescence. "Point well taken. So you're collecting evidence, and when you get enough, the senator will call for a hearing."

"Right. And a verifiable cover-up into the facts surrounding the death of an American airman couldn't be more perfect. The media and the Senate investigators can concentrate on the cover-up, making the involvement of a UFO secondary. Instead of being labeled a UFO nut, the senator becomes a hero for exposing a scandal."

"And you really believe that this will shut Brewster down?"

"Oh, yes," she said, her voice turning harsh. "With the information my father and I have collected on him, the Senate will have to make him the center of their investigation. I may not be able to put him in prison, but I can expose him for the monster he is and close the bastard down for good."

The hatred in her voice startled Kit. "I thought your father was dead."

She didn't look at him. "Brewster's been around a long time." She pulled her sun visor down again and that seemed to put an end to their conversation for the moment.

Kit didn't mind. He needed time to think, because there was something she wasn't telling him. He could sense it. The witty, vivacious woman he'd come to expect even when they were arguing wasn't in the car with him right now. This Brenna Sullivan was filled with cold rage, and all of it was directed at Elgin Brewster.

What was it she'd said last night when he asked why she'd never married? Something about being too single-minded.

Kit had thought she meant single-minded in her quest to prove the existence of UFOs. Now he wasn't so sure. Like the Senate investigation hearing she hoped to engineer, UFOs were strictly incidental to Brenna. She wanted Brewster.

What on earth had he done to earn such hatred?

Kit decided it was time to do some digging and learn more about Brenna Sullivan than the gems of wisdom she chose to share with him when it suited her. His investigation could only benefit from a little extra knowledge about his partner, after all. But there was a more important reason, too.

Given his growing affection for her, it seemed prudent to make sure her life expectancy extended into next week.

BREWSTER STOOD at the window as the air force DC-10 taxied down the runway for a smooth takeoff. He watched until it was airborne, wishing that all his problems could be solved as easily as these two. Captain Ryan Terrell was on that plane, as was Sergeant Glenn Nash. In forty-eight hours, the pilot would be assuming his new position as commander of an active-service strike team stationed at McKinley Base in Leistig, Germany. By this time tomorrow, Nash would be tracking radar signatures in the South Pacific.

Since neither man had been willing to deviate from his insistence that an unidentified flying object had been involved in "The Incident," as it had come to be known, Brewster had assured their silence by invoking national security. Repeating their stories now would result in court-martial. The destruction of a man's career was usually adequate incentive to keep quiet, but with so many UFO rumors flying around the base, and so many tabloid reporters sniffing at those rumors, the transfers had been a logical added precaution.

The other participants in The Incident didn't worry Brewster in the least. Avery and Munroe were career officers who would take the details of the encounter to their graves, and no one else had been privy to the entire scenario. General Avery would have complete deniability if any of those peripheral participants made statements; he would simply claim that they had misinterpreted the facts.

As for the tabloid reporters who were clamoring for Avery to open the base and allow them to snoop at will, Brewster knew only too well how to handle them. He'd learned long ago that the best place to conceal the truth was inside an enormous lie. That's why his men were actively planting bizarre stories among the enlisted men. By the time the tabs got on base, there would be soldiers eager to relate the exotic rumors of how an alien UFO had "beamed" Lieutenant MacKenzie Lewis out of the cockpit of his F-16, causing the crash of the pilotless jet.

Brewster could hardly wait for the resulting hue and cry when the tabloids demanded the return of the "kidnapped" airman. It would make for entertaining headlines. And all of them completely harmless, since Lieutenant Lewis was being buried in Arlington in two days.

The DC-10 disappeared into the hazy canopy of clouds just as someone knocked on the door of Brewster's makeshift office.

"Come."

"Colonel?"

"What is it, Lincoln?" he asked his aide without turning.

"Delta team just reported in, sir."

Brewster nodded as though he'd been expecting this, when in fact he really hadn't given it any thought one way or the other. "This is the team assigned to Powers, the Knoxville tower chief, correct?"

"Initially, they were, sir. But Powers had a meeting

this morning and Delta transferred targets. Baker has assumed surveillance on Powers.''

Brewster turned. ''Who did he meet?''

''The Sullivan woman, sir.''

''Damn,'' the colonel muttered as he moved to his desk. ''I thought she'd be busy with that ranger we released.''

''That was her next stop, sir. She left the meeting with Powers and went straight to Dearbourne, where she talked to Winston for nearly two hours before heading north again. Delta is on the road with her now—destination unknown at this time.''

''Did we get audio surveillance set up on Powers?''

Lincoln looked distinctly uncomfortable. ''Not total coverage, sir. We got taps on his phones and bugs in his car, office and home yesterday. This morning, we even got his girlfriend's phone, but we haven't had time or an opportunity to get a body mike on him.''

''Damn it, I want total coverage on that man! Powers is our weakest link! It is imperative that we know everything he says and does. If he made copies of the Knoxville tower recordings and passed them to Sullivan—''

''Delta team feels certain that didn't happen, sir,'' Lincoln reassured him. ''They performed a thorough search of Powers's house when they planted the bugs last night, and they found no copies. And today, he was carrying nothing with him when he appeared at the meeting with Ms. Sullivan. The clothing he was wearing would have made concealment unlikely.''

''But we have no idea what he said to her?''

''No, sir. The men on Delta are both known to her.

Once they realized who Powers was meeting, they deemed it unwise to attempt close surveillance."

Brewster took a seat, shaking his head as he reached into his humidor—the only piece of personal property he ever took with him when he went into the field. "In the last dozen years, I have expended more energy discrediting that damn woman than I spent on all other civilians, reporters and UFO investigators combined," he said as he went through the ritual of preparing his cigar. "I should have swatted her like the little gnat she is before she connected with Senator Hanson."

"Yes, sir. That might have been wise."

Brewster was about to put a light to his smoke, but that stopped him. "Oh, really? You don't usually agree with me on the use of Option Four, Mr. Lincoln. Why the change of heart?"

The attaché paused, looking even more uncomfortable than he had earlier. "I believe she may be more dangerous this time out, sir."

"How so?"

"She has someone with her, Colonel. That's why Delta transferred surveillance from Powers onto her— they wanted to be certain that their identification of her new associate was correct."

"Who is it?"

"Dr. Christopher Wheeler, sir."

Brewster glared at Lincoln. "That's absurd. They must be mistaken," he scoffed.

"With all due respect, sir, they're not. While the Sullivan woman and her associate were interviewing Dale Winston, our men lifted a clean fingerprint off the door handle of Sullivan's Mountaineer. They checked it against Wheeler's service record, and it was a match, sir.''

"This is ridiculous. Why would a mainstream journalist and respected scientist like Wheeler involve himself with a UFO fruitcake like Brenna Sullivan?''

"I don't know, sir, but a review of our own video footage of yesterday's press conference shows that Kit Wheeler was at Lion's Head with a GNN camera crew. They may have connected after that. We're checking the tape more closely now to see if we can find the two of them together.''

"Damn! If Avery hadn't been such an incompetent ass, we'd have known about this! He should have ordered the Sullivan woman detained after the press conference!''

"Yes, sir, but he didn't. And now Kit Wheeler seems to be showing an interest in the UFO connection.''

"But why? There has to be a reason, and I want to know what it is. Check with everyone who might have been in a position to see Sullivan and Wheeler together yesterday. I want to know how they met. And get me every scrap of information the Pentagon has on Wheeler. If he's got skeletons, I want to know where they're buried.''

"He's been in the public eye a lot of years without any hint of scandal attached to him,'' Lincoln reminded the colonel.

"Doesn't matter,'' Brewster said with a wave of his hand to send Lincoln on his way. "No one is scandal-proof. If Wheeler doesn't have any vulnerabilities, I'll make some.''

"Yes, sir.'' Lincoln turned on his heel to depart,

and almost made it to the door before the colonel stopped him.

"And, Lincoln..." He waited for the attaché to turn. "Get me a copy of Brenna Sullivan's master file a.s.a.p. It's just possible that Kit Wheeler doesn't fully understand what a huge mistake it is to ally himself with a dangerous, obsessive head case like our Ms. Sullivan."

"I'll see to it, sir." Lincoln turned again and departed, leaving Colonel Elgin Brewster alone with his cigar.

CHAPTER TEN

WHEN KIT AND BRENNA reached the cabin late that afternoon they saw immediately that Cy Coleman had dropped by. A foot-high stack of UFO reports containing copies of nearly every photograph that had been taken by Clear Lake's residents Thursday night was piled on the porch.

And sitting next to the stack was Janine Tucker, pretty as a picture, with reports and photographs spread out around her, and a pair of designer eyeglasses perched on her nose. At the table behind her, Stu Clendennan was leaning back in a chair with his feet propped on the porch railing and a book in his lap.

Kit parked Brenna's Mountaineer beside the white GNN van, shut off the engine and sat staring at the porch. For the first time, he was grateful for Brenna's tinted windows. "Oh, brother. Are those papers she's looking at what I think they are?"

Brenna nodded. "Yep. Apparently, I overestimated your ability to control Janine."

Kit ignored the dig. "What are the chances that our friends in the black sedan will pay us a visit while she's here?"

"Next to nil," Brenna replied. "We lost them in that traffic jam around the marina and this place isn't easy to find without directions. Besides, they won't force a confrontation without Brewster's okay, and I don't believe he'll make a move until he's had time to figure out how you and I connected.''

"So what do I tell Janine?"

"Why don't you wait and see what Janine tells you?" she suggested.

"Good idea."

Unable to avoid the inevitable, they got out and moved toward the porch. Kit looked from Janine to Stu and back again. "Remind me never to entrust my privacy to Cy Coleman again," he said to Brenna.

"Will do."

Janine smiled at them brightly. "Cy Coleman? Would that be the same person who filed this report?" she picked up an envelope labeled with Cy's name. "I've never met the gentleman, but he tells a whale of a story." Janine pulled the *Gazette* article from the envelope and dangled it in front of her by two fingers.

"The very same," Kit affirmed. "But if he didn't give you directions up here, who's the snitch who told you how to find me?"

"Ross Jerome."

"Ross!" Kit looked at Brenna again. "Remind me never to invite my boss up here to go fishing again."

Brenna grinned. "When did I become your personal secretary? Should I start taking notes, sir?"

"That depends." Kit turned his full attention on the reporter. "What are you doing here, Janine?"

"Well, you were behaving very strangely at Lion's Head, Kit. I suppose it's part of your Boy-Scout charm, but frankly, you're not a very good liar," she said matter-of-factly. "When I got back to Atlanta, my boss was as curious as I was to know what you were doing at the crash site. Since the shortest distance between two points is a straight line, he called Ross and asked.''

Janine's smile made Brenna want to start looking around for canary feathers as the woman continued, ''Of course, Ross didn't know anything about this mysterious investigation you were so sure I wouldn't be interested in. Since you told him you were taking a few days' vacation, he couldn't imagine any reason why you would be at Lion's Head.''

Janine looked at Brenna. ''So next, I did a little checking on your friend here, and lo and behold, what do I find?'' She pointed over her shoulder to a stack of books and magazines on the table. Stu grinned and waggled a paperback at them. Brenna recognized it immediately as one of her own. ''The woman who's helping Kit Wheeler do background research is one of America's foremost authorities on the subject of UFOs!''

Kit looked at Brenna and she shrugged. ''I told you my books were bestsellers. They're not hard to find.''

''No, they weren't,'' Janine said smugly. ''And you two were pretty transparent yesterday. Brenna forgot to rewind that video, so it wasn't hard to figure out which segment of it you were interested in. I saw three military types escorting a guy in a forest ranger uniform off in a helicopter, and I had to ask myself, is he the missing eyewitness General Avery didn't want to talk about?''

Kit sat on the step below Janine. There didn't seem to be any point in lying to her. ''The ranger's not missing anymore.''

"Have you talked to him?"

He nodded. "That's where we just came from."

Janine batted her eyelashes at him. "We'll argue later about whether you're going to give me his address," she drawled, then held up Cy's article. "At the moment, I have bigger fish to fry. Did you take pictures of a UFO as this suggests?"

Kit glanced at Brenna again, but she only shrugged. It was up to him. "Yes," he said after a moment.

Though that was the logical conclusion based on everything she'd learned, Janine seemed nonplussed by his answer. "You have honest-to-God photographs of a UFO—like these?" she asked, handing him two three-by-five snapshots that had been lying on one of the report envelopes.

Brenna moved around to the side of the stairs and leaned close, resting her hand on Kit's shoulder. "These are good, Kit. Much better than the Polaroid Cy printed."

"Yeah, they are."

Brenna glanced up and caught the speculative look Janine was giving her. She straightened self-consciously. "I'd better check and see if there are other good ones."

Kit handed her the pictures, and Brenna navigated her way up the stairs, took a stack of the report envelopes to the table, to see how many other Clear Lake residents had captured the UFO.

"I want in on this story, Kit," Janine said.

"Are you insane? Janine, this kind of story could be death to a serious reporter's career."

"That depends on whether or not there's fire to go along with the smoke. If there's a connection between this UFO and the F-16 crash, this could also be the story of the century," she argued. "Is there a connection?"

"Very possibly," Kit admitted reluctantly. "But we've got nothing yet to prove it." In broad strokes, he explained what little they knew, only leaving out Justin Powers's confidential statement and Brenna's Senate connection.

"You're being followed?" Janine asked. "My God, what better proof do you need that you're on to something big?"

"Much better. And a division of labor may be the best way to get it." Kit sighed heavily. "Wait here, Janine. It's time I checked in with Ross," he said as he came to his feet and moved up the steps.

Brenna looked up at him as he reached her. "Are you sure you're ready?" she asked softly.

A wry smile teased his lips. "You're the one who dragged me to this point, kicking and screaming all the way. Don't you think it's time I accepted the inevitable?"

"It's what you think that counts, Kit."

He cocked his head to one side and studied her face tenderly. After a long moment, he gave a little shake of his head. "Not anymore."

He unlocked the front door and disappeared inside, leaving Brenna a little breathless.

"Tell me, have you seen the pictures Kit took?" Janine asked.

"Uh, yes. I have. They're the most remarkable UFO photographs ever taken, but it hasn't been easy for Kit to accept what he saw."

Janine seemed surprised. "Really? I've always

thought of Kit as eager to embrace new ideas. He's a very open-minded guy.''

Brenna chuckled.

Janine frowned. "What's so funny?"

"Nothing. I guess even open-minded people have their limits.''

Janine clearly didn't understand what Brenna meant, but she didn't question it. "How long have you and Kit known each other?''

"I was on my way to Lion's Head when I saw that *Gazette* article and tracked him down.''

"You met him yesterday? You're putting me on, right?'' she asked.

"Why would you think that?''

Janine shrugged. "The two of you have a very interesting…rapport. And you really know how to push his buttons. I've seen Kit deal with a lot of stressful situations, watched him maneuver around infuriating bureaucrats. I've even seen him face down a loud-mouthed drunken bully who was determined to pick a fight with him, but I've never seen him as angry as he was after you left Lion's Head without him. He was so furious, I almost bought his lover's-quarrel story.''

Brenna was surprised. "That's what he called it?''

"Yes.''

"Oh.'' There was no reason for Brenna's pulse to quicken just because Kit had said they were lovers. But it quickened all the same.

"How long have you been writing about UFOs?'' Janine asked.

"I published my first book twelve years ago, but I've been studying them most of my life.''

"When I was looking for the books you've written, I ran across a couple by someone named Daniel Sullivan. Any relation?"

"He's my father."

"Is he—"

"Ooh, this is intense." Both women shifted their attention to Stu Clendennan. He lifted Brenna's book, a paperback entitled *The Conspiracy Factor.* "This document…'Manipulation of Civilian Witnesses.' Scary stuff."

"What is it?" Janine asked.

"It's a four-stage process for dealing with people who claim to have had encounters with UFOs," he replied. "Option One is surveillance. Option Two is to discredit the person—you know, make him look like an idiot. In Option Three, they buy the witness's silence with threats or rewards…"

"And Option Four?" Janine said.

"Termination," Brenna said as she stood and moved down the stairs past Janine.

"Murder? You're kidding, right?" Janine said.

Brenna stopped and looked back at her. "No. I'm not," she said, then moved on.

Janine frowned as Brenna stalked off to the Mountaineer, where she opened the hatch and disappeared from view. "Is it just me, Stu," the reporter said quietly, "or is Kit's girlfriend a little too intense for a laid-back guy like Kit?"

"It's just you," Stu replied, scratching his silver beard. "That is one hot tamale, I don't care how laid-back you are."

"How very P.C. of you," Janine said drolly as she came to her feet and moved closer to Stu.

"Hey, you're the one who asked."

She leaned against the wall, keeping her voice low and one eye on the Mountaineer so she wouldn't be caught gossiping. "Well, I expected you to back me up and remind me that she can't be his girlfriend because he's only known her for two days."

Stu looked up at her, grinning. "Jannie, baby, some of the most meaningful relationships of my life came and went in less time than that."

Janine sighed heavily. "You and most of the other men on the planet. I guess I just expected better from America's favorite hero."

"Sorry to disillusion you, Jannie, but Kit Wheeler's a card-carrying, red-blooded American male. He doesn't chase every hot tamale who comes down the pike, but he's itching to take a bite out of that one, I guarantee it."

ELGIN BREWSTER didn't like computers. If he was going to read something, he wanted to see it in a book or on a piece of paper, not on a TV screen. That's why he left retrieval and manipulation of information in the capable hands of his computer-savvy aide. Thirty minutes after Brewster had requested information on Kit Wheeler, Lincoln brought him a file an inch thick. An hour later, the aide had presented him with a stack of files four inches thick on Brenna Sullivan.

Now, all he needed was intelligence from Delta team so that he could start piecing together the sequence of events that had brought a mainstream media personality together with a woman so paranoid she made Oliver Stone seem naive.

Brewster had read through Kit Wheeler's file twice

by the time the team reported in at 8:00 p.m. He didn't need to read Brenna Sullivan's—she'd been buzzing around his head for so long that he knew more about her than she knew about herself.

"Well?" he said expectantly when Lincoln appeared in his office with yet another file, this one so thin it could only contain one or two sheets of paper at most. The file was tucked under the aide's arm, and he made no attempt to hand it over yet.

"Intelligence from Delta, sir. Two hours ago they lost Sullivan and Wheeler in a traffic jam at a resort community known as—"

"Clear Lake," Brewster finished for him somewhat impatiently. Based on the information in Wheeler's file about his cabin in the mountains, the colonel had already guessed the former astronaut's destination. He hadn't expected his men to suddenly become incompetent, though. "How the hell could they lose their target in a resort the size of a postage stamp?"

"Apparently, all roads lead to one main intersection at the marina, sir, and there's a massive influx of traffic due to a fishing tournament that's being held there this weekend. In addition..." He hesitated.

"What?"

"Clear Lake has apparently become something of a tourist attraction due to a recent UFO sighting."

Brewster bowed his head in disgust. "Damn."

"A very impressive sighting, sir." Lincoln handed Brewster the file he was carrying. "Delta faxed this."

Brewster opened the file and saw the fuzzy photo on the fax copy of the front page of the Clear Lake *Gazette*. "Son of a bitch," he muttered. "How many saw it?"

"The article says dozens, but the people Delta team has been talking to at the resort say at least a hundred saw it, and many of them photographed it."

"Does Sullivan have their pictures?"

Lincoln nodded. "As near as they can tell, sir. When Kit Wheeler's name was mentioned, every person Delta spoke to clammed up, but they all made reference to having filled out a UFO report. I think we can safely assume that it was Sullivan's doing. I don't think those are the pictures we need to worry most about, though."

Brewster frowned. "Oh?"

Lincoln leaned over the desk and pointed to the fax. "Near the end. Here, sir. A disturbing piece of speculation that we would be foolish to dismiss."

Brewster's frown deepened into a scowl as he read the section Lincoln indicated. "The son of a bitch has pictures of Mother," he muttered, dropping the file, though he'd much rather have thrown it.

"Yes, sir. That's the conclusion I would come to, as well."

The look in Brewster's eye would have sent a chill down Lincoln's spine if the aide hadn't been so accustomed to it. "Wheeler has to be silenced. Immediately," Brewster announced.

"Yes, sir."

The colonel came to his feet. "Move to Option Two immediately. We'll continue from there."

"How far, sir?"

"As far as we have to go to bury those pictures." Brewster raised his dark eyebrows expectantly, waiting for a protest from his aide, but there wasn't one.

Even a pacifist like Lincoln understood that occasionally deadly force was necessary.

"ALL RIGHT, JANINE. It's done." The door slammed behind Kit. Brenna had her computer set up on the table and was already cataloguing the reports Cy had dropped off. "Ross thinks I'm crazy to be chasing a UFO story, but he's given me carte blanche. You're mine to do with as I will for the duration."

Janine practically purred. "Ooh, I do like the sound of that."

"We'll work the story together, with me producing," he said, pointedly ignoring her innuendo. "And I want absolute secrecy on this thing for as long as we can maintain it. No one at GNN or anywhere else is to know what we're working on, clear?"

"Of course it's clear, Kit," Janine replied a trifle impatiently. "I'm not in the habit of giving away stories to my competition."

Kit laughed shortly. "Believe me, Janine, the competition wouldn't want this one. I just want to stay out of tabloid range for as long as possible."

Brenna looked up from her computer. "Then you've got until Tuesday if you want to do your broadcast before the tabloids tell the world that you took those pictures. That's when most of the major tabs hit the supermarkets."

Kit shook his head. "I'm not going to rush this story. There's still way too much that we don't know or can't prove."

"Where do we start?" Janine asked him.

"With Dale Winston, the ranger. Brenna taped his statement, but it's only amateur video. I want you and

Stu to get down to Dearbourne and interview him tonight.''

"He's the ranger?" Janine guessed.

"Yes. I just called him and he's expecting you. Make sure you get the details of his sighting and detention. And Brenna—" he turned to her "—have you got a picture of Elgin Brewster that Janine can show Winston, the way you did? I want that identification on camera."

"Sure." She dug into her briefcase and came up with the same photo she'd shown Winston earlier.

"What about tomorrow?" Janine asked as she accepted the picture.

"Find a motel somewhere around Dearbourne tonight and start interviewing everyone who knows Winston—his boss, colleagues, whoever. See what they say about his character, his reliability... We'll find out if he's really as good a witness as Brenna and I think he is."

"Done."

"After that, I'll be in touch to give you instructions on where to go next. I'm going to try to arrange interviews with General Avery, the tower personnel at Longview and that other pilot." He bent to pick up the remaining stack of UFO reports Cy had brought, and put them on the table for Brenna. "Until I get those interviews set, we'll film the statement of everyone in this valley who filed a sighting report."

Brenna stayed in the background with her computer as Kit issued instructions to Janine and Stu. With every order he gave them, she felt control of their investigation slipping out of her grasp. She wasn't in charge anymore, but she was astonished to realize that she didn't mind. Somewhere between her argument with Kit this morning and their arrival at the cabin this evening, he had accepted the reality of the situation.

By the time Janine and her cameraman drove off, the sun was hanging low on the horizon, and to the west, thunderheads were beginning to form great towers above the mountains.

Kit stopped at the bottom of the steps to look at the gathering storm clouds. "Looks like we might get some rain in an hour or two. I doubt we'll be able to do any stargazing tonight."

"That's probably for the best. I have a lot of reports to write and paperwork to catch up on."

He moved up the steps. "You're not going to key all of those into the UFONet tonight, are you?"

Brenna shook her head. "No. I just want to get a list of the witnesses in case something happens to the originals. Tomorrow I'll make copies, then express them to Randall so that my assistant Claudia can key them in."

Kit came to the table and stood over her. He picked up the photograph that was lying on the top file. "Some of these are amazing, aren't they?"

"Not as good as yours, but with pictures from all these angles, taken with different types of cameras on varying sizes of film, you don't need any more validation." Brenna craned her neck to look up at him. "Do you understand what that means, Kit?"

"Well, it's certainly a relief," he said with a smile.

"That's not what I mean," Brenna said pensively. "You don't have to engage Brewster now."

Kit frowned as he backed up to the porch railing and sat. "I'm not following you."

Brenna picked up another set of photographs. "Every one of these reports supports your sighting, Kit. Nearly one hundred people throughout the valley saw exactly the same thing you saw, and many of them photographed it. There's even a man who says he has a videotape he wants to give you as soon as he gets a copy made."

"That's wonderful!"

"Of course it is, but the point is that with this much hard, physical evidence, your sighting can't possibly be debunked. Even a Hollywood special-effects wizard couldn't manufacture this kind of variety of photographs. You can't possibly be accused of fraud."

"I'm glad you think so," Kit said with a touch of caution, "but I still don't understand what you meant when you said I don't have to engage Brewster."

"As you've pointed out loudly and quite often, we don't have a shred of evidence to connect the Clear Lake UFO to the one that caused the death of Lieutenant MacKenzie Lewis."

"But we've got a pretty clear indication that the military is trying to suppress any suggestion of UFO involvement in the crash."

"Why make that your problem?" Brenna asked.

Her face was so blank and her voice so bland that Kit couldn't read her emotions, and he found it frustrating. "Wait a minute. Are you suggesting that I bow out of the investigation?" He stood up. "You've got to be kidding. You beat me over the head with your off-the-wall theories and convince me that I'm smack in the middle of a UFO conspiracy. Then just when I finally get with the program, you tell me to get lost. What's the name of the game *you're* playing, Brenna?"

"It's no game, Kit," she said. "I just want to be certain you know where you stand. When I suggested that we work together, I never dreamed that the Clear Lake sighting would prove to be this conclusive. What's more, I believed wholeheartedly that we'd find a direct link between your sighting and the F-16 crash."

"And now you don't think there's a link between the two sightings?"

"Of course I do. But without evidence, it's nothing but speculation. Which basically means that you have *two* stories here, Kit. The Clear Lake sighting, and the F-16 encounter."

"So?"

"So if you forget about the F-16 and the military cover-up, Brewster will probably leave you alone. Forget about Dale Winston. Broadcast some interviews with your Clear Lake neighbors, show the American public their pictures and yours. Don't say that you saw an extraterrestrial craft. Say you saw something you can't explain, and let the sheer volume of the evidence speak for itself. You'll be free and clear if you do, Kit," she promised.

"And if some other reporter finds it impossible to believe that there's no relationship between the crash and the Clear Lake UFO? What then?" Kit asked.

"Let him—or her—risk his career, and possibly even his life trying to prove it. But I guarantee you, no one will—not even Janine Tucker. My UFO colleagues and I will dig and poke and prod, but Brewster will find ways to discredit us, as he always does. Without the power of Kit Wheeler's integrity behind this story, the incident will become just another entry in the mythology of UFOs.''

''And you won't get your Senate hearing.''

Brenna pursed her lips thoughtfully. ''No. I won't.''

''Then why point out this option at all?''

''Because you might not realize it exists if I don't,'' she replied. ''Seeing that UFO put you in deep, uncharted waters, and before you had the chance to figure out how to swim, I came along and presented myself to you as a life preserver. But instead of helping you, I've dragged you into the shark tank.''

''So you're going to save me by pushing me out of the tank?''

Brenna shook her head. ''I'm not pushing, Kit. I'm just showing you where the ladder is located.''

Kit turned and leaned against the table beside Brenna's chair so that he was facing her, looking down into her upturned face. Her offer was so generous that all the emotions he was feeling for her doubled in intensity, making them very powerful, indeed. ''Thanks for the offer, partner, but there are still too many questions. I'm not going to bail out until I've got answers to them.''

''But remember where some of those questions came from, Kit,'' she said, tapping her own chest. ''This morning you were accusing me of manufacturing evidence.''

Kit sighed impatiently. ''This morning I didn't

want to believe in UFOs or cover-ups, or anything else that challenged my beliefs.''

"But now?"

"I believe in you," he said softly, then grinned at her. "Though God only knows why.... You're stubborn, outspoken, paranoid, opinionated, independent and generally infuriating—" he reached out and cupped her jaw in his hand "—but you're also a lot more vulnerable than you'd ever want anyone to know."

Brenna found she was having difficulty breathing. "What does that have to do with our investigation? Or the price of rice in China?"

"It doesn't mean anything to the investigation..." Kit reached for her hand. He tugged on it gently, pulling Brenna to her feet—and straight into his arms. "But it has a lot to do with this."

He brought his lips to hers, and like last night, the reaction was immediate and stunning. She let the sensual, sexual feelings she usually denied herself mix and swirl in all directions.

She shifted in his arms so that their bodies fit together like pieces of a puzzle, and when she pulled her mouth away from his because she had a desperate need to test the flavor of the skin on his throat, Kit began to caress her breasts. Brenna gasped at the intimacy of his touch, and when he captured her mouth again, she knew she was lost. Making love with Kit Wheeler was as inevitable as the thunder rumbling in the distance.

Kit seemed to read her mind. With a groan that expressed all the hunger Brenna felt, he dragged his lips away from hers and looked into her eyes. "If you want me to stop, Brenna, say so now," he whispered, his voice hoarse with hunger. "Because I've never wanted any woman as much as I want you."

With her eyes locked on his, Brenna answered him by sliding her hands across his chest and down his abdomen. She felt the muscles contract as he sucked in his breath, but that didn't stop her from unfastening the buckle of his belt and the button of his trousers. As she lowered his zipper, Kit grabbed her wrists, closing his eyes as he sucked in another breath.

"I get the message," he said thickly, his jaw clenched in an effort to control the out-of-control sensations Brenna had created inside him. When he finally dared to open his eyes, the look on her gorgeous face was the sexy, self-satisfied cat-and-the-cream look of a woman who knew she had her man in the palm of her hand—literally.

Kit dragged Brenna's hands up to his chest and pinioned them there. "Shall we move this inside, or do I ravish you here on the porch?"

"Take me to bed, Kit," Brenna whispered, pressing a soft kiss to his lips. "You can ravish me later on the porch, maybe on the lawn...in the lake...in the back seat—"

CHAPTER ELEVEN

A REPORTER FOR the *National Inquisitor* arrived in Clear Lake the next morning. When Cy Coleman called to report the fact, Kit and Brenna were still lounging in bed, not sleeping or talking, but not quite making love, either. Mostly, they were just savoring each other and the leftover emotions from the night before.

It wasn't the kind of morning meant for dealing with crises.

"But what should we do, Kit?" Cy wanted to know. "He's here at the Catfish Grill, interrogating everyone in sight about my article. No one knows what to tell him."

"Tell him the truth, Cy," Kit replied. "Or just say no comment. I'm sending a reporter down this afternoon to take statements on camera, and people can do the same thing then. No one has to go public if they don't want to. Just do me one big favor."

"I know. Don't tell that bloodsucker from the *Inquisitor* how to get to your cabin."

"Right. Thanks." He hung up and slid the phone onto the nightstand.

Brenna was lying on her side facing Kit, with her head propped on her hand, and the sheet drawn up loosely around her torso. "Where one slimy tabloid goes, half a dozen more soon follow," she said philosophically.

Kit nodded. "We may have to move our base of operations before the weekend is over. I hate the thought of being run out of my own home, but they'll find us eventually, and we are a tad out of the way here. We should probably start scouting motels or a rental cabin closer to Longview."

"Oh, not until we absolutely have to, please," Brenna pleaded, running her fingers through the short curly hair that ran down the middle of Kit's chest in a provocative vee.

Kit chuckled and captured her hand when it came to the end of the vee. "All right. We'll stay here for the time being. I guess I can live with the headlines."

"What headlines?"

Kit nibbled on Brenna's fingertips. "Former Astronaut Caught In Love Nest With 'Alien' Beauty," he intoned.

Brenna yanked her hand away and scrambled off the bed. "Oh my God. You're right. We can't let that happen, Kit."

"Brenna, I was joking," Kit said, laughing as he made a grab for her and succeeded in pulling her back into the bed.

"Well, it's not funny," she replied, squirming only halfheartedly to escape him. "Your reputation is precious to you, Kit. I won't be responsible—"

"Oh, for crying out loud. You're not an 'alien,' and I'm not a married politician cheating on his wife. I'm one of America's most eligible bachelors—or so the magazines keep telling me. I don't think anyone will be particularly scandalized to learn that I find you irresistible. In fact, I expect I'll be applauded for my good taste.''

Brenna smiled and touched Kit's face lovingly. "You are the most naive grown-up I have ever met."

Kit chuckled. "Not naive. Just optimistic."

"Well, I'm realistic, and I don't want to be photographed naked in your bed when that *Inquisitor* reporter bribes one of your neighbors for the directions up here.''

She tried to climb off the bed again, but Kit wouldn't let her. "The reporter is at the Catfish Grill right now, and no one there will sell me out as long as Cy is standing guard. I figure that gives us at least two hours.'' He ran his hand lightly down Brenna's hip as he nuzzled her ear. "Don't you think we can find something constructive to do with that time?''

"Oh, what the heck.''

As it turned out, they did indeed make excellent use of the time. They concentrated on each other with decidedly sensuous and satisfying results, and then flipped a coin to determine who got to shower first, and who got to start breakfast. Brenna won.

Her hair was still damp when she came out of the bathroom and followed the tantalizing smell of coffee down the hall, through the living room where her computer and the UFO reports had been dumped after she and Kit rescued them from last night's storm. When she passed by Kit's office, she heard the unmistakable whir of his fax machine, and she stepped in to retrieve the sheets that were lying in the paper tray.

The temptation to glance through them was fleeting, at best. They were Kit's communications, and therefore deserved privacy. More than that, though, they represented work and responsibility. A return to reality. And that was someplace Brenna was in no hurry to go.

Except for a few phone calls, they'd gotten very little work done last night, and Brenna couldn't have cared less. She felt better than she had in years— *happier* than she could ever remember feeling, in fact. Brenna had no idea where her fledgling relationship with Kit was headed, but she was falling in love and she intended to enjoy every second of it for as long as it lasted.

Humming merrily, she stepped to the kitchen door and found the object of her affections clothed in nothing but the delightfully disreputable faded blue jeans he'd been wearing when they met. He was in the little U-shaped cooking area, balancing a tin of hot biscuits in one hand while groping around the top cupboard shelf with the other, looking for God only knew what.

It was the first time Brenna had ever thought of culinary skills—even ones as limited as Kit's—as sexy.

"Look! Up in the kitchen! It's a bird! It's a plane! It's...Breakfast Man!"

Kit finally snagged the basket he knew was on the top shelf. "Breakfast Man?" He turned a skeptical eye on her as he dumped the biscuits into the container. "What kind of a superhero is that?"

"He rescues starving damsels and serves them orange marmalade."

"Then I'm afraid you've got the wrong guy, lady," Kit said with a grin as he moved to the refrigerator.

"This superhero is fresh out of marmalade. You'll have to settle for honey or strawberry preserves."

"Oh, how the mighty have fallen," Brenna moaned. "Can I at least get a cup of coffee?"

"What do I look like now? Waitress Man?"

Brenna came around the counter wiggling her eyebrows and doing her best to affect a salacious leer. "Not like any waitress I've ever seen, cutie pie." She punctuated the compliment with a lingering caress of Kit's derriere.

"Ooh. I'm glad to see you're a big tipper. Just for that..." Kit snagged a mug off the wooden tree and poured Brenna a cup of coffee.

"Thank you. Now, what can I do to help?"

"Nothing. Breakfast is served. It's not much, but most of the major food groups are represented."

Brenna looked at the counter. Canned biscuits, honey, preserves, butter, two apples and a paring knife, two glasses of orange juice, a carton of milk... "Protein?" she queried.

"Oh, if you insist." Kit turned to the cupboard, retrieved a jar of peanut butter and plopped it beside the biscuits. "Protein."

Brenna grimaced. "For breakfast? I'll survive without protein this morning."

Laughing, they settled at the bar and attacked the biscuits. "Well, should we be silly a while longer, or get down to work?" Kit asked.

"I'd prefer silly, but sensible has its strong points, too," Brenna replied, resigning herself to the fact that playtime was over. "Did I hear the phone ring while I was in the shower?"

Kit nodded as he drizzled honey onto a biscuit.

"Janine checked in. She has one more interview in Dearbourne this morning, then she and Stu will come back to Clear Lake and start taking statements. She said it would be helpful if we could look over the report forms and make a list of the most promising witnesses."

"She's right. Are you going to go down and do the interviews with her?" Brenna asked.

Kit shook his head. "Not with that *Inquisitor* reporter hanging around."

"What are you going to do today, then?"

"I thought I'd make another stab at getting an appointment with General Avery. When that fails, I'll catch up on my reading. I still haven't put a dent in that background material you gave me."

Last night during the brief period before Kit and Brenna gave up trying to work, he had succeeded in reaching the public information officer at Longview. Unfortunately, all the snooty lieutenant had been willing to do was assure Kit that his request for an interview would be passed along to the general first thing Monday morning.

"Oh, speaking of reading, you might want to start with these," Brenna said, sliding the faxes across the table to him as she popped the last honey-coated bite of biscuit into her mouth.

"Thanks." He leafed through the pages, then stopped, frowning, and went back to study them more closely.

"What is it?"

"I thought you said it was impossible to find background information on Elgin Brewster."

Brenna sipped her coffee. "It is."

"Well, you and I have different definitions for the word *impossible*." He held up the sheets. "Yesterday afternoon when I was talking to Ross Jerome, I asked him to put one of the station researchers on it. He's come up with this already."

"Let me see that," she said, snatching the faxes out of his hands. She glanced through them, unable to believe her eyes. "An air force colonel?"

"Attached to the Accident Investigation Unit," he said with a nod. "That would explain his presence at Lion's Head, and his interest in Dale Winston."

"There's nothing here about the DIS," Brenna muttered as she continued to scan the lengthy service record. "This is all garbage for your benefit. You're a new player in the game, so he's rewriting the rules."

"I'm flattered. I guess."

"You should be." She scowled at the paper. "Stationed in Germany from 1980 to 1988? That is totally bogus! I know that Brewster assumed control of Project Chariot in 1981. He's been active in the U.S. ever since."

"Project Chariot?"

"That's the code name for his recovery and investigation unit," she replied, still studying the papers. "Unbelievable! According to this, all he does is investigate accidents—the air force equivalent of an insurance adjuster."

"What would you expect him to put in his service record?" Kit asked, taking back one of the sheets. "At least he's admitting that he's stationed in D.C. at the moment."

"That's because I can thoroughly document his

presence there going back ten years," she told Kit. "He's trying to establish a plausible cover for his activities."

"Then why lie about being in Germany if he was in the U.S.?"

A familiar weight and an even more familiar pain came crashing in on Brenna. "There was a particularly volatile period of UFO activity in the early eighties. He has to dissociate himself from it. Being out of the country gives him deniability."

Kit frowned. That cold, lifeless tone had returned to her voice. He cocked his head to one side. "Brenna, what is it about Brewster that turns you into a different person?"

She looked at him, startled. "What do you mean?"

"Every time that man's name comes up, it's as though—" he paused, fighting for a way to describe it "—as though someone flipped a switch and drained all the life out of you. The temperature around you drops ten degrees."

Brenna stood stiffly and moved across the kitchen to pour herself another cup of coffee. "Sorry. Maybe you should wear a parka."

"Maybe you should tell me what Brewster did to make you hate him so much."

Kit could see only a sliver of her profile as she stood at the counter, not moving. Not doing anything. Yet he could sense the conflict in her, as though she was wrestling with the hardest decision of her life.

And it was. *One* of the hardest, anyway, because Brenna knew that Kit wasn't ready to hear about the "truth" that governed her life. It was too extreme, too radical. Brenna had friends who spent their vacations at UFO hot spots, hoping to witness a saucer "fly-by." She knew people who were convinced that the Pyramids at Giza had been built by aliens. She had colleagues who believed wholeheartedly that the UFO cover-up wasn't just a national issue, but one of global proportions....

But of all the UFO "extremists" she knew, there was only one—Randall Parrish—who believed as Brenna did that her father's death hadn't been an accident.

To say that Kit wouldn't believe her was an understatement. Of course he wouldn't—he was only one night of passionate lovemaking away from his belief that she was a paranoid UFO nut. In fact, for all Brenna knew, he still believed that. At the very least, his respect for her was fragile.

Brenna didn't want to look into Kit's eyes and see doubts about her sanity. But she couldn't lie to him, either.

Dreading the inevitable, she finally turned and looked at him. "Elgin Brewster murdered my father."

Exactly as she had expected, Kit recoiled. "What? Wait a minute. You told me your father died in a car accident."

"No, I said a car *crash*. You assumed it was an accident. The *police* assumed it was an accident. The *world* assumed it was an accident! But it was murder."

Kit could see how upset she was, but he had no idea how to comfort her. The idea that someone would commit murder to cover up anything having to do with UFOs was absurd. Yet Brenna obviously believed it with all her heart and soul.

He had to know why. "Do you have any proof?" he asked.

She lifted her chin defiantly. "Not even the tiniest sliver. But I know Brewster was directly responsible for my father's death."

Kit nodded slowly. She was challenging him to call her a liar. To tell her she was nuts. "What makes you so certain?"

"Because my father had *pictures* that Brewster wanted," Brenna said pointedly.

Whoa!

Kit felt as though the pocket of air around him had just been sucked away. The feeling passed quickly, but not before a chill ran down his spine. Brenna certainly knew how to deliver a bombshell.

"Pictures of a UFO? Like mine?" he asked her.

She shook her head. "Not quite. He was investigating a wave of sightings in the Southwest when a UFO crashed in a valley in the southern Colorado Rockies. He got to the site, slipped through a military cordon and photographed the crash-recovery operation. I don't know exactly what he got on film, but Brewster was there. Daddy told me so when he called from a pay phone in the little town of New Vista. He'd just left the recovery zone and was on his way to the airport in Cortez when he stopped to call. He was elated by what he had seen, but I think he was scared, too."

Kit saw that Brenna had her fingernails buried in the palm of her hand. He couldn't bear seeing her in this much pain, but when he moved across the kitchen to her, she shied away. He stopped and leaned against the counter. She leaned against the counter opposite him.

They were close enough to touch, but they didn't.

She went on with her story. "When he didn't call me back that night as he'd promised, and I couldn't find anyone else who'd seen or heard from him, I notified the police. It was too soon to file a missing person's report, of course, so I had to fly to Cortez and start the search myself. While I was making my way to New Vista, a highway patrolman spotted a damaged section of guardrail."

Brenna cleared her throat "A search-and-rescue team found his car and retrieved the body. The next day, when the car was brought up and examined, there was nothing wrong with the brakes or the steering. And there wasn't a single roll of film or a camera in any of Daddy's belongings."

Her eyes were cold and lifeless when she looked at Kit. "That may not be proof of murder to the police, the courts or to you, but I know that Elgin Brewster murdered my father. I'll never *prove* it, so I'll never have justice, but no matter what it takes, I'm going to destroy that man. I'm going to bring his sick little monarchy crashing down around his ears."

Kit had never seen so much pure, undiluted hate in anyone's eyes before. It was a frightening thing to behold—a woman of intelligence, beauty, and passion whose life was ruled by hatred. She was so consumed by it that Kit had to wonder if there was room for anything else in her life.

He looked away because he didn't want that image of Brenna seared too deeply into his brain. Instead, he studied a worn spot in the floor, looking for a tactful way to express his doubts. The old linoleum didn't offer anything constructive.

"You think I'm crazy, don't you?" she asked when the silence got too large for the small room.

"Of course not." He managed to look at her again, and was relieved to find that she'd recovered her composure. "But it is hard for me to accept the premise that someone would kill to keep the existence of UFOs a secret."

"Really?" Brenna folded her arms across her chest. "Remember the Cold War, Kit? The paranoia? The insane things intelligence agencies did to keep secrets?"

"Yes."

"Well, pretend you're back there, and you're getting reports from reliable witnesses that saucer-shaped aircraft utilizing amazing advanced technology are being seen near nuclear weapons silos. You don't know what these things are—you may not even be absolutely convinced that they exist, but you're damned sure of two things... One: If they're real, you want one of them to study. And two—"

"I'll do anything necessary to keep them out of the hands of the Russians," Kit finished for her.

Brenna nodded. "Exactly. The simple fact is that during the Cold War, awful things were done. Things like the murder of my father.

"Brewster's cover-up isn't about UFOs," she continued. "It's about capital crimes...life sentences in prison... Careers destroyed—careers that go a lot higher up than Elgin Brewster! A serious, official investigation into the subject of UFO secrecy would start peeling the veil off a conspiracy that goes back forty years. Once Congress starts digging for the truth, the media will follow suit and eventually Brewster's house of cards will come tumbling down. That's all I want. It's all I've ever wanted. Can you understand that, Kit?"

"I don't know, Brenna."

"Well, do you at least believe me, Kit?" she asked him. "About my father, I mean."

"I know that *you* believe," was the best answer he could give her.

"And you think I'm wasting my life because I believe it." She didn't phrase it as a question.

"It's your life. I don't have the right to make that decision for you."

"But you don't want any part of it, do you?" she pushed away from the counter, her breakfast cold and forgotten.

Her lay-it-on-the-line candor was one of the first things that had attracted Kit to her. That's what made it so hard to tell her, "I'm not sure you've got room in there for me, Brenna."

The pain in her eyes was even more difficult to look at than the hatred had been. Kit opened his mouth to call back the words, but the ringing phone stopped him.

"I should get that. It's probably Janine."

"Sure."

Brenna stepped out of the way so that he could pass. How quickly things could change, she thought. From passion to pain in the space of a heartbeat. From hope to sorrow, straight down to an aching sense of loss that was going to be hard to get over.

But she had no choice. Staying here with Kit was

out of the question now. She moved into the living room and began gathering the reports and stacking them beside her computer. She would compile the interview list for Janine as quickly and efficiently as possible, then collect her belongings and get out. Kit had started his own investigation; he wouldn't need her anymore—wouldn't *want* her. She'd escape as soon as she could go somewhere to lick her wounds. Have a good cry, tell herself he wasn't worth the tears, and eventually forget about their one-night stand.

Yeah. And pigs could fly.

Brenna felt Kit's return and knew something was wrong even before she turned to look at him. When she did, his ashen face and stricken expression confirmed it.

"What's wrong?" she asked, moving to him.

"A friend of mine is in the hospital," Kit said, still reeling from the news and its implications. "In critical condition."

Brenna laid her hand on his arm. "Oh, Kit. I'm so sorry."

"I have to get home immediately."

"Of course. Is there anything I can do to help?"

He nodded. "You can come with me."

"Me?" He was asking for her moral support after what had just passed between them? "Of course. But isn't there someone—"

"The friend is Sandy Kirshner," he told her, his voice taking on a harshness that almost made her take a step back from him. "He's the man who developed my UFO pictures, Brenna. He was shot during a robbery at his lab. The pictures are gone."

Brenna caught her breath. "Oh, Kit..."

"Get your things together," he commanded. "We're going to D.C."

CHAPTER TWELVE

WHEN BRENNA AND KIT entered the ICU waiting room, a woman in her mid-thirties, her face pale and drawn, stood immediately. Kit dropped his overnight bag onto a vacant chair and took Sandy Kirshner's wife into his arms and hugged her close. "Is there any word, Maura?" he asked her.

"Nothing since we talked on the phone. He's still critical," she replied.

"Has he been able to speak yet?"

Maura stepped out of Kit's arms, but kept a tight grip on his hand. "No. He's been on a respirator ever since he came out of surgery, and he couldn't tell us anything even if he wasn't. He's drifting in and out of consciousness—I don't think he's even aware of where he is or what's happened." Her voice caught in her throat and she quickly changed the subject. "I can't believe you got here this quickly. It's only been a couple of hours."

It was closer to five, but Kit didn't correct her. Time didn't have any meaning in places like this. "We got lucky and caught the early-afternoon flight out of Knoxville," he explained.

"Maura, this is my friend, Brenna Sullivan," Kit said.

Brenna stepped forward. "I'm sorry we're meeting under these circumstances. I hope I'm not intruding."

"No, of course not. I'm glad to have the company," she replied.

"Maura, what happened?" Kit asked, guiding her back to the corner conversational area.

"Sandy couldn't sleep last night, so he was in his office at our condo doing some paperwork when the alarm at the lab went off. It must have been very late because I was sound asleep."

Tears filled Maura's eyes. "The alarm is supposed to ring through to the security company and then to the condo office but apparently the burglar had disabled the primary alarm, and somehow missed the secondary. Sandy drove straight to the lab, but the security company was never alerted."

Kit remained silent, lightly caressing his friend's shoulder when she released his hand so that she could search for a tissue in her purse. "The custodial service found him early this morning. He'd...uh...he'd been shot twice in the chest." She brought a trembling hand to her face, and Kit gently pulled her into his arms.

Brenna felt helpless.

"It's just so unreal, Kit," Maura murmured. "Why would someone kill for those pictures?"

Brenna saw Kit stiffen. "My pictures? That's all that was taken?" he asked.

Maura pulled back and looked at him blankly. "Yes. Didn't I tell you that earlier?"

Kit shook his head. "You said they were gone, but you didn't say they were the only ones. I guess I didn't want to know." He took her hand. "I am so sorry, Maura. I never imagined—"

"Kit, I don't blame you," she said forcefully, squeezing his hand hard. "How could you know that some UFO fanatic would be willing to kill for a stupid set of pictures?"

"A fanatic?" Kit asked, frowning. "What are you talking about?"

"The police have the man in custody," Maura explained. "When Sandy and some of the guys from the lab went to lunch yesterday, a man followed them to the restaurant, then back to the office. Like an idiot, Sandy confronted him, demanding to see some identification."

"And the man cooperated?" Kit asked incredulously.

"Yes. That's why Sandy didn't call the police. The guy was very polite about showing his driver's license. He fed Sandy some bogus story about having a new job in the area, and convinced him that the man hadn't been deliberately following Sandy. Sandy was laughing when he told me about it last night. He even made some offhand comment about how paranoid he'd become since he got your pictures."

Maura's composure collapsed and she pressed her fingers against her mouth to hold in another bout of tears. It was a moment before she could continue, "I...I told the police about it, and the guys from work gave them a description and the man's name. He was arrested a few hours ago. He's a nut from some UFO group, uh...the Center for UFO Research, I think."

Brenna gasped. "What?"

Kit's startled, furious gaze flew to Brenna's face. "One of your people? *You* did this?" he demanded.

"Of course not!"

Kit turned to Maura again. "What was his name?"

"Uh...Randall Parrish."

Brenna shook her head vehemently. "That's not possible, Kit. Randall would never do anything like this."

"But you told him about my pictures," he accused.

"Yes, but I didn't tell them where they were. How could I have? You didn't tell me! How could Randall know—" Brenna caught her breath. "Oh my God."

"What?" Kit demanded harshly.

"What is going on?" Maura chimed in, looking back and forth between them. "What are you two talking about?"

"Brenna is the director of the Center for UFO Research," Kit explained, his voice cold with rage. "Randall Parrish works for *her*."

"You?" Maura came to her feet. "You did this?"

Brenna stood. She didn't blame Maura for thinking the worst of her, but Kit was a different story. Kit's distrust cut through her like a knife. "Maura, I had nothing to do with what happened to your husband," she tried to assure her. "And it couldn't have been Randall, either."

Kit was on his feet now. He took hold of Brenna's arm. "What were you going to say a minute ago? When you murmured, *Oh my God?*" he asked.

Brenna pulled her arm away, then faced him squarely. "When you refused to tell me where your pictures were, I was concerned that they weren't safe. Randall offered to do a background check to see if you had any association with a photo lab in D.C., and I told him to go ahead. He never mentioned it again, and I forgot all about it. If Randall really *was* following your friend yesterday, that's undoubtedly why.''

She looked at Maura, begging her to believe her. ''But he never would have broken into the lab—with or without a gun! He didn't shoot your husband, you must believe that!''

For just a moment, Brenna was certain Maura Kirshner was going to slap her, but she didn't. Instead, she stepped back and turned away. ''Get her out of here, Kit! Just get her out.''

Brenna looked at him and found him every bit as angry as Maura. ''You heard her. Get out.''

The look in his eyes killed something inside Brenna. ''I didn't do this, Kit. Neither did Randall, I swear it,'' she told him, her voice soft but urgent. ''Please believe me.''

''Just go, Brenna,'' he said flatly.

That was all. No trial. No jury. Just the verdict: Guilty. Brenna dug her fingernails into the palm of her hand trying to fight back tears. The relationship that never should have begun, was ending with Kit's cold, accusatory glare. It was a look she'd never forget.

''All right, Kit. Have it your way. But be careful,'' she warned him, her voice taking on a harshness that was as cold as the ice in Kit's eyes. ''This is Elgin Brewster's handiwork, not mine. I hope you figure that out before it's too late.''

She turned and hurried out of the room without looking back.

"CLAUDIA! Randall? Marsh? Where the hell is everyone?" Brenna tore through the cramped central room that was CUFOR's main office. She made a full circle through the two smaller offices that flanked it. No one was there.

"Damn it, where are you people?"

It was Sunday, but that didn't mean anything around here. When there was a crisis, everyone worked—even the freelancers. So why wasn't there at least one person in the office? This is what she got for mixing business and pleasure. This, and a broken heart.

She pushed thoughts of Kit Wheeler aside and focused on what was important. She hadn't talked to Randall since yesterday morning. While she and Kit were en route to Dale Winston's, she'd related Powers's story to him and authorized him to put one of their part-time investigators on the trail of the airline pilots Powers had mentioned. Randall had assured her that he'd put Marsh Edwards right on it.

Nothing had been said about Kit's pictures or Randall's search for the lab where they were being held. Whatever investigation Randall had initiated must have paid off after they'd talked. Brenna couldn't imagine why Randall had followed Kirshner, but she was certain he hadn't broken into the lab.

Would they be able to prove it, though? The thought that this could be one of Brewster's setups terrified Brenna. If Randall had been framed for the break-in...

She didn't want to think about it. Jumping to conclusions wouldn't get Randall out of whatever police precinct he was being held in.

Brenna moved to Claudia's desk and looked for a message, a note, a doodle, anything that might give her a clue where her staff had gone, but there was nothing. And nothing on Randall's desk, either. She couldn't get into his computer files without a password, which he changed daily.

Maybe upstairs, then...

Everything in her living quarters was exactly as she'd left it—a chaotic mess.

"Damn..."

Frustrated, she sat at the cluttered desk in her cluttered living room, fighting the urge to cry. Tears weren't going to help Randall, and they wouldn't make her last meeting with Kit any less painful. She had to think clearly.

In the cab on the way here, she'd called the Central Division police station and two of its satellites, but no one had been able to tell her anything. It was probably going to take a lawyer to get the answers she needed.

Brenna reached for the phone to call one, and that's when she heard the voices. She was on her way downstairs in an instant.

"Claudia? Is that you?" she called out.

"Brenna?" It was a man's voice that returned her hail, and Brenna almost stumbled down the last few steps in her haste to get to him.

"Randall?" She grabbed the newel post to slingshot around the banister, and ran straight into her friend's arms. Their questions tumbled over each other.

"Brenna! What the hell are you doing back?"

"How did you get out of jail? Have you seen a

lawyer? Have you already been arraigned? What about bail?''

"Why didn't you call? Arraigned? No—"

An ear-piercing whistle shut them both up and they stared at the diminutive Claudia Zukowski, who was removing her thumb and forefinger from her mouth. "This would probably go better if you talked one at a time," she advised them. "And can we do it upstairs? My stomach hasn't seen anything but lousy police-station coffee since breakfast. I'm starving."

"You were arrested, too?" Brenna asked.

"No one was *arrested,*" Randall told her. "Where did you hear that? We were taken in for questioning."

"Did you call a lawyer?

"Yeah. Dewey Baumgartner," Randall told her. "He says the police don't have a case."

"Well, don't believe everything that he tells you," Claudia said as she moved up the stairs. "It may only be a matter of time. If you hadn't been so stupid—"

Randall turned to follow her. "I was not stupid!"

"Oh, yeah? You got tagged by your surveillance target and then showed him your real ID. If that's not stupid, I don't know what is."

"Enough! Let's take this one step at a time." Brenna felt like the parent of squabbling siblings— not an unusual predicament for her when it came to Claudia and Randall. How they related to each other usually depended on whether their on-again-off-again romantic relationship was on or off. Apparently, it was off today.

The three of them settled in the kitchen, and while Claudia scraped together a meal, Randall and Brenna talked.

The facts surrounding Randall's escapade were pretty straightforward. After Brenna had authorized him to look for a connection between Kit and a D.C. photo lab, Randall cross-referenced a background check on Kit with D.C.-area business owners of photographic services. When Sandy Kirshner's name had shown up along with Christopher Wheeler's on a list of ROTC graduates from William and Mary College, Randall had decided to take a look at the photo lab and Kirshner.

He'd arrived there around lunchtime yesterday, just as four men were leaving. Randall followed them to a restaurant and sat at the next table, trying to pinpoint which one was Kirshner, and eavesdropping to see if anything would be mentioned about Kit's pictures. Then he made the stupid mistake of following them back to the lab, and that's when Kirshner had confronted him.

He'd talked his way out of the incident, and had even shown Kirshner his ID to prove how harmless he was.

"His own ID!" Claudia exclaimed on her way to the sink with a colander full of limp broccoli. "Everyone in this den of rampant paranoia has at least two sets of phony identification cards, and this genius flashes his real driver's license."

"And it's a damn good thing he did," Brenna told her.

"What? Why?" Claudia turned on the cold water and stuck the colander under the faucet.

"Because it illustrates his lack of criminal intent. He lied about the fact that he was following Kirshner, but no one forced him to flash his ID. Why would a man who planned on committing a break-in give his name to his intended victim in front of three witnesses?'' She looked at Randall. ''Did the police say anything about me?''

He nodded regretfully. ''I'm sorry, Brenna, but I couldn't keep you out of it.''

''I wouldn't expect you to. What did you tell them, exactly?''

''Everything. Apparently, Kirshner's wife had already told them about Wheeler's pictures, so I didn't have to dance around that subject.'' He related what he'd told the police, which was essentially a repeat of the conversation he'd had with Brenna on Thursday.

''Then I can probably expect a visit any time now,'' she said, wondering how she was going to survive a police grilling.

''But they think you're still in Tennessee,'' Claudia said.

''Oh, I'm sure Kit has let them know that I'm available and where to find me.''

''Why would he do that?'' Randall asked.

''Because he thinks I ordered you to shoot his best friend and steal his pictures.''

Brenna explained the call Kit had received from Maura Kirshner and their subsequent return to the city. When she realized that her colleagues didn't know yet about anything that had happened after her meeting with Justin Powers, she caught them up on the facts as succinctly as possible.

She said nothing, of course, about the romantic side trip she'd taken into Kit's bed, but Claudia looked at her once or twice as though she was reading between the lines.

"Well, now what?" Randall asked when she had finished her narration.

Brenna shook her head wearily. "I don't know. I guess my first order of business will be to hire someone to drive to Knoxville to pick up my Mountaineer. I left it at the airport."

Claudia was at the stove now, simmering a sauce for the steaming broccoli. Brenna couldn't imagine where she was finding ingredients since she hadn't shopped in weeks. "You're not going back to Tennessee?" Claudia asked her.

"No."

"But there's still so much to do," she told her. "No one has gotten onto the air base yet. And you just said you left the Clear Lake sighting report forms with that newspaper guy, Coleman, so that he could give them to Janine Tucker—"

"Yeah, we definitely need to get those back," Randall chimed in.

"No," Brenna said more forcefully this time. "I'm stepping back from anything that has to do with the Clear Lake sighting until I know whether or not Kit is going to finish his investigation."

"But—" Randall began.

She held up her hand to silence him. "No! I don't want to hear anything about it. I don't care right now."

"Brenna!"

"Well, I don't!" She slid off the bar stool, and strode out of the kitchen, through the living room, into her bedroom. She dropped onto the bed and wasn't at all surprised when Randall appeared at the door a moment later.

"Okay, what gives?" he asked as he stepped inside and closed the door behind him.

Brenna gestured broadly to their surroundings. "Do you mind? I'd like a little privacy. This is my bedroom."

He made a big show of looking around. "So it is. Do I get a prize for being the first man to ever set foot in it?"

"Don't start with me, Randall. I've had a really crappy day," she warned him.

"No kidding. Join the club."

She sighed heavily. "Sorry. I guess an afternoon at the police station wasn't a lot of fun for you."

"No, it wasn't. What's your excuse? I don't think I've ever seen you like this. It's as though you've given up."

"Never. You know me better than that," she said with as much force as she could muster. "But it's time to proceed with caution, Randall. That attack on Sandy Kirshner proves that Brewster is playing for keeps. I don't want anyone else to end up in the hospital."

"That's not it," Randall said with a shake of his head. "You got involved with Wheeler, didn't you? You're in love with him."

"Don't be ridiculous." She got off the bed and began collecting clothes from the chair in the corner.

"Did you sleep with him?"

"That's none of your business!" Brenna snapped, moving past him into the dressing room.

"Oh my God. You did." He followed her. "Well, did you at least practice safe sex?"

Brenna threw the clothes into the hamper and whirled to her friend. "Several times! In fact, we made it out of the practice stage! Now mind your own business! Leave me alone!"

She brushed past him again, but she didn't have anyplace to run to, which made it easy for him to catch up with her and very gently take her into his arms. "He really got to you, didn't he, pal?"

His kind, sympathetic voice and comforting embrace were too much for her. Brenna suddenly felt a sob welling in her throat and, a moment later, tears coursing down her cheeks. She dropped her head onto his shoulder and cried.

Neither of them spoke until she pulled herself together and left his arms to search for a tissue. "Does that answer your question?" she asked, trying for a light tone but failing.

"Brenna...Brenna...Brenna..." Randall dropped onto the newly vacant chair in the corner. "How could you be so foolish? Falling in love with a buttoned-down, unimaginative, flag-waving Boy Scout? I thought you had more sense than that."

"So did I." Brenna found a tissue and blew her nose.

"Then why'd you do it?"

"How the hell should I know? I got up on his damn mountain, took one look at him in a pair of skintight, faded blue jeans, and it just felt...I don't know...inevitable, I guess."

Randall shook his head. "Sex might have been inevitable, but you're in love, my friend."

"Sorry. I don't know how to do one without the other. I've had a busy life that hasn't included a lot of romance."

A busy life consumed by hatred, conspiracies, and revenge. A life Kit had condemned even before he'd accused her of trying to kill his best friend. Brenna felt like crying again.

"Well, look on the bright side," Randall suggested. "Once the police clear me of responsibility for the attack on Sandy Kirshner, Wheeler will see how wrong he was and come crawling back to apologize."

Brenna laughed humorlessly. "No, I don't think so. For one thing, we'd reached an impasse even before he learned about Sandy. And for another, I wouldn't have him back, no matter how far he crawled to get to me. We're too different." She disposed of her tissue and flicked another one out of the box. "Thanks for the sympathy and the shoulder, but I'd really like to be alone for a minute. Do you mind?"

Randall heaved to his feet. "Okay. Splash some water on your face and get your act together. Claudia should have supper ready soon." He opened the door and turned to her. "Oh, and thanks."

"For what?" she asked.

There was nothing teasing in his tone or expression when he said, "For not asking me if I did it."

Brenna felt like crying again. "I didn't need to," she said simply. "You couldn't mastermind a break-in to a Cracker Jack box."

"Gee, thanks." He grinned and made a vague gesture toward her head. "Don't forget to fix your makeup. You're not one of those lucky women who cry well.''

JUSTIN POWERS took the first of his three mandatory breaks from work at 1:30 a.m. He didn't mind the time away from his job. The Knoxville air traffic control tower wasn't the greatest place in the world to work these days. The pressure was more intense than normal, and paranoia was running rampant. A. J. Conchlin, for example, swore that he'd heard the telltale clicks of a surveillance tap on his home telephone yesterday. Jim Nakamura said that a stranger had been canvassing his block, questioning his neighbors about the company he kept and the odd hours he worked.

Justin had listened to their complaints, wondering if he should confess that he was pretty sure someone in a black sedan had been following him yesterday. He hadn't said anything to his colleagues, but before their shift was over, he might. Probably would, in fact.

But for now, he would take his twenty-minute break alone.

At 1:37, Andy McGinty came into the break room. The maintenance man smiled a toothy greeting, bought a diet cola from one of the vending machines behind Justin, poured it over a cup of crushed ice and started toward the door.

At 1:39, he tripped over the leg of a chair and dumped the entire cup of cola—ice and all—down Justin's back.

Justin yowled at the cold and Andy apologized profusely as he looked for something to sop up the mess, but the only roll of paper towels in the room was empty and they wouldn't have done much good anyway. The damage was too severe. Justin's shirt was drenched from collar to tail, and the seat of his pants was soaked. When he stood, he squished.

Fortunately, Andy had an extra pair of coveralls in his locker at the maintenance shed, and he dashed off to get them, still apologizing as he went out the door. Justin followed more slowly, squishing his way to the men's room, where he stripped out of his shirt, unzipped his trousers and rescued his soggy wallet from his back pocket.

Even his cash was wet, and he took everything out, laid it out on the shelf above the bay of sinks and wondered whether a bath in diet cola would destroy the expensive leather wallet, which had been a gift from his girlfriend last Christmas.

The answer seemed pretty obvious when he noticed that one corner of the leather was already peeling up. He pressed the spot down, but it refused to stay. He pressed a little harder, and felt a strange bump under his thumb. He stopped pressing, peeled the corner up and found a fine sliver of wire with a shiny silver ball at one end.

Microtechnology at its finest. Justin Powers was wired for sound.

His break was long over by the time he figured out what to do about it.

His hands never did stop shaking.

CHAPTER THIRTEEN

BRENNA WASN'T SURPRISED that she couldn't sleep. At this time last night, she and Kit had been making love. She had been happy and free. She had felt warm and safe.

It was a long drop from there to the lonely, miserable place she was in now, and she was pretty sure she hadn't hit bottom yet. It was going to take a long time to get Kit Wheeler out of her system.

On the plus side, though, her interview with the police had been short and sweet. Since she'd been out of town last night—a fact confirmed by Kit—there was little to connect her to the robbery/assault. They hadn't even been able to order her not to leave the jurisdiction.

Not that she wanted to go anywhere. Her brain was totally numb and she felt paralyzed. There were a million and one things she needed to be doing—not the least of which was filing a report with Senator Hanson to bring him up to date on Brewster's activities. But she couldn't make herself do the report or anything else. She didn't know what to tell the Senator. She also didn't know who to talk to next, or what door to open....

Her investigation into the F-16 crash shouldn't be at an impasse this early in the game, but Brenna just couldn't make herself focus on what had to be done. For the first time in fifteen years, cornering Elgin Brewster didn't seem worth the effort or the sacrifices she'd made to get this far.

Unable to sleep, she poured a glass of wine and called the hospital. The ICU nurse told her that Sandy Kirshner was still listed as critical.

Brenna almost asked if Kit Wheeler was still in the waiting area, but she restrained herself. What good would knowing that do? She didn't want to talk to him. Not now, not ever. He was a man with a lot of good qualities, but he wasn't the man for her. He had too much power to hurt her, and Brenna had gone as far down that road as she intended to go.

She thanked the nurse, hung up the phone and nearly jumped out of her skin when it rang before she could retract her hand. She could still feel the tingle against her fingers as she snatched up the receiver. "Hello?"

"Brenna Sullivan?"

It was a man's voice. It had a familiar ring, but she couldn't identify it. "Speaking. Who is this?"

There was a short pause. "You said this phone call couldn't be traced. Were you telling the truth?"

She recognized the voice. Justin Powers.

Brenna's heart started to pound, and the enthusiasm for the hunt came pulsing back. Reluctant witnesses like Powers didn't call her in the middle of the night just to chat.

"Are you calling from a public pay phone, as I suggested?" she asked.

"Yes."

"Then no one but the two of us knows about this

conversation," she assured him. "I swept the phones and my apartment for listening devices earlier this evening."

There was another pause, and Brenna finally prompted, "It's safe for you to talk to me, Mr. Powers. I think I understand what you're going through. You're being followed, aren't you?"

He didn't seem alarmed that she used his name. "I think so. Yes," he told her.

"What else?" She could see that this was going to be like pulling teeth. "What made you decide to call?"

"I found a radio transmitter in my wallet about an hour ago—someone has me wired for sound."

"Can you think of when it might have been planted?" she asked.

"It could only have been last night, just before this shift. On my way to the tower, I stopped at my health club to work out. I put my wallet in my locker, but I guess someone could have tampered with the padlock."

"Where's the bug now?"

"I took it into my office and turned on last Monday's tower audiotape. Whoever is at the other end is getting a boring earful of tower-to-air chatter."

Brenna grinned. "Very smart. Now, what can I do for you?"

"I need to speak to Kit Wheeler."

Damn. Now what? Telling him that she and Kit weren't exactly on speaking terms anymore didn't seem prudent. But she could tell him the truth without divulging the *whole* truth. "I'm sorry, but Kit's not here, and even if I could track him down for you, there's no way to guarantee that his phones are clean. Can I give him a message?"

"Yeah. I want him to come get those backup tapes I made of the UFO incident."

It was everything Brenna could do to keep from shouting for joy. "You did make backups, then."

"That's right. And now I want to go public."

"What made you change your mind?"

"That bug—along with everything else." He told her about the suspicious goings-on his colleagues had reported, and about the pressure they had all been getting from their boss about the reports they had filed. All three of them had recanted their stories, but all three still feared that their jobs were in jeopardy.

"I figured once I retracted my statement, that would be the end of it," Powers told her. "But that bug was planted the day *after* I withdrew my report. These people still want something from me, and the way I see it, if you and Wheeler could figure out that I have backups, they could, too."

"I'm sure you're right, but I still don't understand why you decided to come forward."

"I'm not coming forward," he corrected her. "I'm giving Kit Wheeler copies of everything I supplied to the FAA, but there won't be anything in what I hand over that proves where these copies came from. He can air all of it—even my original report—but he can't say where he got it."

"I understand. I promise you, Kit will honor that condition," she assured him.

"He'd better. I figure once the truth is out, nobody will have any reason to follow me or bug me, or harass the guys who work for me. And if no one can prove who leaked the tapes to the press..."

"You'll be in the clear," she finished. "You're doing the right thing, Justin. Where are the backups you made?"

"In my safe-deposit box at the bank," he told her. "But I don't know how to get to them without being spotted. If the backups are the reason I'm being followed, what's going to keep those guys behind me from grabbing them as soon as I pick them up?"

"Me."

He snorted derisively. "Yeah, right."

Brenna laughed. "I wasn't thinking of a physical confrontation, Justin. But I can tell you how to ditch a tail so that you can get the tapes and we can meet without being watched. What's the biggest shopping mall in Knoxville, and where's the main entrance located?" she asked, reaching for pencil and paper.

"Mountain View on Glenriver Boulevard."

"What kind of parking area does it have?"

"A big three- or four-story garage that's attached to the back."

"Perfect. What time do the shops open?"

"Nine in the morning."

She jotted down his replies. "All right. After you get off work, I want you to find a logical way to kill time until nine-thirty."

"All right."

"Shortly before nine-thirty, I want you drive to the mall and park in the garage. Get out and stroll into the mall. Don't look behind you, but make sure you give your tail plenty of time to keep up. Go straight through the mall to the front entrance—don't ever rush or run, just be casual. I'll have a cab waiting for you there. Have him take you directly to your bank. Got it?''

"Yeah. Where will we meet?''

"On the interstate just east of the city. You name the place.''

"Uh...there's a truck stop called Checkers at Route 96—you can't miss it. It has gigantic red-and-black racing flags all over the front.''

Brenna glanced up at the clock on her living-room wall. It was a quarter to three. She had more than enough time to charter a plane, pick up her car at the Knoxville airport and meet Justin. "I'll be there this morning by ten-thirty. Is that enough time for you?''

"Plenty,'' he assured her.

"At some point before you meet me at Checkers, you'll have to switch vehicles—get into a different cab or borrow a friend's car. Do you have a relative or a girlfriend who can do you a favor?''

"Yeah. My girlfriend, Rayna.''

"Good. Arrange for her to meet you someplace public, like a hospital parking lot. Dismiss the cab before you rendezvous with her. You take her car, and she can call for a cab and go to the mall. She can pick up your car, drive it around for the rest of the day, then meet you at your place tonight. If anyone asks why you switched cars, just tell them that you promised to give your girlfriend's car a tune-up.''

There was a short pause. "You have an answer for everything, don't you?''

Everything except how to fix a broken heart. "Not quite,'' she replied. "You'd better go now. We both have some arrangements to make.''

"Thanks, Ms. Sullivan. I'll see you later," he said, then added, "Oh, and thank Kit Wheeler for me, too."

"Sure." They hung up and Brenna started making phone calls.

Kit Wheeler wasn't one of them.

THE LIGHTS were turned low now in the ICU waiting room, and Kit was alone. Maura and those visiting other patients were taking advantage of the ten-minute 3:00 a.m. visit the hospital allowed them.

Since he wasn't a family member, Kit wasn't permitted inside to see Sandy, so he remained outside pacing the carpet, waiting for Maura to come back and give him the latest news.

The waiting was murder. The guilt was even worse.

And not only the guilt he felt about Sandy. A police detective had dropped by in the middle of the evening to see if the victim was able to answer questions yet. He wasn't, of course, so Detective Vance had questioned Kit instead. That's when Kit learned that Randall Parrish hadn't been arrested. Though the CUFOR employee was the prime suspect in the ongoing investigation, there wasn't a shred of physical evidence to tie him to the attack.

There was nothing to tie Brenna to it, either, and once Kit's initial shock had worn off, he had been sick about the way he'd treated her. But every time he convinced himself that she couldn't possibly have been involved in the break-in at Sandy's lab, he remembered the hatred he'd seen in her eyes when she'd told him she'd do whatever it took to bring down Elgin Brewster.

He didn't know what to believe. His heart was telling him she was innocent, but his logical self kept coming up with arguments to the contrary.

He devoutly wished his logical self would shut the hell up.

WHEN MAURA CAME back into the waiting room she had a thin white hospital blanket folded over one arm. She looked so tired that Kit couldn't imagine what was keeping her going. He moved to her and escorted her back to the little corner they'd carved out for themselves.

"How is he?" Kit asked her, taking the blanket.

"The latest catchphrase is 'guardedly optimistic,'" Maura replied. She sat down on the little sofa and Kit sat next to her. "He's sleeping now, the nurse still doesn't know when they might take him off the respirator."

"Let me take you home, Maura," Kit begged. "You can get a couple hours' sleep and be back by the 8:00 a.m. visit."

"No. Not tonight. I'll sleep better on this sofa, a stone's throw away from Sandy, than across town in my own bed."

He knew it was pointless to argue. "All right." He held out the blanket and let gravity unfold it. "Lie down and start sleeping."

Maura managed a half smile. "I will if you'll go home."

Kit shook his head and patted his shoulder, indicating that he intended for her to use it as her pillow. "Sorry. I'm here for the duration."

Too tired to argue, she curled her legs under her

and laid her head on Kit's shoulder. They maneuvered around a bit until they found comfortable positions, and Kit slipped the blanket over her.

"It was nice of your boss to drop by tonight," Maura said for the third or fourth time since Ross Jerome had left.

"Yes. I appreciated it," Kit replied. Ross had come by to pick up the fax photos Kit had brought with him from the cabin. "He's a good guy."

"He was shocked by your pictures."

Kit nodded. "A common reaction."

"How true. I certainly couldn't believe my eyes when Sandy showed them to me."

Another wave of guilt washed through Kit and he was grateful that Maura fell silent. She was still for so long that he thought she was asleep until she said very quietly, "It's not your fault, you know."

Kit rubbed one hand lightly up and down her arm. "I'd really like to believe that, Maura," he whispered.

"Then do."

He couldn't, of course, and her attempts to comfort him only increased his guilt.

There was another long silence before Maura asked, "You really cared about that woman, didn't you?"

He didn't need clarification about which woman. "I barely knew her," he replied evasively.

"But you cared," Maura pressed.

"Yes."

"Did you love her?"

Kit closed his eyes and there was Brenna's face. He had the strongest feeling that it was going to haunt him for as long as he lived. "I don't know. This sure as hell feels like it."

"You know, Kit, the heart is a pretty good judge of character," Maura said softly. "It's hard to imagine you falling in love with someone evil enough to do this to Sandy."

"Not evil," he replied. "Obsessed. Brenna wants to take revenge against the man she thinks murdered her father. I don't know how far she's willing to go to get it."

"I think you do, Kit. Otherwise, you wouldn't be torturing yourself over the way we treated her this afternoon. If I'd had my facts straight, this might not have happened."

"Parrish wasn't arrested, but that doesn't mean he's innocent," Kit said.

"And it doesn't mean your friend told him to do it, either."

"I know." His voice was a lonely, hollow sound in the still room.

Maura sat up and the blanket fell off her shoulder. "There's something I don't understand, Kit. Explain it to me."

"If I can."

"You said that Brenna wanted your pictures because she's obsessed with vengence? Well, how would they help her get it?"

"It's very complicated, but basically she wants to be certain that the pictures are made public in order to prove the existence of UFOs. That's why we teamed up in the first place. But Brenna was never sure that I would air them."

Maura frowned thoughtfully. "Well, how can she

possibly make them public now? Police will assume she's responsible for the lab break-in. She'd be arrested for attempted murder.''

Kit frowned, too. He hadn't considered that factor. ''True. But she could always pass them to someone else anonymously,'' he said tentatively, hating himself for even trying to think up reasons why Brenna could be guilty. His heart knew better. Why wouldn't his head listen?

''I don't know, Kit. The more I learn about your friend, the less sense this makes,'' Maura told him. ''I know how carefully some of Sandy's government work has to be documented. Once you lose chain of custody, you risk accusations of tampering. Doesn't she know that?''

Of course she did! Kit suddenly felt like ten kinds of a fool. Not only did Brenna know it, she'd preached it to him the day they met. She'd told him in no uncertain terms that unless the chain of custody was carefully documented, the pictures were useless.

Stealing the pictures certainly counted as disrupting the chain of custody, which meant that Brenna wouldn't have wanted them stolen. She had only wanted to make certain they were safe—and obviously her concerns had been correct.

''Oh God, Maura, you're right,'' he said with a groan. ''Brenna warned me that someone might go after them, but I didn't listen.''

''Why not?''

''Because she was spouting conspiracy theories, and I didn't want to hear them.'' Kit's head fell back and he gritted his teeth in anger. ''God! Why didn't I listen to her? If I hadn't been so damn determined to deny what was right in front of my face, Sandy wouldn't be in—"

"Don't, Kit," Maura said firmly. "Don't get on that merry-go-round."

He looked at her, his eyes filled with torment. "But don't you see, Maura? I didn't believe in Brenna, even as I was falling in love with her. This morning she told me how this man, Brewster, murdered her father, and I all but accused her of being a lunatic for believing that someone would kill to keep UFOs a secret."

"Well, you have to admit, that is difficult to believe," Maura replied. "Even after what's happened to Sandy, it sounds ludicrous when you put it in those terms."

Kit shook his head. "But that was Brenna's point, and I just didn't get it. The *cover-up* has become the secret worth killing for," he explained. "UFOs are incidental."

"Then what are you going to do?"

"I'm going to go see Brenna tomorrow, and beg her to forgive me."

"You could go right now," Maura suggested with a wistful smile. "That's the kind of thing a woman doesn't mind being awakened from a sound sleep to hear."

Kit smiled, but shook his head. "No, I'm not leaving you until your sister arrives from Chicago tomorrow afternoon. I don't want you to be alone."

"Kit, I'm fine. I don't need a baby-sitter."

He shook his head resolutely, putting an end to the discussion. "I'm not letting you go through this alone, Maura. Don't argue with me. Brenna will still be there tomorrow. I just pray she'll forgive me."

THERE WAS SOMETHING about the phone call with Justin Powers that nagged at Brenna all the way to Knoxville, but she couldn't put her finger on what it was. His voice had sounded okay; she didn't get the sense that he was setting her up for something, and the quality of their connection had seemed normal. She had believed his reason for changing his mind about turning over the tapes.... So what was it that kept poking her just below the level of consciousness?

Whatever it was escaped her. She made all her arrangements, briefed Randall, made the flight to Knoxville, picked up her Mountaineer and reached the rendezvous point at Checkers without figuring it out—and without being followed. Every step of the way, she used at least two different tricks that were guaranteed to make even the most invisible surveillance visible, but no one had been watching her.

At Checkers, she was even more careful, parking her Mountaineer in an out-of-the-way niche between two big tractor-trailer rigs so that she could watch for Powers and anyone who might be following him.

Visibility was terrible—a gray, rainy day that even a duck wouldn't have enjoyed—but when the air traffic controller arrived in his girlfriend's sporty red coupe, got out and began looking for her, Brenna waited from the shelter of her Mountaineer until she was certain that he was alone. Only then did she approach Powers and make the pickup—quickly and cleanly. She called Randall at the office to let him know that things had gone off without a hitch, and started back to Washington.

As she pulled back onto the interstate, Brenna wished for the thousandth time that Kit was with her—particularly now when she was home-free and faced with a six-hour drive through the steep, winding Appalachians. Kit would have called the whole escapade "James Bondish." He would have teased her about her excessively paranoid precautions, and made fun of the black pageboy wig she was wearing as a disguise. They'd have passed the time with a lively debate that would have distracted Brenna from the nagging feeling that there was still something about that phone call with Powers that hadn't been right.

But Kit wasn't here. He didn't even know that she had gone to Tennessee—and he *wouldn't* know until she got back, made her own copies of the tapes and could deliver a set to him in person in a safe, protected environment.

And then they'd go their separate ways. Now that she had possession of these tapes, she didn't need Kit for anything. If he didn't air this story, she could easily find some other television journalist who would. The tapes from the Knoxville control tower showed that the air force had lied about the circumstances surrounding the F-16 crash. This was unimpeachable proof of a cover-up, and it was more than enough to get legitimate journalists asking hard questions—and probably enough for Senator Hanson to get Congress involved.

Kit's photographs were irrelevant now—at least as far as Brenna's investigation was concerned. And Kit was irrelevant, too. She wouldn't have to put up with his skepticism, his quicksilver temperament, his doubts and uncertainty. She'd never again have to bear the brunt of his irrational anger or have him judge the choices she'd made in her life and find her lacking. She'd never again be hurt because he was so quick to believe the worst of her.

But no matter how many times she told herself that she was better off with Kit Wheeler out of her life, she still found herself wishing that he was here with her.

A steady drizzle chased her out of Tennessee and patches of fog ghosted up from the deep gorges and hillsides that flanked the highway. Forty miles southwest of Roanoke, the rain picked up, and even in the light midday, weekday traffic Brenna didn't feel comfortable driving the newly revised seventy-mile-an-hour speed limit. She took the Mountaineer off cruise and slowed to a more sensible sixty. Several cars and a huge eighteen-wheeler passed her almost immediately, but some of the traffic was going even slower than Brenna. This might be a four-lane interstate, but it wasn't Kansas. The road cut through rugged mountains that demanded more than a little respect.

Brenna wasn't sure of the precise moment when she realized she was in trouble. She seemed to experience more of a gradual swelling of fear than a swift attack of panic. The semi that came up on her left at first seemed like any other. And so did the one behind it. When the first one passed, blinding her with spray from every one of its tire sets, she slowed a bit more and readied herself for another onslaught as the second semi pulled alongside her.

Her windshield wipers were no match for the fierce

spray, and she could barely make out the taillights of the first semi that had pulled into the lane in front of her. She tapped her brakes again, desperate to get away from the deluge of black, grungy spray from the semi on her left.

She expected the semi to surge ahead as she slowed, but that didn't happen. Instead, a horn blared behind her, and Brenna had to hit the gas to keep from being rear-ended by a third tractor trailer.

She was pinned on three sides, and on her right was the narrow, paved shoulder, an aluminum guardrail and the steep slope of an Appalachian mountain that disappeared downward into a haze of mist.

It wasn't as steep as the Colorado mountain that had killed her father, but it would do the trick.

She was caught in a death trap.

In tandem, the three vehicles picked up speed, leaving Brenna no choice but to do the same. They were going downhill, and the semis used gas and gravity to increase their speed to seventy, then eighty miles an hour. They started uphill again, but their speed didn't slow appreciably. Their trailers must have been light-loaded, carrying enough weight to keep them balanced but without making driving uphill laborious. On the next downhill grade, they'd top ninety miles an hour, Brenna guessed.

Between the rain, the spray and the barricade created by the semis, she was virtually blind. And even worse, she had no options. The truck behind her wouldn't let her slow down, the one ahead would swat her off the road like a fly if she tried to pass him on the shoulder. All she could do was clutch the steering wheel, hang on and pray for an act of God.

When her cellular phone started ringing on the seat beside her just as the trucks guided her around a sweeping right-hand curve at ninety miles an hour, Brenna almost laughed. She needed a third hand, an answering machine or maybe her own personal operator.

"Sorry, but this line is about to be dead," she muttered, wondering if Saint Peter gave points for gallows humor. And on the heels of that thought, she wondered if this was the same method Brewster had used on her father. Had Daniel Sullivan seen what was coming? Had he been as frightened as she was now?

Well, at least he hadn't had a damn ringing phone jangling his nerves further and driving him to distraction.

The road began a sweeping turn to the left. The space between the pickup and the lead semi increased suddenly, and Brenna realized that this was it. They were making their move. The front and back trucks were making room for the semi on her left to edge in between them. Never mind that that was Brenna's only corner of the world right now. The left semi wanted it, and he was big enough to take it. He swerved toward her, leaving her no choice but to take the shoulder. He edged even closer, and Brenna's right front fender set sparks off the guardrail.

The road curved more sharply to the left, and suddenly the mountain fell away to nothingness. The tractor trailer scraped Brenna again, and this time there was nothing she could do. Her Mountaineer smashed into the guardrail, shearing it in half, flipping the vehicle end over end—straight down into chasm.

It happened with such a bone-jarring jolt that Brenna thought her head might snap off, but she was conscious through it all—conscious of pain, of the vehicle tumbling through the air, of flashes of green, of the stomach-churning roller-coaster sensation of falling. She was even aware that the damn phone was still ringing as it tumbled with her.

And that's when it all crystallized in her mind—in that moment of stunning clarity before the earth slammed into her—that's when she realized what had been wrong with her conversation with Justin Powers. They'd had one long, uninterrupted telephone call, but if he'd used cash, as she'd told him to, a mechanical operator would have broken in at some point and demanded more money.

But that hadn't happened. Justin had used his telephone credit card. The credit card had displayed her phone number. Brewster had been watching the air traffic controller's card transactions.

The colonel couldn't have known what they were discussing, but it wouldn't have been hard for him to guess. He'd been ready for them, and all Brenna's careful subterfuge had been for naught.

A telephone credit card.

What a stupid thing to die for.

That was Brenna's last clear thought before the world came to an abrupt end.

CHAPTER FOURTEEN

KIT COMPARED the address on Brenna's CUFOR business card with brass numbers on the Mulhull Avenue brownstone. It looked more like an office for a historical preservation society than a UFO investigation facility, but then, nothing about Brenna Sullivan had ever been predictable. The sun slid behind an approaching gray rain cloud as Kit moved up the walkway. When he rang the bell, a man's curt, impatient voice immediately responded through an intercom, "Who is it?"

He hesitated a second, knowing he wasn't going to receive a warm, fuzzy welcome. In fact, he'd be lucky if Brenna was willing to speak to him at all.

"Is someone there?" the man demanded harshly. "Come on! I don't have time for games!"

Kit frowned. There was almost an edge of hysteria in the man's voice. "This is Kit Wheeler."

There was a lengthy pause before the telltale click of an electronic lock opened the door. Kit pushed the heavy oak door and heard the same male voice in a heated monologue.

"No, don't! Don't put me on hold again! I've been waiting ten minutes already, damn it. Yes, but... No, I can't tell you exactly what her location should be—

she's somewhere on Interstate 383, traveling
north...."

Kit moved down a long corridor to a small central
office that held three unoccupied desks. From there,
he followed the voice into the first of two offices.
Standing behind the desk was a tall, thin man with
dark hair and angry, intense blue eyes. A gold placard
in front of him read, Randall Parrish.

"Knoxville," Parrish was saying. "About ten-
thirty this morning... Look, I know something is
wrong. An hour ago her cellular phone was ringing,
but she didn't answer it. When I called again ten
minutes later, all I got was a 'Sorry, your party is out
of range' message."

Parrish paused, listening, then, "But she's *not* out
of range! That's my point! The cellular company
claims that that area is fully covered. Something is
wrong, I'm telling you... No! Don't put me on
hold—" Kit thought Parrish might throw the receiver
through the wall. "Damn it!"

Randall glowered at Kit. "What do you want,
Wheeler?"

The response left no doubt that Brenna had told
him about what happened at the hospital. "I came to
talk to Brenna," Kit replied, his forehead creased in
concern. "What's happening? What was that you said
about Knoxville?"

"Brenna's out of contact, and I'm afraid something
has happened to her. She flew back to Tennessee early
this morning to meet with Justin Powers."

"Powers? Why?"

"The backup control-tower tapes," Randall answered. "Powers discovered that he was being

bugged last night, and it shook him up so badly that he decided to let you and Brenna use them, after all.''

"So she went to Knoxville to get them? Alone?" Kit asked, his heart pounding in his throat. If Brewster had been willing to kill to get his hands on Kit's pictures, he wouldn't think twice about killing Brenna to get those radar tapes. "Why didn't you go with her, Parrish?"

Randall was looking at him in surprise, as though this reaction was the last one he would have expected. "I'm a suspect, remember? I can't leave the jurisdiction. And besides, Brenna insisted that she had taken all the proper precautions."

"So why is she missing?" Kit asked, then went on before Randall could frame an answer, "Who are you talking to?"

"The Virginia State Highway Patrol. I'm trying to find out if there have been any accidents along the interstate. Both her cell-phone line and her computer-modem line are down. I can't—" He stopped abruptly when the highway-patrol dispatcher came back on the line. As a courtesy to Kit, Randall put the call on the speakerphone.

"I suggest you call Post 462 at Roanoke," the dispatcher was saying. "They are currently responding to a vehicular accident south of the city. I don't have anything on it, but they might be able to connect you to an officer at the scene who can tell you whether or not your friend is involved."

"Thank you," Randall said.

"If you've got a pencil handy, I'll give you that number."

"Go ahead." Randall wrote down the number

and disconnected the call. He glanced at Kit. "How's your friend?" he asked as he punched in the new number.

"Still critical but showing improvement."

"Then I'm still under threat of imminent arrest?"

"I'm afraid so. But I'm sure you'll be cleared soon," he added.

Randall met his gaze squarely. "So am I. Let me show you something, Wheeler." The phone was ringing at Post 462, but no one was answering. Randall opened the lower left-hand drawer of his desk, took out a wallet and tossed to Kit.

Kit opened it and found a picture of Randall Parrish on a driver's license, but all the identification bore the name of Tony DiCiccio. "I've got two more of those under other names. If I was planning armed robbery, why did I give your friend my real name? Why didn't I wear a disguise?"

Before Kit could come up with any kind of answer, the phone stopped ringing.

"Virginia State Highway Patrol, Post 462. Trooper Adams speaking."

"Hello, sir. My name is Randall Parrish and I'm trying to determine whether a friend of mine might have been involved in an accident on I-383 in your jurisdiction sometime within the last one to two hours. Her name is Brenna Sullivan, and her Washington, D.C., vanity license plate reads C-U-F-O-R-One."

"CUFOR-One," the officer mumbled. "Uh, would that be a silver 1995 Mountaineer?"

"Yes."

"Mr. Parrish, are you a relative of Ms. Sullivan?"

Kit's heart slammed into his rib cage, and Randall had to take a deep breath before replying, "Ms. Sullivan doesn't have any immediate family. I'm her friend, and in the event of an accident or her incapacitation, I hold her medical and legal powers of attorney. Has Brenna been in an accident? The patrol post at Wyatt said you had just started working an incident."

"Yes, Mr. Parrish. Ms. Sullivan's silver Mountaineer went off the highway thirty-eight miles south of Roanoke. Her car went through a guardrail, down a steep embankment into a wooded ravine."

"Oh my God. How is she?" Randall asked at the same time Kit demanded to know, "Was she seriously hurt?"

"I'm afraid I can't answer that, Mr. Parrish."

"Damn it! I told you! I have her power of attorney!" Randall exclaimed. "You can tell me—"

"Please calm down, sir," the trooper responded. "I'm not refusing to tell you anything. I don't have any information to give. When the EMTs succeeded in reaching the vehicle, Ms. Sullivan was gone."

The trooper hesitated a second. "It appears that she just vanished."

TROOPER ADAMS DIDN'T have much information to give them, but he did know that the Mountaineer was totaled, and there was quite a bit of blood in the front seat, on the air bag and on what was left of the shattered windshield.

They were guessing that Brenna must have been disoriented and wandered off along the base of the ravine looking for a way up the steep incline to the highway. Being hurt and, very likely, confused, she had gotten lost. Currently the officers were searching on foot, fully expecting to find her at any moment, but if she wasn't located within the next hour, they would bring in tracking dogs and a helicopter.

"I have to get down there," Randall muttered as he ended the call. He turned to his computer and began searching for the telephone number he needed.

"Wait a minute. You can't go," Kit argued. "Remember the investigation? The police want you—"

"To hell with the police! Brenna needs help."

"How is getting arrested for leaving this jurisdiction going to help her?" Kit demanded. "*I'll* go."

Randall laughed sarcastically. "You're kidding, right? You have no idea what's happening. If she's not already dead, you could get Brenna killed! If this had been a genuine accident, Brenna would have stayed with the car and waited for help. Somehow, Elgin Brewster found out that Justin Powers gave her those control-tower tapes. He set up this so-called accident, and right now, Brenna is running from his men, trying to get to shelter and a phone. I have to get down there and be ready to pick her up when she calls."

"I understand all of that," Kit retorted. "But if the police are watching you, you'll never get out of the city. It makes more sense for me to go."

Randall studied him doubtfully. "I don't know. You did a real number on Brenna yesterday. I'm not sure she'd want—"

"What she wants is irrelevant, Parrish. She needs help and we're all she's got! We have to work together on this!"

"Then you believe that Brewster is responsible?"

"Yes! That's what I came here to tell Brenna. I finally got it through my stupid, thick skull that she's been right about Brewster all along. Now, are we going to argue, or are we going to figure out what we have to do to help her?"

Randall still looked a little suspicious, but he finally nodded in agreement. "All right. Let's get to work. We've got to get you out of D.C. without Brewster knowing about it."

"How do we do that?"

"I'll show you."

They got to work.

THE RAIN had finally stopped, but it was a moot point. Brenna was soaked to the skin from head to toe. Using a tree as support, she knelt to catch her breath and take stock of her position. She was exhausted, and there wasn't a spot on her body that didn't ache, throb or outright scream with pain.

Still, she was alive, and that was more than she'd thought would be the case five hours ago as she'd plummeted down that mountainside.

Thank God for seat belts, air bags and miracles. Not to mention reinforced chassis and roll bars. Her father's murder had taught her an unforgettable lesson about lifesaving precautions. The only reason she survived the crash was because of all the special modifications she had made to her vehicle.

Once she'd climbed out of the Mountaineer through the opening where her windshield used to be, basic first aid had stopped the bleeding of a dozen or more cuts, but she knew she needed a doctor to treat her broken ribs. At the moment, though, she was a long way away from any medical facility listed on the maps she'd stuffed into her survival kit before abandoning her demolished vehicle.

In fact, she was miles away from anyplace that she thought Elgin Brewster might expect her to be. She'd left enough blood in and around her car to convince Brewster's men that they needed to watch the area hospitals and clinics. Airports, bus terminals, taxi services and rental-car agencies would be put under surveillance, as well. Beyond that, it was anyone's guess what Brewster might do to find her. Her worst fear was that he had put out a fake arrest report on her, making her a wanted felon.

Basically, it meant that there was no one she could trust. So she stayed away from anything that resembled a road or even smelled of civilization, working her way toward a remote little state park at a place called Fulton Lake. Her guide was a compass and a topographical map for western Virginia that she'd torn from the copy of the *U.S. Geological Survey Atlas* she carried as standard equipment. A commercial tour guide for the mid-Atlantic states was helpful, too.

The little resort area was the only place she'd seen within a fifteen-mile radius of the wreck where Brewster might not think to look for her but where she was certain she could find a telephone and maybe even shelter from the rain. And it also provided camouflage. In town, a woman who looked like something the cat dragged in would stand out like a sore thumb, but if she ran across anyone out in the woods, she could claim to be a camper who'd gone for a hike and taken a bad fall.

Leaning heavily against the tree, Brenna took a look around. For the last half hour, she'd been on a hiking trail that followed the shoreline of one of Fulton Lake's many inlets. If she had gauged her position correctly, she was only a quarter mile from a recreational beach area that had picnic and rest-room facilities. With any luck, the rain had discouraged swimmers and picnickers. With a lot of luck, the rest area would also have a pay telephone.

She hit the jackpot on both counts. There wasn't another living soul in view when Brenna finally limped onto the man-made beach, a two-hundred-foot-long strip of imported sand, with a dozen picnic tables anchored under the trees that grew well back from the shore. In the middle of the area sat an undistinguished concrete building with doors on either side labeled Men and Ladies.

Tucked deep under the eaves between the two doors were a water fountain and a pay phone.

And the pay phone worked.

She wondered how many more miracles she dared hope for today.

It was all she could do to stay on her feet as she dug into her survival kit—the black, waterproof backpack that she hoped contained everything she needed to make it through this ordeal alive. Aside from a first-aid kit, compass, flashlight and basic survival gear, it also held two sets of alternate identification, cash, credit cards, a versatile change of clothes, a wig, makeup and a few toiletries.

She found a telephone credit card for her Marla Gainsborough alias and used it to call CUFOR. Randall's curt "Hello," was like hearing sweet, comforting music. She sank down the wall onto her knees, fighting back tears.

"Hello? Who is this?" he demanded again, more forcefully this time.

"A wayward traveler who could use a lift."

"Brenna! Thank God. Where are you?"

"It's Marla Gainsborough right now. And I'm in the middle of nowhere. I presume you know about my so-called accident."

"Yes," Randall confirmed. "I've been in touch with the highway patrol several times today. What the hell happened down there?"

"I'll fill you in on the details later. At the moment, I need to get to someplace safe, and preferably dry. What have we got in the area? Did you send Claudia to get me?"

"No. Not exactly. Kit Wheeler was here when I got the call about—"

"No! You didn't!" she exclaimed. Her head fell back against the wall and she winced with pain. "Tell me you didn't send Kit! My God, Randall, are you trying to finish what Brewster started? Kit thinks the man is a pussycat. He'll lead the bastard right to me."

"No, he won't. Kit's finally gotten with the program. He knows your life is in danger and he's taking every precaution. Besides, he was so worried about you, I couldn't have stopped him from going down there even if I'd wanted to."

"Damn." Brenna felt like crying all over again. She had enough problems as it was—she didn't need the emotional stress this was going to place on her.

"I'm sorry, Brenna," Randall said with genuine

regret. "You know that I'd have come myself if it hadn't been for this damn police thing."

"Kit's friend isn't any better?"

"Not that I've heard, but I haven't called the hospital since this morning."

"Then what was Kit doing at CUFOR in the first place?" she asked, then quickly retracted the question. "No, don't answer that. I don't care. Where is he now?"

"At a motel in a little town south of Roanoke called Belmont, waiting for a call from me. I wanted him to choose something closer to the wreck, but he pointed out that he'd be more likely to be spotted by Brewster's men if he did."

"Kit thought of that?" Brenna asked in surprise.

"Uh-huh. Like I said, he's now with the program."

"How did he get down here?"

"We chartered an executive jet to Roanoke and he leased a black Cherokee."

"Not under the name Christopher Wheeler, I hope."

"Of course not. Matthew Lawrence."

Brenna remembered when Randall had put that identity packet together for himself, and a short bark of laughter bubbled weakly in her throat. "Lawrence? Isn't he the one—"

Randall was chuckling, too. "Yeah, but it was the best disguise we could come up with to keep him from looking like Kit Wheeler."

"How did it turn out?"

"Oh, it's priceless. With that long blond wig and flashy clothes, he looks like a first-class surfer dude.

Or maybe a rock star. If he gets asked for an auto-graph, it won't be as Kit Wheeler."

Brenna put the images together and laughed again. Even as tired as she was, it felt good. It made things seem a little less bleak. "And Kit actually went along with it?"

"Oh, yeah."

"Well, I'll believe it when I see it."

"Sorry. You're the one who taught me that you never hang on to a flashy identity like that any longer than necessary. If he's following instructions, he's al-ready switched to Alexander Durbin. I hope you like beards."

"I'll like anything that gets me back to D.C."

"You're covered there," he assured her. "I've got a charter on standby at the municipal airport in Lynchburg. I'll set it up so that it will fly to Roanoke as soon as the pilot gets a call from Marla Gainsbor-ough. He can be there in under thirty minutes. Now, tell me where you are so that Kit can pick you up."

Randall had all the bases covered, for which Brenna was immensely grateful. "Okay. You got your maps?" she asked as she pulled hers from her backpack.

"Maps, travel guides, and I downloaded the area phone directory to my computer," he informed her. "All I need is your location."

Brenna gave it to him, and after several minutes of consultation, they agreed on a meeting place. It was only a half mile or so from the beach. She figured she could make it that much farther before dark—and before she collapsed of total exhaustion.

She thought they were ready to sign off, but Randall had something else on his mind.

"Brenna..."

She heard the hesitation in his voice. "What?"

"How badly are you hurt?"

She'd been working so hard at ignoring her pain that she really didn't want to think about it now. "I've walked at least ten miles over rough, wooded terrain in the last five hours. Could I have done that if I was badly hurt?"

"If you had to, yes."

"I'm okay, Randall," she assured him. "You can see that for yourself real soon."

"If Wheeler doesn't get you home safely, I'll kill him," Randall swore mildly.

"I doubt you'll have the chance," she replied. "If Brewster finds us together, he won't leave either of us alive."

CHAPTER FIFTEEN

KIT CHECKED the directions again as he turned off
Scenic Route 15 onto Scenic Route 42. Apparently,
everything in this part of the Blue Ridge was a scenic
route, but even if it hadn't been getting too dark to
see, Kit wouldn't have been able to appreciate the
countryside. Brenna was out there waiting for him,
and the closer he got to her, the more frightened he
became that Brewster would get to her before he did.

It couldn't be much farther, though. His headlights
flashed briefly over a sign that said Fulton Lake State
Park, and a few yards later illuminated a larger, gaud-
ier one with an arrow that pointed to Wyler's Marina
where one could purchase "Bait, Tackle, Groceries
and Beer."

Kit slowed, looking for the turnoff indicated by the
arrow. He was supposed to meet Brenna at Wyler's—
or, more accurately, he was supposed to leave the
Cherokee unlocked while he went in to the little country store to inquire about boat rentals. He would visit
with the proprietor for five minutes, giving Brenna
time to sneak into the back seat of the car. They had
a contingency plan, as well, but Kit was counting on
the first one working.

He made the turn indicated on the billboard and his
sheet of directions. It took him around a hairpin curve,

and he saw Wyler's immediately. It was at the base of a steep incline, and behind it, just beyond a stand of trees, he could make out Fulton Lake.

He drove down the hill slowly, wondering where Brenna was hiding, and by the time he reached Wyler's parking lot, he was furious. Brenna wasn't a criminal. She shouldn't have to hide out like one. He should be able to step out of the car, call to her and have her come into his arms. He should be able to hold her close without worrying that the wrong person might see them.

This was insane.

No, *Brewster* was insane. And he had to be stopped.

As planned, Kit parked the Cherokee so that Brenna could approach the passenger side without being seen by anyone inside the store. He made sure the doors were unlocked, and went inside, praying that his fake mustache, dark-rimmed eyeglasses and Atlanta Braves baseball cap would keep the proprietor from recognizing him. Five minutes later, he came back out as anonymously as he'd went in, but with a six-pack of beer and an earful of information about the best fishing spots on the lake.

Kit forced himself not to look in the back seat when he climbed in and shut the door.

"Brenna?"

"Don't forget to fasten your seat belt."

Kit's stomach constricted painfully as it hit him how very desperately he would have missed that dry, wicked sense of humor if Brewster had succeeded in killing her. God, how he needed to take her into his arms.

He turned his head a little, barely glancing over his shoulder as he buckled up. "I can't see you."

"Thank your lucky stars," she said as she gingerly got up from the floorboard to lie on the seat. "I look like someone who walked ten miles in the rain through the Blue Ridge Mountains of Virginia after she fell down a three-hundred-foot cliff."

"That good, huh?"

"My beauty is truly blinding to behold."

"I can believe that." He looked in the rearview mirror, but couldn't see her. "Brenna, I—"

"Don't, Kit. If it's personal, I don't want to hear it right now."

Kit swallowed his disappointment—and the things he needed to say to her. "All right. Later, then."

"Yeah."

"Randall said to take my next instructions from you. What should I do?" he asked as he started the car.

"Are you sure you weren't followed?"

"Positive."

"And Brewster doesn't know you came down here?"

"I don't see how he could."

There was a short pause before she pleaded softly, "Then take me someplace safe, Kit. I need to rest." Her voice was suddenly choked with emotion. "I need to stop being scared for a while."

"You are safe, Brenna," he swore. "I won't let anything hurt you."

"Don't make promises you can't keep, Kit," she said softly. "We're a long way from home."

KIT DROVE BRENNA to the Chalet Motor Lodge, where he had a rented room on the back side of the small, well-kept motel. He parked in front of the door and shut off the engine, but Brenna didn't stir. She'd fallen asleep almost before they were out of Wyler's parking lot, and he hated to wake her now.

Kit got out, opened the back door and crouched, with his head close to hers. Light from a single lamp at the other end of the parking lot filtered weakly onto her.

"Brenna?" He reached out to touch her, and found her hair damp and matted. He brushed a tangled lock off her face, and got his first real look at her. "Oh my God," he muttered. A blackening bruise discolored her face from her cheekbone to her temple, and there were too many cuts and scratches for Kit to count.

"Brenna," he said more forcefully, touching her shoulder.

This time, her reaction was instantaneous. She came awake with a startled cry of pain, cringing from his hand.

Kit withdrew it quickly. "I'm sorry."

"Don't do that again," she scolded as she struggled to sit up.

"No, lie back down," he ordered. "I'm taking you to a hospital."

"You can't. Brewster will be watching them," Brenna argued, managing to get upright. "Just stand back and let me out. And don't touch anything—except maybe the door to our room."

Wincing and groaning, she crawled out of the back seat, dragging her pack behind her. Kit took it and stayed at her side until she was safely inside, then he hurried to the Cherokee and retrieved the suitcase Randall had helped him pack in Brenna's apartment this afternoon.

By the time he got back inside, Brenna was nowhere to be seen, and the shower was running. Kit locked the door, put the suitcase on the double bed closest to the bathroom, took out the well-stocked first-aid kit Randall had packed and waited impatiently, feeling like a helpless idiot because Brenna needed more medical attention than he was going to find in that box of bandages and ointments.

The shower finally stopped running, and Kit sprang toward the bathroom door a moment later when he heard an agonized groan.

"Brenna! Are you all right? Answer me!"

"I'm okay," she assured him. "But why do they put mirrors in bathrooms? There ought to be a law against it. I could give Medusa ugly lessons."

Kit sagged against the wall in relief. "Well, I won't turn to stone, I promise. Now get out here and let me take care of those cuts."

The door creaked open and steam rolled out. She stepped out with one towel wrapped turban-style around her head, a smaller one tied around her left forearm and another knotted around her torso, covering her to midthigh. It left her shoulders bare, vividly displaying the swelling and contusions around her left shoulder. Streaks and splotches of blood stained all three towels.

"Oh, Brenna."

She stopped just outside the bathroom door, and momentarily forgot all about her cuts, bruises and broken ribs when she saw Kit's Alexander Durbin "disguise." "Oh, Kit," she said, parodying his tone. "Clark Kent you ain't."

"What? Oh." He took off the baseball cap and glasses. "There was supposed to be a beard, too, but I couldn't get it on right. I figured no beard was better than a lopsided one."

"I'll fix it for you later," she said as he stepped closer and began inspecting the deep cut in her hairline and another on her cheek.

He was scowling when he told her, "Brenna, these need stitches."

She gestured toward the towel on her left arm. "So does this one. But we're going to have to make do with butterfly bandages and gauze until we get to D.C."

"Even if it means you'll be left with scars?"

She looked up at him. "There's very little I won't do to facilitate my obsession," she said with a hint of sarcasm.

"There's a difference between obsession and a determination to see justice done," he said firmly. And he made sure she was looking at him when he added, "I'm sorry I didn't realize that sooner, before I turned on you at the hospital."

She seemed completely unfazed. "If you volunteered for hazardous duty just to tell me that, you're a fool, Kit Wheeler," she said lightly as she limped around him to the suitcase.

Kit frowned at her. "Brenna, why are you making a joke out of everything?" he asked testily.

"Because this is an emotionally charged situation, you're very concerned, and it would be incredibly easy for me to dissolve into tears, throw myself into your arms and let myself be comforted by you,'' she replied matter-of-factly.

"And this would be a bad thing?"

"Very bad." She reached into the suitcase and pulled out an oversize black cotton T-shirt with a logo that read: The Truth Is Out There.

"Would you care to explain why?"

Brenna sat on the bed. "Because I don't envision myself in the role of helpless damsel in distress. It might make you feel better to see me that way, but it won't help me."

"That's unfair, Brenna." Kit moved to her with a bottle of antiseptic and a handful of cottonballs. "You're about as helpless as a great white shark swimming through a school of tuna."

"What a lovely image."

"Thank you. You know, accepting a little comfort doesn't make you helpless."

"No," she agreed, wincing as Kit began swabbing at the cuts and abrasions on her face. All traces of humor left her voice. "But it might promote the false illusion that we have a relationship."

"We *do* have a relationship, Brenna," he insisted.

"Not one with a future," she countered.

Kit paused a moment to let that digest. "Because of the things I said at the hospital?"

"Because of who you are, and who I am. Opposites may attract, but oil and water don't mix. Pardon the clichés." She reached up and stayed his hand as her eyes met his. "Don't get me wrong, Kit," she said softly. "I'm grateful to you for coming here, but I refuse to pretend that what we felt for each other back in Tennessee was anything more than lust."

"Lust."

She released his hand. "Lust."

Kit's imagination had conjured several different versions of what might happen when he was reunited with Brenna, but this didn't bear a resemblance to any one of those scenarios. It was so typically Brenna, though, that it would have been funny if she hadn't been giving him the big kiss-off.

He moved to the first-aid kit to get an assortment of bandages. "Then I guess you don't want to hear how sorry I am for the way I reacted at the hospital."

"No, I don't. At every crossroad we've come to, you've always believed the worst of me," she reminded him. "Give me one good reason why I should leave myself open to the pain those doubts and accusations cause me?"

"Because I love you."

Brenna looked up at him again, and when her eyes met his, she knew that he meant it. There was love, compassion, warmth and even a measure of respect in his eyes...everything that Brenna could ever want or hope to see. Her heart automatically opened, reaching toward that love, but she quickly slammed the door closed.

Kit was in love with her, but for how long? Until this crisis was over, the danger gone and their very different lives returned to what passed for normal; that's how long. What he was feeling was an utterly predictable "guy thing." His former lover was in trouble. He wanted to rescue her, be her protector.

Brewster's attack today had brought them back together, but it was only temporary.

Brenna wasn't going to be sucked in. "I'm sorry, Kit," was the only thing she could manage to say to him.

"What does that mean exactly, Brenna?" he asked, scowling. "That you don't love me? You can't forgive me?"

"It's not a question of forgiveness, Kit. We're just too different. You're still the pragmatist, and I'm still the obsessed conspiracy theorist who believes that her father was murdered because of a set of UFO pictures."

"And you don't think I might have come to believe that you're right?" He lightly touched her chin and tilted her head up until she was looking at him as he told her, "Maybe I realized that believing you was as simple as believing *in* you."

"No, no. I've heard enough." Brenna shook her head. This was too intense. Kit was breaking through barriers that she didn't want lowered. "Look, just slap a few butterfly bandages on some of these cuts so that we can plan what we're going to do next. Brewster is still looking for me, and I don't have time for this right now."

"Brenna—"

"I said, enough! All right?" she practically shouted. "In case you haven't noticed, I've had a tough day."

"Yeah, I noticed," Kit said quietly.

He didn't try to tell her again that he loved her. If

she wouldn't believe his words, he'd have to find the right actions to convince her that he had no intention of living without her.

CHAPTER SIXTEEN

"WELL, WHERE DO we stand?" Elgin Brewster asked as his aide hurried into the office. Brewster was back in his own little corner of the Pentagon, but his troops were deployed in western Virginia. He didn't like directing this type of operation long distance, but there were people in D.C. who had needed assurance that their careers had not suddenly been placed in jeopardy because of an air traffic controller and a lucky ufologist who'd gone from aggravating to dangerous in a matter of hours.

"We may finally have a lead, sir," Lincoln said, handing his boss a folder.

"She's been spotted?" Brewster asked hopefully, flipping the folder open.

"Not exactly. But I believe we were wrong in our assumption that the attack on Sandy Kirshner drove a wedge between Sullivan and Kit Wheeler."

Brewster glanced down briefly at a fax photograph, but barely saw the long-haired hippie in the picture. "What do you mean? Isn't Wheeler still at the hospital with Kirshner's wife?"

"No, sir. We had to pull our woman out of the ICU waiting room this morning when the situation with Sullivan went critical. Our resources were stretched too thin. But a few minutes ago I found that picture among the other surveillance photographs taken at the Roanoke airport this afternoon, and I did some checking. We've lost Wheeler completely. He hasn't been at the hospital since late this morning. The wire in his apartment indicates that he was there for two hours at midday to shower and change clothes, but he hasn't been back since. Nor has he checked in with his office at GNN.''

"Then where is he?"

Lincoln pointed to the picture.

Brewster sighed and looked at the photograph of a blond surfer with long fuzzy hair, a silk shirt opened to his waist and mirrored sunglasses. Kit Wheeler? A conservative, respected American hero disguised in a getup like this...?

But the facial structure did bear a striking resemblance to Kit Wheeler's...

"This was taken at the Roanoke airport, you said?"

"Yes, sir. At approximately 3:00 p.m."

"What name was he using?"

"Unknown, sir. We have no idea whether he came in on a scheduled flight or a charter. The airport team is making inquiries. I'm hopeful that someone will remember a passenger that...distinctive."

Brewster leaned back in his chair and smiled for the first time all day long. "Well, well, well. I wonder if Mr. Wheeler has had any more luck finding her than we've had?"

"It seems likely."

"Why?"

"Since she has eluded the police search for this long," the aide said, "it might be reasonable to assume that she had a functioning cellular phone with her when she left the scene of the crash. If she was able to call from the scene, she could have gone into hiding until Wheeler arrived.''

The colonel frowned. After the Sullivan woman had been forced off the road, Brewster had arranged for his own team of "Emergency Medical Technicians" to be first on the scene. When they'd discovered Brenna and the Knoxville tower tapes gone, they'd also found a damaged cellular phone that had been thrown from the vehicle, and a smashed cellular-modem hookup in what was left of the mangled cargo area.

Lincoln's suggestion stretched the colonel's credulity. "*Three* cell lines? Isn't that a little excessive, even for Brenna Sullivan?''

He shrugged. "She's a very resourceful woman.''

"She's a pain in the ass,'' Brewster barked, glaring at his aide. "Don't tell me you admire her.''

Lincoln didn't bother looking apologetic. "She's managed to make herself a serious threat to Project Chariot, and eliminating her has not proved to be a simple task,'' he said. "I think it would be a mistake to underestimate her.''

As much as he hated to admit it, Brewster knew his aide had a point. "How many men do we have at the Roanoke airport?'' he asked.

"Three, sir.''

"Double that,'' he ordered. "Wheeler got past our men at the airport once—it may give him confidence that he can do it again if the Sullivan woman makes contact with him,'' he said, then added sarcastically, "And be sure that every one of those men knows how resourceful she is.''

Lincoln didn't blink. "Yes, sir. Anything else?"

He thought it over. "Yes. Adjust the distribution of our manpower. If Wheeler has been in the area for five hours, it's possible that they might have connected already. Shift some of our surveillance onto the Roanoke targets we discussed earlier."

"Yes, sir."

"Dismissed."

Lincoln departed, closing the door behind him, and Brewster reached for a cigar, completely ignoring the fact that smoking was prohibited in government buildings. He'd been operating outside the law for so long that rules didn't seem to apply to him anymore. Little ones like "No smoking" weren't worth thinking about, and it had been a decade since even the big ones—like "Thou shalt not kill"—had cost him any sleep.

He felt no remorse for the shooting of Sandy Kirshner. Getting those pictures and negatives had been essential; and the only emotion associated with the attempt on Brenna Sullivan's life was intense irritation, coupled with a twinge of fear that he couldn't quite control. But that would go away as soon as he got his hands on Sullivan and those tapes.

It was a moment he was looking forward to immensely.

It was a moment he couldn't afford to have his men screw up.

That realization brought him to his feet. As long as he was redistributing manpower, he might as well do it right. He stubbed out his cigar and hurried around his desk to the door. "Lincoln!"

"Yes, sir."

"Get me a chopper to Langley and a jet to Roanoke," he barked. "I'm going to take charge of this capture myself."

"Yes, sir."

BRENNA WAS FAST ASLEEP. After Kit had finished tending her wounds, they'd argued briefly over when to leave, and Brenna had won. Kit had wanted her to get immediate medical attention, which meant getting her onto a jet to D.C. a.s.a.p., but Brenna wanted to wait until the passengers started arriving for the commuter flights early tomorrow morning so that they could blend with the crowd.

She was also concerned with having the strength to continue this deadly game of hide-and-seek. She was past the point of exhaustion, physically and mentally. Crowd or no crowd, if they ran into any trouble at the airport, there was no way she'd be able to think clearly enough to outwit Brewster or muster the energy to outrun him again.

She needed rest, so Kit was watching her sleep.

This day had given him a little better understanding of the obsession that had been pushing her for so long. Before he'd left CUFOR this afternoon, he'd talked to the highway patrol two more times. He'd listened to their horrifying descriptions of the "accident" site and the condition of Brenna's Mountaineer. He had contemplated their opinion that it was a miracle she had lived, let alone walked away under her own steam. And then he had spent what seemed like at least two lifetimes waiting for news from Randall.

What he had been through today couldn't compare to what Brenna had suffered when her father had been killed fifteen years ago, but it had given Kit a very unhealthy hatred for Elgin Brewster, all the same. The man had to be stopped.

Now that she had the tower tapes, Brenna finally had the ammunition to do it. All she needed was to find a weapon to fire it from as soon as she got the tapes to safety. Fortunately, Kit had that weapon, and he'd spent a good part of the evening formulating plans to implement Brewster's downfall.

As he watched her sleep, knowing it would be several hours before they could make a move to get out of Roanoke, one of those plans came clearly into focus.

This delay could work to their advantage in more ways than one.

Smiling at the thought of what he was about to do, Kit used Randall's scrambled CUFOR cellular phone to call Ross Jerome. The GNN news director answered his home phone on the second ring.

"Ross? It's Kit Wheeler," he said, keeping his voice low so he wouldn't wake Brenna.

"Kit? It's about time you checked in. I've been trying to reach you all day. I thought you were coming into the office this afternoon."

He sounded agitated, but that was nothing unusual. Ross was famous for his temper. "I got sidetracked," Kit replied softly.

"Doing what?"

"Rescuing the woman I love."

That took a little of the wind out of Ross's sails. "Oh, really? When did you take time out from chasing UFOs to fall in love?"

"I'll tell you a secret, Ross. If you fall in love with

a UFO chaser, you don't have to take time out," Kit replied. "Why were you trying to reach me?"

"Your friend, Maura Kirshner, started calling me when she couldn't reach you."

Kit's heart jumped into his throat. "What's wrong? Is Sandy worse? Is he—"

"He's fine, Kit," Ross reassured him hastily. "They took him off the respirator this afternoon and he was able to make a statement to the police."

"Thank God," Kit murmured. "He told them Randall Parrish had nothing to do with the break-in, right?"

Ross sounded surprised when he asked, "How did you know that?"

Kit looked at Brenna. *I started listening to my heart,* he almost said, but didn't. He needed Ross's help, and the news director was already skeptical of the story Kit was pursuing—it wouldn't do to have Ross think his science correspondent had gone all the way around the bend.

"Never mind. What else did Sandy tell the police?"

"That the whole break-in scenario was a lot more complicated than they figured," Ross replied. "It was no accident that that secondary alarm sounded in Sandy's office. It was set off deliberately to bring Sandy to the scene because the thieves couldn't find what they were looking for."

"You mean, my pictures," Kit murmured as his guilt swelled and his hatred for Elgin Brewster grew.

"Yeah."

Brenna stirred in her sleep, and Kit moved into the bathroom where he could talk without disturbing her.

"Does Sandy think he can identify the men if he sees them again?"

"No, they were wearing ski masks, but both men were under six feet tall. Apparently, Randall Parrish is well over that, which put him in the clear," Ross told him. "Listen, Kit, I think you ought to know that I brought Janine and Stu up here this evening to cover the attack on Sandy because it's so obviously related to this cockamamy UFO story of yours."

"They're in D.C.? That's great! How did Janine do with the interviews yesterday?"

"Oh, she's in hog heaven—she did the Clear Lake interviews and even managed to get onto Longview Air Force Base, where she found out that several of the people involved in that crash last week were transferred to posts out of the country."

Kit remembered the prediction Brenna had made last week. "Including the other F-16 pilot, right?"

"And two men who were in the control tower at the time of the incident," Ross confirmed. "Janine's caught the scent of a cover-up, and it's everything I can do to rein her in."

"She's got a good nose," Kit replied. "Just make sure she knows that the man behind that cover-up is willing to kill. He tried again today, and we're not out of the woods yet."

"What do you mean?"

Using broad strokes, Kit explained what had happened to Brenna and the fix they were in because of the Knoxville tower tapes.

"My God," Ross said with a touch of awe in his voice. "Kit, this is unbelievable. I mean, *literally* unbelievable. I don't care how much evidence you have, if we go on record with accusations like these, we're going to take a lot of heat—and most of it will be directed at you."

"I know, Ross, but this has to be done, and it has to be done fast," Kit insisted. "Until those tower tapes are made public, Brenna's life is in danger, so you're going to help me make them public. And soon."

"All right, all right."

"I'm just sorry that I'm going to have to do this story with nothing but the fax copies of my Clear Lake photographs. It was going to be hard enough to defend their authenticity when I had original pictures and clean negatives. Without them, it may be impossible."

"Didn't I tell you?" Ross asked.

"Tell me what?"

"The reason why Maura was so determined to reach you this afternoon. Sandy put your pictures and negatives in a safe-deposit box at his bank—all the thieves got was a set of negatives from a fireworks display and an extra set of UFO pix that Sandy printed to show Maura," Ross explained. "When Maura learned about the safe-deposit box, she wanted the originals out of their bank immediately before the bad guys figure out that they've been duped."

Kit couldn't believe what he was hearing. Sandy was a genius. And fortunately, a *live* one. "Ross, can you take care of that first thing tomorrow morning if I'm not back by then? Go to the bank with Maura—"

"We've already done that. We took an armed escort with us there this afternoon—your UFO pictures and negatives are in one of the vaults at GNN."

"Then I've got everything I need to do this report."

"We'll be ready here when you are," Ross assured him. "But how are you going to get back here? And when?"

"I've got a few thoughts on that. In fact, that's why I called," Kit replied. "Here's what I want you to do."

It only took a few minutes to lay out his plan.

CHAPTER SEVENTEEN

"STOP TWITCHING or I'm never going to get it in position," Brenna said testily. She was trying to get Kit's beard glued into place so that they could get out of the Chalet Motor Lodge and to the airport, but the beard wasn't cooperating.

"But it itches," he complained.

"Live with it."

Kit was sitting on the vanity in the bathroom so that Brenna didn't have to bend to reach him. Their heads were close together, and Brenna's battered face was scrunched into a very pretty frown of concentration. Unfortunately, seven hours' sleep hadn't improved her disposition. If anything, it was worse.

But that didn't change the fact that he loved her.

"You know, I don't remember you being this grumpy when we woke up together Sunday morning at the cabin," he commented lightly. Her eyes darted toward his, then back to the spot by his ear where she was trying to get the beard to stick, but she didn't comment. "From the way you were behaving then," he said finally, "I figured you were a morning person."

Brenna's jaw stiffened and her spirit-gum brush "accidentally" stabbed his chin as she forcibly turned his head so that she could work on the other jaw. But she still didn't take the bait.

Kit let a moment go by before he tried again. He leaned forward just an inch or two and sniffed. "You smell good."

Brenna pulled back with an exasperated sigh. "If you're trying to flirt with me, your timing stinks, Wheeler."

"Because it's 6:00 a.m.?"

"Because I dumped you last night. Remember? Don't you recognized dumping when you see it?" she asked irritably. "I certainly did when you told me to take a hike at the hospital."

"I tried to apologize for that and you wouldn't let me," he reminded her.

"I heard the apology and I accepted it," she said, grabbing his jaw and yanking his face to the right. "Now, *you* accept the fact that it doesn't matter. When we get back to D.C., we're going our separate ways."

Kit grinned. Brenna was weakening—he could tell he was starting to crack through the wall she'd built up against him. It was only a matter of time.

Providing that they got out of this alive, of course.

They were actually about ready to make their move. As soon as Brenna woke up, she'd called Randall and told him to have the standby charter at the Roanoke airport at six-thirty. She wanted to arrive shortly thereafter, make a smooth walk through the terminal out to the tarmac, board the plane and take off. If all went well, the whole operation would take less than five minutes.

But they had to get there first.

"All right. I think that's got it," Brenna announced, stepping back from the sink.

Kit slid off and turned to look in the mirror over the lavatory. "Not bad," he said, turning his head from side to side. "Maybe I'll grow a beard when this is all over."

"Not a good idea," Brenna said. "It makes your face look too long, and hides your square jawline."

Kit looked at her and grinned. "You like my jawline, huh?"

Brenna retreated from the bathroom. "Of course not."

He leaned against the door. "Then why do you care if I grow a beard? You won't be around to see it."

Brenna stopped and faced him, arms akimbo. "What the hell has gotten into you, Kit? You're behaving as though we're getting ready for the Junior/ Senior Prom! Will you get serious?"

He took a pair of eyeglasses from his pocket, slipped them on and regarded her gravely. "How's this?"

Brenna closed her eyes and took a deep breath. When she opened them, she said, "Are you getting punchy? Is that the problem? Why didn't you get some sleep while I was resting?"

"Because I had plans to make."

"What plans?"

He grinned at her. "It's a surprise. You're not the only one with friends in high places, you know."

"We can discuss that later. Right now I just want to get out of here." She stepped around him and checked her hair in the bathroom mirror. What she saw wasn't encouraging. Her short, curly blond wig was styled so that it hid the damage on her forehead, and theatrical makeup had covered the horrible bruises around her left eye and cheek, but nothing was going to camouflage the tiny butterfly bandages on her cuts. She'd covered them with makeup, too, but if anyone got too close it would be painfully obvious that she had recently had a close encounter with a windshield.

What she needed was something that would take the focus off her face and put it on something else. For a moment, she considered having Kit get back into his surfer disguise so that people would look at the hairy hunk she was with instead of her, but Randall was right. Using an outlandish disguise twice was just asking for disaster.

So what could she use for a visual diversion? She looked herself up and down in the mirror and hit upon the obvious immediately. "Got it!" she said, hurrying from the bathroom as quickly as her battered body would move.

"Got what?" Kit asked as she moved around him and grabbed the pillows off both beds. "What are you doing?"

"Making you a father," she said. She began stuffing all the pillows into one pillowcase.

Kit grinned. "Gee, that has a nice ring to it. Shouldn't we get married first, though?"

"I prefer being a single parent, thank you very much." She pointed to the suitcase. "Throw me that long white T-shirt."

He did, then stood back and watched appreciatively as Brenna transformed herself into an expectant mother. "You know, it's funny, but I thought procreating would be more fun than this."

"You're having all the fun you deserve," she told him.

"Do I at least get to choose the name for our baby?"

"Knock yourself out."

"Uh...Christopher, Jr., if it's a boy, obviously. And if it's a girl...um... If it's a girl, we'll name her Christine."

Brenna looked at him. "Your modesty knows no bounds."

"Thank you."

Shaking her head, she finished tying a knot in the tail of her camp shirt, effectively securing the stuffed pillows in place over her midriff. She put the oversize T-shirt on over that and pulled her shirt collar out, creating the popular layered look.

"Well?" She turned sideways. "How do I look?"

"You're positively glowing."

"Thanks. Then throw some extra money for the pillows on the bureau with the room key and let's get out of here."

A HEAVY FOG that had developed overnight was just beginning to burn off the mountains as they headed for the airport. As soon as they got on the road, Brenna called Greg McMillian, who was supposed to have his jet on the Roanoke tarmac by six-thirty, but when she reached the pilot on his onboard cellular phone he was in a holding pattern somewhere over the city. The fog had socked in the airport, and flights had only just begun to be cleared for landing. They calculated the time and figured that Brenna and Kit would be strolling through a very crowded terminal at about the time McMillian reached the charter area.

They couldn't have asked for a better situation.

Brenna's heart was pounding double-time when they parked the Cherokee and got out. She carried her backpack in one hand, Kit took charge of their only suitcase, and they started inside.

"Do you suppose it would help if we tried to look a little less like a couple walking in front of a firing squad?" Kit asked.

Brenna looked up at him and forced a laugh that was strictly for the benefit of anyone who might be watching. "But that's exactly what we *are* doing," she said gaily, taking Kit's free hand in hers. "Brewster has men here somewhere, I'm certain of it. Maybe we should drive back to D.C., instead. The possibility that he has the license number of your rented Cherokee is slim. We might make it."

She was smiling up at him, but Kit saw the fear that was sparked by the thought of going head-to-head with Brewster's road warriors again. He returned her smile fondly, hoping he looked like a doting husband. "Not a chance. It's too late to turn back now. It'll be all right, Brenna. I promise."

"If you say so." She squeezed his hand tightly as they approached the terminal door. The gesture had nothing to do with their happy-couple charade. "Thank you, Kit."

"For what?"

"Putting your life on the line for me," she said softly.

"I didn't have a choice. I love you." He dropped

her hand and opened the door, stepping back to let her pass.

The terminal was like most regional airports—a long, narrow cavern. This one had a bay of half a dozen ticket counters to the left and a snack bar to the right, with the center area occupied by rows of connected airport chairs.

All Kit and Brenna had to do was make it around the seating area, through the back door, down to the gate marked Charters, across a long stretch of tarmac and onto Greg McMillian's jet.

But the minute Brenna stepped through the front door, she saw one of Brewster's men standing at the back door, studying every face that passed him. And there was another man on the other side of the door doing the same thing. Both had telltale coils of a microphone cable running from their ear into their shirts. They were wired for sound, in constant communication with each other.

She flashed Kit her brightest, most sincere smile. "We're in trouble, darling," she said sotto voce.

He grinned at her. "You mean the bookends at the back door? I see them."

"Any suggestions?" Brenna put a hand to the small of her back and rubbed, hoping it was a good approximation of a pregnant woman with a backache.

"Just keep moving," he said as they stepped in behind a cluster of people moving toward the exit. He raised his voice to a conversational level and reached for her backpack. "Here, honey, let me carry that. It's too heavy for you."

She let it go, but reluctantly. The tapes were inside. "Thank you. Just be careful with it, darling."

Someone announced over a PA, "Appalachia Flight 467 from Richmond to Raleigh-Durham has arrived at gate two. Passengers may begin boarding immediately."

A dozen people stood as one and started for the doors. The miniflood slowed Kit and Brenna's progress, but they didn't mind. The more people the bookends had to look at, the less likely they were to spot their quarry.

A different voice came over the PA, announcing, "This is the last call for Coastal Flight 21 to Washington, D.C. Repeating...this is the last call for Coastal Flight 21 to Washington, departing from gate one. As a reminder, Coastal Flight 38 to Atlanta is currently boarding at gate three. We apologize for the delay, and thank you for flying Coastal Airlines."

The bookends took their eyes off the crowd and glanced outside, as though they thought maybe they'd missed something. Brenna issued a silent prayer that they'd abandon their posts to take one last look at the passengers getting on that Washington flight, but she wasn't that lucky. The bookends stayed where they were, searching faces.

Brenna and Kit kept moving, doing nothing that would call attention to themselves. Neither of them looked directly at either of the men, but as she neared the door, Brenna was keenly aware of them in her peripheral vision. She knew exactly when the one on the left looked at her, then glanced over to Kit's face, then on to the couple behind them. She knew when the one on the right did the same.

But his glance didn't move on. He studied her face a moment too long, then looked at Kit. A second later, he raised his fist to his mouth and said something into a handheld mike.

She and Kit were only a step away from the threshold when the one on the left looked at them sharply, scrutinizing them all over again.

Kit put his hand on Brenna's back. "Keep going," he muttered, edging behind her as she went through the door. "Get ready to run."

"No."

"Just do what I say. Trust me."

The bookends started to move toward them.

Kit shoved the backpack into Brenna's hands and pushed her toward the charter gate. The McMillian jet was only sixty yards away, its door open, its short staircase lowered.

"Kit Wheeler?"

The bookends were right behind him.

"Run!" he ordered her.

She didn't have a choice. She ran.

"Freeze! This is the FBI!" a voice behind her shouted, and she heard Kit growl, "Like hell you are," and then all hell broke loose.

Passengers started screaming and scrambling for cover, and Brenna heard the sound of a struggle behind her, but she kept running.

When she became aware that someone was behind her, she strengthened her grip on the backpack so that she could use it as a weapon. She glanced over her shoulder, ready to spin and swing, but it was Kit...with two of Brewster's men not far behind him...and two more right behind *them*.

"Keep going!" he commanded as they burst through the gate onto the apron. One of their pursuers shouted again for them to stop, and coupled it with an "Or I'll shoot!"

When she heard the two gunshots, Brenna stumbled, but Kit grabbed her arm and propelled her forward. She looked over her shoulder again and saw the "FBI" man who had fired into the air. He was bringing his gun down now, taking aim.

They were more than halfway to the plane, but Brenna couldn't risk it. She was willing to give her own life in her quest for justice, but she wouldn't sacrifice Kit's.

She slowed down, but Kit still had hold of her arm. As he yanked her forward, she gasped, "I'm giving it to them!"

"No! You don't have to. Look at the plane," Kit commanded.

Brenna looked again and saw a man coming toward them with something huge lumped on one of his shoulders. "What?"

She glanced over her shoulder again, and realized that their pursuers were falling behind.

They, too, had seen Stu Clendennan and the big GNN camera that had been filming the entire chase.

"Surprise!" Kit said, grinning from ear to ear as they dashed toward the plane.

OF COURSE, they were anything but home free, even after they reached the safety of the plane and Janine Tucker raised the stairs and secured the door behind Stu. The jet immediately began taxiing toward the runway and Kit ordered everyone to get seated and buckled in, but when he hurried into the cockpit, he found that leaving wasn't going to be easy.

Greg McMillian was on the radio with the tower supervisor who was informing the pilot that he had just taken federal fugitives aboard his aircraft and he was to taxi immediately to apron marker B6 and await boarding by the FBI.

McMillian looked over his shoulder at the bearded man behind him. "Kit Wheeler?" he asked skeptically.

Kit began pulling off his beard. "That's me. And I'm no federal fugitive."

"Well, that may be, sir, but I can't take off without clearance. I could lose my license."

"That's true. So here's the deal." Kit sat in the copilot's seat and extended his hand with his thumb in the air and his forefinger pointed at McMillian. "Pretend this is a gun and think of this as a hijacking. You can't lose your license if I'm doing the flying." Kit lowered his hand. "Please. This is important. Those men have already tried to kill two of the people I love most in the world. I promise, you won't get into trouble."

McMillian took his hands off the controls. "Hey, if you could fly the space shuttle, I guess you can fly this. It's your license, not mine."

Kit settled a headset onto his head, and took the controls, not bothering to point out that he'd lost his pilot's license when he developed vertigo problems. But that didn't mean he'd forgotten how to fly.

"Roanoke tower, this is Dr. Christopher Wheeler of Global Network News," he informed the supervisor on the other end of the radio. "I am not a fugitive, federal or otherwise, and the men who are in your terminal posing as FBI agents are not, in fact, the FBI.

I have commandeered this jet from Greg McMillian, and I *am* taking off. You'd better make room for me."

"Uh...Dr. Wheeler...please. Stand down your aircraft until we can sort this out," the supervisor said.

"No, sir. There is too much at stake. I'm on my way to Washington, and I'll do my sorting out when I arrive. Put Elgin Brewster on the horn," he said, playing a hunch.

He turned the jet onto the end of the runway, jockeyed into takeoff position, set his instruments and had his hand on the throttle by the time he heard a deep growling voice say, "This is Elgin Brewster."

Kit's hand tensed on the throttle. "Hi ya, Colonel. This round is mine," he said, then switched off the radio and proceeded to prove his claim by putting the jet into the air. He'd forgotten how much fun it was, and this takeoff was particularly sweet.

He turned the radio back on. "Still there, Colonel?"

"You haven't won anything, Wheeler," Brewster informed him. "As soon as you land—"

"By the time I land, your goose will be cooked, Colonel. I've got a camera crew on board, ready with a satellite hookup to GNN in Washington. We'll be on the air, live, around the world, in fifteen minutes, and there's not a damn thing you can do about it."

Kit didn't wait for a response. He yanked the headset off and looked at McMillian. "It's your bird. You take it now. I've got work to do."

The pilot nodded respectfully. "Yes, sir."

BRENNA SAT in the most out-of-the-way corner she could find and watched the professional newspeople prepare for their broadcast. Janine had explained it all to her, and Brenna still didn't believe it—that Kit would do all this for her... That he would take these risks, with his life, with his career, with his precious reputation...

But that's exactly what he was doing. Stu had the feed in place and Kit was going over some papers. Janine was talking nonstop to someone at GNN, and before Brenna could fully comprehend what was happening, she was splitting her focus between Kit in the plane, and the GNN news anchor on the television set that Stu had set up.

Harry Stanton, the morning news anchor, announced that they were cutting away live for a breaking story, and then Kit was on TV.

"Good morning, Harry. I'm coming to you from an aircraft in flight somewhere between Roanoke, Virginia, and Washington, D.C., with a story that I at first found impossible to believe," Kit said into the camera in his professional broadcaster's voice. "It was thrust upon me last Thursday night while I was photographing the Segrid meteor shower. I got more than I bargained for, as these pictures will attest."

Brenna heard Janine mumble something unintelligible into her headset connection to GNN, and a dazzling, crystal-clear photograph of the large UFO appeared on the TV screen. Kit continued to talk over that image and several more that followed.

"This is not a late April Fools' joke, Harry," he told the anchor—and the world. "And it's not a still from the latest Hollywood science fiction blockbuster. Frankly, I can't tell you what it is. I only know that

I saw it. I took thirty photographs of it, and my neighbors in the resort community of Clear Lake saw it and took twice that many pictures.''

"Kit, these are simply astonishing," the anchor commented.

"Yes, they are," he agreed. "But what is even more astonishing, Harry, is that I believe there may be a connection between the unidentified craft in this photograph, and the crash of an F-16 jet fighter that killed a young American airman last week in what the air force has up until now called a 'routine training accident.'''

Brenna watched as Kit laid it all out methodically, occasionally referring to notes in his lap, and she realized he must have written them out last night—another of the ''surprises'' he had said were in store for her.

He put it all out there for the public, complete with pictures and the film clips Janine had edited and left at GNN headquarters...the Clear Lake sighting and the interrogation of Dale Winston by government officials who had refused to identify themselves to the eyewitness...the transfer of military personnel involved in the incident...and finally, the Knoxville radar tapes, which Janine cued up so that they ran concurrently with the audiotapes of Justin Powers talking to the pilots who had witnessed the object in the sky.

Whether it was for real, or effect, the GNN anchor let a moment of silence stretch after the tapes played through. Then, he commented in a hushed voice, "You know, Kit, I don't think I've heard anyone actually say the words yet, but we're talking about unidentified flying objects here, aren't we?"

"Yes, Harry, we are," Kit said without hesitation. "I'm making no contentions about what they are or where they come from, but it's clear that something with flight capabilities beyond my own personal comprehension was operating in the sky over the American Midwest last week. Yet government officials told thousands of people who witnessed this phenomenon that they had mistaken UFOs for meteors."

"You realize how fantastical this sounds, don't you?"

"Of course, Harry. Believe me, I resisted this story for days, but it is something that simply cannot be ignored. Since I began investigating, hoping to find a logical explanation for what I photographed last week, the man who developed my pictures was shot and left for dead in his lab by gunmen who demanded that he hand over the original photographs and negatives.

"And just yesterday, an attempt was made on the life of the UFO researcher who first made me aware of the wide-ranging implications of this story. While attempting to transport certain pieces of the evidence I've shown you, Brenna Sullivan was deliberately forced off Interstate 383 in the Blue Ridge Mountains by three tractor trailers. She barely escaped with her life, and just minutes ago, men posing as FBI agents attempted to prevent us from boarding this plane."

Kit grinned at the camera, but on the monitor Brenna saw that Janine was running a clip of their brief airport chase.

"Frankly, Harry," Kit said over the clip, "that's why we're coming to you from twenty thousand feet.

As soon as we land, I expect to find myself in a little legal hot soup.''

"We'll send you a lawyer," Harry promised.

The TV returned to the image of Kit. "Make it a good one," he replied.

"I have a feeling we've only touched the tip of the iceberg on your story, Kit. Is that right?" the anchor asked.

"Absolutely," Kit told him. "This is a story that will go on for quite some time because we're talking about an official conspiracy that spans decades, Harry."

For the first time, Kit glanced away from the camera to Brenna. "In fact, as the investigation continues, I hope to be able to prove that the covert operatives of an organization known by the code name Project Chariot were responsible for the murder fifteen years ago of UFO researcher Daniel Sullivan. His death is listed officially as an accident, but he was killed in a manner strikingly similar to the attack that was made yesterday on his daughter, Brenna Sullivan."

Brenna was stunned and she couldn't stem the flow of tears that rushed into her eyes. Why? Why had Kit done that? There was no proof that her father's death had been murder. After fifteen years, Kit could investigate until the cows came home and he'd never find a scrap of evidence that Daniel Sullivan had been murdered. He knew that. Brenna had told him as much.

Yet he had told the world that it was so. He'd put his integrity and his reputation even further out on a limb, and for what?

For her. To prove that he believed her. That he

loved her. That he understood what the last fifteen years of her life stood for.

Damn him. How could she possibly dump a guy who loved her that much?

She was still pondering that question and trying to dry her tears when Kit ended his report. Stu turned off the camera, and the four of them looked at each other.

"Congratulations," Janine said to them both, then focused on Kit. "We might just turn you into a journalist yet."

He shook his head. "No thanks. From here on out, this story is yours," he said, unclipping his microphone. He moved across the cabin to Brenna's corner and knelt beside her.

"You okay?" he asked.

She nodded. "Fine. But did you have to show the clip of me in that awful wig? I looked like Little Orphan Annie running the Boston Marathon." She picked up the wig and the pillow stuffing she'd removed a few minutes before the broadcast. "A *fat* Orphan Annie."

He reached out and touched her face. "You look beautiful to me."

Brenna took his hand and pressed a long kiss to it. When she finally looked into his eyes, she asked, "Why did you do that? Why did you bring up my father's death? Even *I* wouldn't have gone that far, Kit."

"I wanted the truth to come out. *All* of the truth. You deserve it."

She felt tears stinging her eyes again. "You mean

you were making a grandstand play to prove to me that you love me.''

He nodded unabashedly. ''And trust you. And worship you, and respect you, and adore you... Shall I go on?''

''Please do.'' He gently pulled her into his arms, mindful of all the injuries that still hadn't been attended to. Brenna went willingly, resting her head on his shoulder. ''I love you, Kit.''

''Does that mean I've been un-dumped?''

''I suppose so. Now that Brewster is out of business, I'm going to need something to fill the void.'' She raised her head and grinned at him. ''It might as well be you.''

August 2
Washington, D.C.

GOOD EVENING, and welcome to Night News. This is GNN news anchor Janine Tucker in Washington.

Today's lead story was the long-awaited arraignment of UFO conspirator, Elgin Brewster, on felony conspiracy and attempted murder charges in the June seventeenth attack on ufologist Brenna Sullivan.

This is the second set of indictments that have been brought against Brewster, who is one of the central figures in Senator Davis Hanson's Senate UFO investigation that began three weeks ago after officials at Longview Air Force Base admitted that the death of pilot MacKenzie Lewis was the direct result of his encounter with an Unidentified Flying Object. Brewster has also been charged with attempted murder in the shooting of D.C. business owner Sandford Kirshner.

Brewster's arraignment comes only one week after UFO expert Brenna Sullivan completed her testimony. Sullivan, seen here leaving the Senate hearing with her husband, Dr. Christopher Wheeler, spent eight days before the investigative body, presenting evidence of a conspiracy that spans three decades. Her charges are being investigated and while no one is certain how extensive this conspiracy will prove to be, it is expected that Sullivan's testimony will lead to other indictments before the hearing is concluded.

Sullivan and Wheeler, who were married yesterday afternoon in a quiet ceremony in Clear Lake, Tennessee, were unavailable for comment about the indictment of Elgin Brewster. The couple are currently vacationing in Gulf Breeze, Florida.

Heartbreak RANCH

Four generations of independent women...
Four heartwarming, romantic stories of the West...
Four incredible authors...

Fern Michaels
Jill Marie Landis
Dorsey Kelley
Chelley Kitzmiller

Saddle up with Heartbreak Ranch, an outstanding
Western collection that will take you on a whirlwind
trip through four generations and the exciting,
romantic adventures of four strong women who
have inherited the ranch from Bella Duprey,
famed Barbary Coast madam.

Available in March,
wherever Harlequin books are sold.

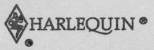

HARLEQUIN ®

HTBK

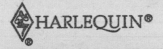

 **HARLEQUIN®**

Don't miss these Harlequin favorites by some of our most distinguished authors!
And now, you can receive a discount by ordering two or more titles!

HT#25645	THREE GROOMS AND A WIFE by JoAnn Ross	$3.25 U.S. ☐ $3.75 CAN. ☐
HT#25647	NOT THIS GUY by Glenda Sanders	$3.25 U.S. ☐ $3.75 CAN. ☐
HP#11725	THE WRONG KIND OF WIFE by Roberta Leigh	$3.25 U.S. ☐ $3.75 CAN. ☐
HP#11755	TIGER EYES by Robyn Donald	$3.25 U.S. ☐ $3.75 CAN. ☐
HR#03416	A WIFE IN WAITING by Jessica Steele	$3.25 U.S. ☐ $3.75 CAN. ☐
HR#03419	KIT AND THE COWBOY by Rebecca Winters	$3.25 U.S. ☐ $3.75 CAN. ☐
HS#70622	KIM & THE COWBOY by Margot Dalton	$3.50 U.S. ☐ $3.99 CAN. ☐
HS#70642	MONDAY'S CHILD by Janice Kaiser	$3.75 U.S. ☐ $4.25 CAN. ☐
HI#22342	BABY VS. THE BAR by M.J. Rodgers	$3.50 U.S. ☐ $3.99 CAN. ☐
HI#22382	SEE ME IN YOUR DREAMS by Patricia Rosemoor	$3.75 U.S. ☐ $4.25 CAN. ☐
HAR#16538	KISSED BY THE SEA by Rebecca Flanders	$3.50 U.S. ☐ $3.99 CAN. ☐
HAR#16603	MOMMY ON BOARD by Muriel Jensen	$3.50 U.S. ☐ $3.99 CAN. ☐
HH#28885	DESERT ROGUE by Erine Yorke	$4.50 U.S. ☐ $4.99 CAN. ☐
HH#28911	THE NORMAN'S HEART by Margaret Moore	$4.50 U.S. ☐ $4.99 CAN. ☐

(limited quantities available on certain titles)

	AMOUNT	$
DEDUCT:	10% DISCOUNT FOR 2+ BOOKS	$
ADD:	POSTAGE & HANDLING	$
	($1.00 for one book, 50¢ for each additional)	
	APPLICABLE TAXES*	$_____
	TOTAL PAYABLE	$_____
	(check or money order—please do not send cash)	

To order, complete this form and send it, along with a check or money order for the total above, payable to Harlequin Books, to: **In the U.S.:** 3010 Walden Avenue, P.O. Box 9047, Buffalo, NY 14269-9047; **In Canada:** P.O. Box 613, Fort Erie, Ontario, L2A 5X3.

Name:_____

Address:_____ City:_____

State/Prov.:_____ Zip/Postal Code:_____

*New York residents remit applicable sales taxes.
 Canadian residents remit applicable GST and provincial taxes.
Look us up on-line at: http://www.romance.net

HBACK-JM4

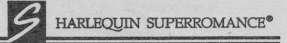

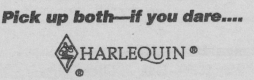

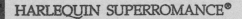

THE OTHER AMANDA
by
Lynn Leslie

Superromance #735

Who Is She?

Amanda Braithwaite has been found nearly beaten to death in a park. At least, everyone *calls* her Amanda—her aunt, her uncle, her grandmother, her doctors. But Amanda remembers nothing, remembers no one. Except Dr. Jonathan Taylor. He saved her life, and he knows more about her than he'll reveal....

Does she really *want* to know the truth, or is the past too painful to remember?

Look for *The Other Amanda* in April wherever Harlequin books are sold.

Look us up on-line at: http://www.romance.net

Loving
DANGEROUSLY

LOVE-497

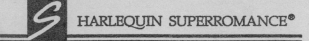

THE
MIRACLE BABY
by
Janice Kay Johnson

If having a baby with a stranger is what it'll take to save her eleven-year-old daughter's life...Beth McCabe is willing to have one.

Is the stranger?

Nate McCabe hasn't seen or spoken to his identical twin brother, Rob, for fifteen years. Now Rob is dead and Nate learns that Rob's widow, Beth, and her young daughter, Mandy, need him—but only because he's Rob's twin. Only because they need a miracle.

Mandy will die without a bone marrow transplant. When Nate's tissue fails to match, Beth persuades him to step into his brother's shoes and father a baby—Beth's baby, a child who has a one-in-four chance of saving Mandy's life.

Watch for *The Miracle Baby* by Janice Kay Johnson.